"Art lights the world," Hemingway said. "And everyone in it."

THE
BOULEVARD

JERROD EDSON

GALLEON BOOKS

First Edition
ISBN 978-1-7780781-5-6

Published by Galleon Books
Moncton, New Brunswick, Canada

www.galleonbooks.ca

Cover artwork by Pamela Marie Pierce, reprinted with permission.
Interior illustrations Adobe Stock.

This is a work of fiction. Any similarity to persons living, dead, or immortal is not at all a coincidence, but the choice of the author to create characters based on such persons living, dead, and immortal.

Library and Archives Canada Cataloguing in Publication
Title: The boulevard / Jerrod Edson.
Names: Edson, Jerrod, 1974- author.
Identifiers: Canadiana 20230453732 | ISBN 9781778078156 (softcover)
Classification: LCC PS8559.D76 B68 2023 | DDC C813/.6—dc23

GALLEON

My father, Paul Edson, read an early version of this story
before he passed away, and when I asked what he thought,
he grinned and said, in typical fashion, "It's different."

This book is for him.

1

T HE EMAIL WAS RECEIVED AT TEN O'CLOCK IN THE MORN-
ING. Received, but not read. Mr. Gregory, a diminutive
demon with a weak chin, round spectacles, and neatly
combed hair, sat perfectly upright in his cubicle, typing away at
his keyboard. He'd heard the computer beep as it always did when
a new email appeared, and although this account was reserved for
the most important messages, often enough junk mail found its
way through and made the computer beep several times during
the day. It was Mr. Gregory's responsibility to determine what
emails were important and what weren't, and though he was very
astute and a very good private secretary, this morning he was
determined to finish the quarterly newsletter to the accounting
department, and so he ignored the beep, deciding it was likely
more junk mail, or at the very least, something that could wait
for later.

An hour passed before he was finished. He sat back in his
chair and reread the last few lines, reminding them to please
check and recheck their work before submitting, and good luck
to all in the next quarter. He stood up, stretched and yawned,
before printing it off and sitting down again.

Then he spotted the email blinking at the bottom of the
screen; he'd forgotten it. He sighed. It was a short email, and as
he read it his eyes widened and his tiny jaw dropped.

"Oh no," he said. "No, no, no!"

He sprung from his chair and scrambled to print it off and
then raced down the hall to the elevator and pressed the button

until the door slid open and he was on his way up to the top floor.

His heart raced. His forehead shone with sweat. He vowed to himself that from now on he would check every email as it came. Every. Single. One. No matter what you're doing, he told himself. If it beeps, you check it. You will never let this happen again. He thought of the email. But this has never happened. Not something as big as this. He could hardly believe it, and he thought there was no way the email was real. It couldn't possibly be. Was it a test? Perhaps. But if so, he'd failed. Which would be better? A test, he thought. Surely a test.

The elevator door opened and he stepped into Satan's office; a vast, wide room with floor-to-ceiling windows on all sides. Satan was at his desk in the far corner of the room.

"Ah, Mr. Gregory," he said.

Mr. Gregory made his way across the room, past the bar and the sitting area with the small library and two wingback chairs facing a fireplace, until he came to Satan's desk and stood, stiffly, and extended his arm with the printed email.

Satan was dressed in a sheer black suit, legs crossed, feet up. His face was gaunt, his cheeks sunken, his eyes black and small. His hair shone dark and was slicked and so thick only the tips of his horns showed.

"I have been thinking of the anniversary celebrations this year. Six thousand years—it is of significance. This requires more than a parade and fireworks."

"Sir, I—"

"I am thinking of something grand," Satan said. "A festival. Music and games. Perhaps a tournament of some kind. We could use the new stadium."

Mr. Gregory's arm remained extended, the paper a terrible weight in his hand.

"Sir, this—I think—"

"The works," Satan continued. "Opening and closing ceremonies. Every city comes. Honest competition." He winked. "Or not."

"Sir…"

Satan lifted his feet from the desk.

"What is it? What have you got there?" He snatched the paper from Mr. Gregory, plopped back into his chair and read it.

His lips tightened to a pucker. He paused. Then he folded the paper and placed it in his pocket and spun around in his chair and looked down upon the sprawling metropolis of Capital City, the endless grey waves of concrete and steel divided by a river, splitting the north from the south. From so high up, the river looked like a snake, slithering along. Straight ahead, stood the mighty Gates at the city's entrance, and beyond them, the black hills and the long winding road to Purgatory.

Satan settled his eyes upon what was simply known as the Boulevard, an illuminated sixty-block route cutting needle-straight from the Gates to the foot of his tower, every building transformed into a giant mural, some as high as fifty stories and so vibrant their glow brightened the entire city. He sat for a moment without speaking, without moving, staring down upon it. And then he sighed. It was not a sigh of tiredness, but a long, deep sigh that came from within; a sigh of sudden defeat.

"Tell me, Mr. Gregory, what do you see?"

Mr. Gregory leaned in.

"Excuse me, sir?"

Satan sighed again, but softly this time.

"It is not a difficult question."

Mr. Gregory looked out the window.

"I see Capital City," he said. He rolled on the balls of his feet. "And the Boulevard, of course."

Satan nodded.

"The Boulevard."

Mr. Gregory perked up.

"Your greatest achievement, sir. Your masterwork. There is nothing like it, nor will there ever be, in this world or any other."

Satan was still nodding.

"The Boulevard," he said again.

He turned and looked to the south, to the suburbs — a flat patchwork of houses and huts — and then beyond them, to the black of the barrens and toward the deepest ends of Hell, all the way to the Foothills and the faint outline of the mountains on the horizon, so far away they were nothing more than a blurred line where land and sky met.

"Fetch Mr. Graves straight away. And get me on the next train to the Foothills."

Mr. Gregory frowned.

"Sir?"

"You heard me," Satan said.

Mr. Gregory bowed and scuttled out of the room.

Satan turned back to the Boulevard. He'd always begun his days looking down upon it, a feeling of pride welling up inside. Indeed, whenever faced with adversity, he'd turn to it and absorb its glow and it somehow made everything better. But not today. And not anymore. Now it is lost, he thought. Forever. A pit settled in his stomach, a dull pit that was hollow and heavy at the same time. And then, out of nowhere, a stitch pricked him in the side, between his ribs, not painful, but just enough to know it was there.

⚶

The elevator door opened and Mr. Graves stepped out. Graves was an old demon with worn horns and a thick stubby nose. He was heavy-set and lumbered across the room. Satan motioned to the sitting area where Graves plopped into one of the wingback chairs in front of the fire. Satan handed him the paper.

Graves read it, then looked up.

"Is this a joke?"

"I am afraid not," Satan said.

"Our anniversary is coming up. Perhaps that's why?"

"Perhaps."

"So, what do we do?"

Satan sat on the edge of the hearth. The black of his shoes shone in the firelight. In the time that he'd waited for Mr. Graves to arrive, he'd accepted what had to be done, and so he was stoic in his delivery.

"We deal with it. We have little time to prepare. Mr. Steel will handle security. Mr. Gordon will oversee, shall we say, *renovations*. He is to eliminate anything vibrant, anything with colour."

"Chinatown has a lantern festival next week."

"Cancel it," Satan said. "Every building is to be stripped of all colours. Everything must go."

Mr. Graves frowned.

"What about the Boulevard?"

The stitch pricked Satan in the side again, a bit stronger this time, enough to make him wince.

"We have no choice."

Graves straightened up.

"What is that supposed to mean?"

Satan simply shook his head.

"But we can't," Graves said.

"We have no choice," Satan said again.

"But we mustn't!"

Satan remained unmoved.

"What do you propose we do?"

"Cover it up," Graves said. "Paint over it. We can restore it later."

"Impossible. It is too vibrant."

"Perhaps he'd paint it again?"

Satan managed a grin.

"Do you really believe that?"

Graves buried his head in his hands.

"I can't believe it has come to this."

"Well, it has," Satan said. "And we have work to do." He paused. "Ms. Victoria will handle the rest. She will know what needs to be done. You are to keep me informed on all progress. Use the others to your discretion and spare no expense."

Graves sat, mouth agape.

"It is only temporary," Satan said.

"The Boulevard isn't," Graves said. "We're destroying the only miracle we have."

Satan frowned.

"Miracle?"

"Don't play me for a fool," Graves said.

Satan sighed heavily.

"And suppose we keep it. What would happen then? It would be the end of us."

"We need to take a stand," Graves said. "Once and for all."

"We would lose," Satan said. "You know that."

Graves huffed and stared down at the floor.

"We need to stop being afraid."

"We are not afraid," Satan said.

Graves laughed sarcastically.

"Remember who you're talking to. At least give me that."

Just then the elevator door opened and Mr. Gregory stepped into the room.

"The next train to the Foothills departs in twenty minutes, sir."

Graves looked up.

"The Foothills? You're going to see him? What for?"

"To tell him," Satan said. "I owe him that much."

"And you think this will absolve you?" Graves said. "Going there and telling him?"

"I don't know."

"You remember how it was in the beginning," Graves said. "Surely you haven't forgotten."

"I have not forgotten," Satan said.

"That's how it will be."

"It will not be like that."

"Oh yes it will," Graves said. He was angry now, a grunt in his voice. "And I shouldn't need to tell you this, but be careful what you're doing, because it's not just you—it's all of us."

2

Satan's private car on the train was a scaled-down version of his office: flamboyant rugs, a sitting area with two wingback chairs, and a fireplace with bookshelves on either side. A dining table and two small chairs lined the windows. The walls and ceiling were of a floral design in black velvet. Near the entrance the hall was narrow, making way for Satan's sleeping quarters which consisted of a large bed with black satin sheets, a nightstand, and a gold-trimmed armoire.

Satan sat, facing the fire, his mind swirling as the train pulled out of the station, the engines heaving slowly and steadily forward against the weight of the cars. He could see out the window the glow from the Boulevard outlining the tops of the buildings and it deflated him so that his only comfort was to sink a little lower in his chair and stare into the fire. He knew Graves was right; that it was an unimaginable thing he was doing; that the Boulevard really was a miracle, how its light shone over the entire city in such a way that it felt as though Hell, in all its gloom, had somehow acquired a tiny piece of the sun. It also bothered him what Graves had said about being afraid. It didn't bother him because Graves had said it, but because he knew, stubbornly against himself, that Graves was right about that too.

Mr. Gregory entered the car.

"Pardon me, sir, but I've just been informed that Mr. Ernest Hemingway and Ms. Jean Rhys are on this train."

Satan perked up.

"Hemingway? Send for him—but not Ms. Rhys."

※

Ernest Hemingway was big and burly with wide shoulders and

a broad chest, and he lumbered across the car, not laboriously like Mr. Graves, but flat-footed, each step a pigeon-toed thump. He sat in the other chair facing the fire, his frame snug between the armrests. He wore a plaid wool shirt, unbuttoned at the top, the girth of his chest stretching the buttonholes. A worn, leather wineskin was flung over his shoulder and he removed it and placed it at his feet.

Satan gave him a moment to settle before he spoke.

"I apologize for not inviting Ms. Rhys."

"No problem," Hemingway said.

"She is a fine writer," Satan said. "But she is—forgive me for saying it—*uncivilized*, and I am not in the mood."

Hemingway grinned.

"You should see her in bed—downright criminal." He looked around the car. "Classy little setup you got here."

Satan nodded, pleased.

"How have you been, Ernest?"

"Doing fine," Hemingway said. "On my way to Cabo San Vito for the *pelea de gallos*."

"I do not see the interest in cockfighting," Satan said.

Hemingway reached down between his feet, uncapped the wineskin, and squeezed a drink.

"Not sure I agree with it, but I like it. Nobody touches the birds once they're in—nobody tells them to fight—they do it themselves—it's in their blood." He squeezed another drink. "It's a hell of a show, though, and whether you like it or not, once it begins you can't take your eyes off it." He crossed his legs and adjusted his body so that his hips were angled, making more room in the snugness of the chair. "What about you? Where you going?"

Satan handed Hemingway the paper. Hemingway read it quickly.

"This is from God."

Satan nodded.

Hemingway scratched his cheek.

"He's coming *here*?"

"Yes."

"He ever been here before?"

"Never," Satan said.

"And he doesn't know about it?"

"No."

"You mean to tell me after all this time he has no idea?"

"Time is irrelevant, Ernest—the blink of an eye."

"He's gonna shit."

"I am expecting as much."

"The Wrath of God," Hemingway said. "You scared?"

"I have no time for that, Ernest."

Hemingway slapped the armrest.

"Horseshit! What are you gonna do?"

"I am working on it."

"You need Hell to look like Hell."

"Yes."

Hemingway thought a moment.

"*A furnace of fire, a gnashing of teeth.*"

"Precisely," Satan said.

"You've got some work to do."

"Indeed," Satan said.

"That means the Boulevard," Hemingway said. "That's a damn shame."

The stitch pricked Satan again, this time biting him, and he winced, and Hemingway saw it.

"You alright?"

Satan waved it away.

"I am going to the Foothills, to see Vincent. Would you like to meet him?"

"*Vincent van Gogh?*" Hemingway said. "Christ, yes. You can drop me off in Cabo San Vito on the way back. The matches don't start for another two days anyway."

Satan stared into the fire.

"As for Ms. Rhys—"

"Don't worry about her," Hemingway said.

"She will be most displeased, I am sure."

"She's always displeased," Hemingway said. "She says she doesn't belong here, you know. *Clerical error*, she says."

Satan shrugged.

"It happens."

Hemingway glanced around the car and lifted his wineskin.

"You got anything stronger than this?"

Satan snapped his fingers and Mr. Gregory approached.

Hemingway, despite being seated, was eye-to-eye with Mr. Gregory, who stood soldier-straight, clasping his tiny hands.

"A bottle of scotch and a bucket of ice," Hemingway said.

"Right away, sir."

Satan sighed.

"What a morning, Ernest. I woke up thinking of the anniversary celebrations and now this. It is a pity how quickly you lose the day when you must deviate from your plans."

"You mean when the shit hits the fan," Hemingway said.

"Indeed," Satan said. He frowned, lightheartedly. It was better to have someone to talk to, to have Hemingway to talk to, whom he admired. "You are a man of words, Ernest. Tell me, why is that the saying? Do you know?"

Hemingway smiled.

"You ever throw shit at a fan?"

"No."

"Me neither," Hemingway said. "But I bet it ain't pretty."

The train pushed on through the outskirts of Capital City and into the suburbs where the light was dimmer, the glow of the Boulevard already fading. Hemingway had gulped down more wine and now sipped on a glass of scotch. He held up the tumbler and swirled the glass.

"Damned fine scotch."

"Do you know about Vincent?" Satan asked.

Hemingway rested the glass on his thigh.

"His life and work, sure. And of course, the Boulevard. Meat and potatoes guy. I respect that."

Satan leaned over the side of the chair, so that there was more of an intimacy between them.

"Do you know what happened to him? What *really* happened to him?"

Hemingway shrugged.

"The *Black Ass*. What did he call it—*la tristesse*? And madness in the end, just like the rest of us."

Satan grinned.

"It is not as simple as that."

"It never is," Hemingway said.

Satan slunk back in the chair and stared into the fire.

"It is a long train ride, Ernest. Let me tell you about Vincent, and how the Boulevard came to be..."

3

EDEN WAS A SPECTACULAR VIRGIN WILDERNESS. BIRDS SANG IN the trees, perched upon tangled branches and vines that twisted and snaked their way through the greenery. Rays of sunlight shone down onto the moss-covered forest floor where flowers bloomed in all colours. A herd of deer grazed in a small, bright opening by the treeline, next to a slow-flowing river with water so clear the pebbles on the riverbed sparkled in the sunlight.

Teams of angels were strewn about, surveying, measuring, and collecting samples. Jars and vials filled with earth, water, and assorted specimens of plants and insects, all neatly organised in containers, littered the landscape. Satan plucked a flower from its stem and studied it. He was called Lucifer then, and he was, in those days, the vision of a young angel: tall and lean, his skin fair and flawless, a head of flowing blonde hair that shone gold, and wings that fluttered effortlessly.

The angel next to him, whose name was Simon, swiped the flower out of Lucifer's hand and tossed it to the ground.

"We are not here to amuse ourselves," he said. "I shouldn't

need to remind you our objective is to collect core samples and nothing more." He then marched off into the brush, tripping over a root before collecting himself and carrying on.

"Never mind *him*," another angel whispered. He was a chubby, youthful angel with fat cheeks and smooth rosy skin. His wings were thick and drooped from his shoulders like weighted branches on a tree. He peered down at the flower at Lucifer's feet. "In case you're wondering, that's a purple violet."

Lucifer gathered it from the ground and held it up to the sunlight.

"It makes its own colour."

Simon turned around, his wings quivering violently.

"God makes colour!"

"God makes flowers," the angel said. "But flowers make colour."

"And so God makes colour," Simon said.

Lucifer still held the flower to the sun.

"Funny, I don't see God anywhere in here."

Simon gasped.

"Blasphemy!"

"Oh, hush up," the angel said. "We're only talking."

Simon mumbled something to himself and carried on, stumbling his way through the brush.

"Heel! Sit! Fetch!" the angel said.

"Obey!" Lucifer said.

The angel chuckled and held out his hand.

"I'm Mr. Graves. This is your first time here?"

Lucifer nodded.

Mr. Graves grinned. His cheeks were flushed red and jolly.

"I was as taken as you are now on my first trip."

Lucifer picked another flower, smelled it and caressed the petals and felt the softness, the delicateness on his fingertips.

"Astonishing."

"That's an iris," Mr. Graves said.

Lucifer pointed.

"Those?"

"Roses."

"And the little yellow ones?"

"Dandelions," Mr. Graves said. "And daffodils and chrysanthemums and delphinium. There are many."

"Get moving!" Simon shouted.

Lucifer dropped the iris into the river and watched it float away.

"Why aren't these in Heaven?"

"I'm sure there's a reason," Mr. Graves said.

Lucifer placed his hands on his hips. The sun was warm on his face, his skin tickled by a cool, soothing breeze that came off the river.

"It is beautiful here."

"It will spoil," Mr. Graves said. "Give it time."

The train chugged along, leaving the suburbs and heading into more open land. It was even more dim here, the light of the Boulevard fading fast. Satan peered out the window.

"Upon my return to Heaven I took it straight to Council, but I was rejected without reason."

Hemingway dropped two ice cubes into his glass and filled it with scotch. He swirled the glass, cooling the scotch and waiting a moment for the ice to melt into it. Then he lifted the glass to his nose, sniffed, then sipped and sighed, satisfied.

"I had a good system in Cuba," he said. "I'd pour water and scotch into glasses and place them in the icebox. The water would freeze on the surface and the scotch would sit underneath it, cold and clear, and you'd drink it and the ice would cool it as you drank." He swirled the scotch in the glass again, watching it, thinking of his system, and of Cuba, before taking another drink, and he was back again. "Well shit, that's too bad," he said. "Flowers in Heaven. I bet they would've looked good."

Satan grinned.

"Indeed, they did."

Lucifer was sitting beside Mr. Graves. They were returning from their third visit to Eden together, on one of the last caravans before Eden was set to officially open. The convoy consisted of a dozen other angels who sat, buckled in, talking amongst themselves. Lucifer's cupped hands rested in his lap. He nudged Mr. Graves, then opened his hands, slightly, just enough to show what he was holding.

Mr. Graves' eyes widened, but the rest of his face remained calm.

"Put it away," he whispered.

"What's wrong?"

"Put it away!"

Lucifer tucked the flower into his wing and sat, staring down at his feet.

"I thought you'd—"

"Be quiet," Mr. Graves said.

"But—"

"Shut up!"

Upon their arrival, Mr. Graves took Lucifer by the arm and led him to a path that snaked along a hillside that climbed up and up until it leveled off and revealed the glow of a valley on the other side. Heaven was not unlike Eden; it had earth and solid ground, but there was a white, warm glow, like a fog, everywhere, and as they hiked, the fog was so dense in places that Lucifer had to hold onto Mr. Graves to avoid stepping off the trail and getting lost. They hiked without speaking for two hours, until they came upon three angels—two males and a female—a hundred yards off the path, huddled in a small circle and talking quietly.

The female angel stood up and frowned. Lucifer was immediately struck by her wings, which curved and sprung from her back in a wide arc, the most beautiful wings he'd ever seen. Her eyes, though angry, sparkled silvery blue.

"Who is this?"

Her beauty, matched with the sternness of her voice, brought a lump to Lucifer's throat.

Mr. Graves nudged him.

"Show her."

Lucifer pulled the flower from under his wing. It was a yellow rose, and to his surprise it now glowed in Heaven's light. He felt it warming in his palm.

The female angel's mouth opened slightly.

"Where did you get this?"

"Eden."

"What's your name?"

"Lucifer."

"You're the one who went to Council."

"Yes," he said, pleased that she'd heard of him.

Her eyes shifted to Mr. Graves then back to Lucifer.

"Give it to me."

Lucifer cupped his hand around the rose. The lump in his throat was gone.

"I will not."

"You don't know what you've gotten yourself into."

"Then tell me," Lucifer said.

Again, her eyes shifted to Mr. Graves.

"He can be trusted," Mr. Graves said.

"How do you know?"

"He's my friend."

"He could be a spy."

Mr. Graves laughed.

"He's no spy. He showed it to me in front of others. If he's a spy, then he's the worst spy I know."

"Did anyone else see it?"

"No."

Ms. Victoria glared at Lucifer.

"Did you show it to anyone else?"

"No."

"Nobody knows you took it?"

"Nobody."

She studied his face for a moment. Then she stepped back and sat down in the circle and made a space for them. Lucifer, with his hands still cupped around the rose, sat beside Mr. Graves. The glow from the flower shone between his fingers.

One of the angels slid a case in the middle of the circle, the same kind used in Eden; a linen-cloth case, bound by leather straps. He opened it, revealing an assortment of flowers housed in small glass compartments, the flowers glowing under the glass.

"It will be safe here," the angel said.

Lucifer peered down at his precious flower.

Mr. Graves nudged him again.

"It's okay."

Lucifer studied it a moment more.

"Do you trust me?" Mr. Graves asked.

Lucifer nodded.

"Then give it to him," Mr. Graves said.

Lucifer placed the rose in the case.

The angel folded the flap over the case, smiled, and offered his hand.

"I'm Mr. Steel," he said. "This is Mr. Gordon, and Ms. Victoria."

"Why did you take the flower?" Mr. Gordon asked. He had big teeth, like a horse, and when he spoke it was all you could see and made him look like he was smiling. Lucifer found it difficult to take him seriously, and it relaxed him. He shrugged.

"I wanted it."

"But you're not permitted," Mr. Gordon said. "A violation with severe consequences if caught."

"I was not caught," Lucifer said. "And what about you?"

The three angels glanced at one another.

"This is only the beginning," Mr. Steel said. He and Ms. Victoria caught eyes and she shook her head ever so slightly. Lucifer saw it.

"What about it then? You have told me this much already."

Again, the angels glanced at one another.

"Let me show you," Mr. Graves said.

He led Lucifer further off the path, into the fog, until they came to a huge stone wall that disappeared up into the whiteness. He stepped out of the way and swept back a curtain of vines to reveal, at his feet, a roughly dug hole, big enough to crawl through.

"It's a tunnel," Mr. Graves said. "We come and go as we please."

"We've already snuck into Eden three times," Mr. Gordon said. He was smiling. Or he wasn't. Lucifer couldn't tell. Those teeth. But one thing he was sure of: these three were not as calm and cool as he'd initially thought.

"We're going to plant them in the valley," Ms. Victoria said. She too had seemed overly anxious, her sternness now replaced with an excitable smile, like a child spilling the details of a very good secret.

"To do what?" Lucifer asked.

"Just as you were going to do with yours," she said, still smiling. "Enjoy them."

⁂

"That's a damned ballsy operation," Hemingway said. His huge frame had finally settled into the chair, his arms draped over the sides. "I knew plenty of smugglers in Key West. A few in Cuba too."

Satan grinned.

"You were not one of them?"

"Nah," Hemingway said.

Satan kept his stare upon him.

"Not really," Hemingway said. "Once the war broke out, I was too busy hunting U-boats."

Satan grinned again.

"Ah yes, your state-sponsored fishing expeditions."

Hemingway grinned back and took a quick drink of scotch.

"Those U-boats reached the mainland," Satan said.

"Never saw 'em," Hemingway said. "But if they'd have showed

their faces we'd have blasted them. *Pilar* could handle any Kraut tin box you'd throw her way."

Satan was still grinning.

"You were too busy fishing."

Hemingway adjusted himself in the chair.

"We were already out there. What were we supposed to do, work on our tans? You ever hook a marlin? Strapped in and it's just you and the fish and you feel him on the line, his ability in his fight; his strength and his desperation as he breaks from the surface and you see each other and he goes under again and you both hold on until one of you breaks? There's nothing like it."

Satan stared out at the land as it passed.

"This was no fishing trip, Ernest." He paused, remembering it. "We smuggled every kind of flower we could find. Others came after me, Mr. Gregory among them, and we were well organized. Indeed, it was a fine operation, for the short time it lasted."

4

They each carried two cases as they trekked through a maze of rock and loose earth down the mountainside and deep into the valley, into the dense glow of white. Their destination had been pre-determined: a small plot of cleared land, hidden by a dip in the valley floor; the perfect spot for a secret garden. They passed a few sentries posted along the route, who stood smiling, excited to see them. Mr. Gregory was one of them, his spectacles sliding down his nose as he offered a quiet salute. By the time they reached level ground their feet were sore, their calf muscles twitching.

"We're almost there," Mr. Graves said. "The land will dip, and then it levels again. Beyond the dip, that's where it is."

Without saying another word, they hurried their pace, one last reserve of energy to push for their destination. Soon they were almost jogging, until Mr. Steel, at the front of the line, stopped and kicked at the ground.

"This is it."

They placed the cases down flat and dropped to their knees and began to claw at the earth, digging holes with their hands. They opened the cases and the small compartments and placed the glowing flowers into the holes and buried them under the dirt.

"Now what?" Mr. Steel said.

Mr. Graves picked the dirt from under his nails.

"We wait."

"For how long?" Lucifer asked.

Mr. Graves shrugged.

"In Eden they can take weeks to push through."

Ms. Victoria had a smear of dirt on her nose.

"We did it," she said. "We really did it!"

Indeed, they'd pulled it off. They sat on the ground, resting before the trek back up the mountainside, smiling to themselves.

Ms. Victoria sat with her arms cupped around her legs, her knees up by her face.

"I'm going to live here, so I can tend to the garden every day. Wouldn't that be lovely?"

Lucifer had never considered this, but it sounded, as she'd said, lovely. They sat in a row, dirtied and sweaty, resting, each quietly pleased, each wondering, dreaming. Mr. Gordon had fallen asleep and was snoring. Mr. Graves leaned over and pinched Mr. Gordon's nose and he croaked and grunted and coughed a little before his mouth opened and he was snoring again, and they all chuckled.

Then, as they chuckled, Lucifer suddenly sat up.

"Does anyone feel that?"

They all remained perfectly still. And they all felt it, the ground beneath them tingling, a tiny, constant tremor.

Ms. Victoria frowned.

"What is it?"

A violet had burst through the soil and glowed brilliantly,

a flash of purple in the whiteness. Then another flower burst through, then another, until all the flowers they'd planted formed a line of coloured lights.

The ground still tingled.

Two more flowers appeared. Then four more. And more after that.

Mr. Steel dropped to his knees and started ripping the flowers from the ground, clawing at the earth. Dirt and stems and petals sprayed about, but each piece, each tiny fragment formed a new flower of its own.

"You're making it worse!" Ms. Victoria cried.

Nobody moved. Mr. Steel was breathing fast, hands dirtied, his face stricken in panic. Flowers surrounded them now, glowing in all colours in the whiteness. The ground was still tingling.

※

"They really took off on you," Hemingway said.

Satan was shaking his head, lost in the memory.

"We had underestimated Heaven's light. They bloomed like wildfire. There was nothing we could do." He paused and sighed, softly, still remembering it. "Their beauty I cannot put into words. To this day Heaven is filled with them, and it is all because of us."

"Heaven for me is two or three *barrera* seats in a big bullring," Hemingway said. "And outside a stream full of trout. And maybe Bergman with me. Naked." Then he paused, and his mouth dropped a little at the edges. "No. Hadley. Hadley with me. And Bumby."

Satan was not listening.

"We lasted but a week before we were found out." He paused, but only because the pleasant memory of a moment ago was suddenly replaced with the dreadful thought of what had come next. "And we paid dearly for it. All of us."

A large crowd of angels whispered amongst themselves, gathering around a guillotine which stood ominously tall, its long, slanted blade sharp and silver and clean. At the base of the guillotine was a huge slab of rock. Leather straps were nailed into the slab and hanging over the sides. On the ground next to the slab was a large, square block of iron, with a heavy sledgehammer perched against it. Twenty feet from the slab was a hole in the ground. The angels kept their distance from it, the blackness of the abyss, of what was down there, too terrifying to approach.

The first group of angels appeared, led through the crowd in chains by four masked angels. These were the main conspirators: Lucifer, Mr. Graves, Ms. Victoria, Mr. Steel, and Mr. Gordon. They were placed next to the guillotine, in a line, facing it.

An older angel with thick legs, a broad chest, and with heavy wings, not drooping like Graves', but powerfully erect, appeared with a scroll. He unrolled it, holding it from the top and the bottom, and with arms outstretched, in a deep and loud and clear voice, he read:

"FOR THE CRIMES OF CONSPIRACY, TREASON, AND INCITING A REBELLION, THE AFOREMENTIONED PARTIES HAVE BEEN FOUND GUILTY AND ARE HEREBY SENTENCED TO BANISHMENT, WHERE THEY SHALL BE CAST DOWN INTO THE PITS OF HELL. HEREWITH, ON THIS DAY, SUCH PUNISHMENT SHALL BE EXECUTED."

Mr. Graves' face reddened then. Grunting and tugging at his chains, he turned to Lucifer.

"What is he talking about?" He tried to keep his voice to a whisper, but it came out in a restrained hiss. "Convicted without council—without trial. It's ludicrous! Everything he says is a lie!"

The train chugged along.

"That's it?" Hemingway said. "But what about the rebellion? About the war?"

"Mere propaganda," Satan said.

"But all you did was plant a few flowers."

"Those flowers wielded power," Satan said. "It was in their best interest that we appeared guilty of more serious crimes. Everyone loved the flowers, and the concern was, would they love us for it?"

"The crime must fit the punishment," Hemingway said.

"Precisely."

Hemingway squeezed a mouthful of wine.

"It's still a damned crooked thing."

"It was to be expected," Satan said. "And I respected it. But yes, it was, as you say, *crooked*."

"You go high enough up any chain of command you'll always find a crooked son-of-a-bitch," Hemingway said. "In Spain during the war all the journalists stayed at the Hotel Florida in Madrid. There was a Russian, Oleg Federov, a sickly bugger who survived on a steady diet of vodka and stale crackers. He thought he was a big shot because he was editor-in-chief of some tid-bit half-ass paper in Moscow, and here he was, in his first war. And he was as crooked as Quasimodo. He was part of our little group who played cards in the evenings and he cheated, we all knew, but he was bright and we could never catch him in the act. Nobody trusted him. He didn't stay at the Florida, but at Gay-lord's—where many Russians stayed, yet he played cards with us every night. We were always sure to be tight-lipped around him; it wouldn't have shocked us if he were a Kraut spy. Anyway, one morning when he was out on the front he got hit by a shell and blown to shit, and that night we played a straight game and drank to the cheating prick and had a laugh. Now I know it's not the same kind of crooked, but in the end it's no different. Crooked is crooked and those bastards deserve what they get."

"They got Heaven," Satan said. "And our flowers."

Hemingway huffed.

"Then the whole system's fucked."

Satan grinned.

"That it is, Ernest. That it is."

❧

The old angel's arms were outstretched so that his bicep muscles bulged, the sleekness of his forearms taut as he held the scroll and continued.

"ANYONE WHO WISHES TO ARGUE THE INNOCENCE OF THE ACCUSED, ALL OR ANY, SPEAK NOW, OR FOREVER HOLD YOUR PEACE." He lowered the scroll and paused. No one spoke.

Mr. Graves tugged at his chains again.

"Everyone knows the truth! COWARDS!"

"Save your breath," Lucifer said.

Graves glared at him.

"How can you be so calm? Don't you see what's going on?"

"I know exactly what is going on."

"They're lying!" Mr. Graves hissed.

Lucifer looked around at the flowers glowing in the whiteness.

"Do you really think they would condemn us for these?"

"And yet you're still calm," Mr. Graves said.

"There is nothing we can do," Lucifer said. "But just look around. Our flowers are here to stay. For that we have made our mark."

Mr. Graves tugged at his chains.

"They have chosen their side," Lucifer said.

"And what side is that?"

Lucifer peered over to the hole.

"Not ours."

The angel rolled up the scroll and turned to another angel posted next to the guillotine.

"PROCEED."

The angel stepped toward them, just as Lucifer, his head held high, stepped forward on his own accord.

❧

"One of us had to do it," Satan said. "Ms. Victoria was crying. Next to her was Mr. Steel, shaking like an infant. Mr. Gordon had vomited, appearing half-mad with his teeth, and though Mr. Graves was brave, he was too angry to think straight."

"Hard to remain calm in a situation like that," Hemingway said.

Satan chuckled.

"We were far from innocent, Ernest. But what could we do? We were hopeless against him. Our plight was so insignificant he did not even attend. That alone was testament to his power, not to mention his lack of mercy."

"And now he's coming here," Hemingway said.

Satan stared into the fire.

"What was done was done. A despicable scene and I was determined to bring some dignity to it."

"And you did."

"I did," Satan said.

"Grace under pressure," Hemingway said. "It's a thing of beauty."

❧

The angel next to the guillotine moved back as Lucifer stepped forward and laid himself onto the slab, onto his side. Two other angels laid out Lucifer's wings and buckled the straps tightly around his shoulders, waist, and legs. He did not fight it. When the angels were finished, they took a few steps back and stood, side by side. The crowd was quiet, focused on the blade, which was high and shone clean and clear. Then, without warning, the blade dropped and there was a quick swish-slice and Lucifer gnashed his teeth and grunted hard and loud. Behind him, on the ground, his wings fluttered erratically, the last of the nerve endings quivering, then sputtering out, until there remained only a lifeless pile of blood-soaked feathers. Lucifer was then rolled onto his stomach and buckled down again, this time across his waist and legs. The two angels lifted the iron block and placed it high on his back, on top of his bloodied, wingless stumps. Lucifer, cringing in pain, struggled to breathe under its weight.

A fifth angel appeared, his shoulders slunk, as though his name had been drawn for the terrible task and he had no choice but to perform it. He took the sledgehammer and reluctantly lifted it over his head, holding it for a moment, mercifully, before coming down in a thunderous blow upon the block. Lucifer grunted hard and the crowd moaned. The angel lifted the sledgehammer again and came down hard, and again Lucifer grunted, and again the crowd moaned. With each blow the slab flattened against the stumps on Lucifer's back, pounding them into his body, blow by blow, inch by inch, until they began to emerge on the sides of his head, first as bumps, but with each blow swelling more and more until the skin broke and glistening white horns burst through the scalp. Lucifer's head hung over the side of the slab, blood trickling from his hairline and down his forehead in a vein-like streak and dripping from the tip of his nose onto the flowers below.

Many in the crowd had turned away. They could no longer watch as Lucifer's limp body was dragged from the slab and dumped into the hole. Feathers were strewn about the guillotine. The blade was hoisted back up to its original place, ready to drop, its silver shining and smeared red with blood that dripped down onto the slab. Mr. Gordon vomited again.

Hemingway finished his glass of scotch then reached down between his feet for his wineskin and squeezed a mouthful.

"Reminds me of what happened in Ronda in '36."

"I was there that day in Spain," Satan said. He bit the tip off a cigar and spit it into the fire. He rolled the cigar between his fingers then leaned forward and placed it in the glow of the coals until it lit. Then he sat back and puffed. "How could I have missed it? Five hundred people beaten and dropped into the gorge. You captured it well, Ernest."

Hemingway nodded, accepting the compliment.

The stitch in Satan's side had gone away, but now there was a tightness in his chest and he adjusted himself in the chair. He took another slow, smooth puff on the cigar in the hopes of loosening the tightness, and he coughed a little, then puffed again.

"It was not easy in the beginning."

5

HELL WAS A LAND OF DARKNESS. THE AIR BLACK WITH SMOKE, the ground layered in ash. Fires ignited sporadically, spurting from the earth. Glowing orange pools of lava bubbled thickly and hissed bursts of steam. In the distance shone the jagged outlines of burning mountaintops. Sometimes an entire mountainside would ignite and light up the valley and glow dimly off the mountains on the other side.

Lucifer awoke with his face pressed into a bed of ash. The plump outline of Mr. Graves lay face-down a few feet away. Next to Graves was Ms. Victoria, a patina of ash accentuating her curves, like a toppled-over statue. Soon he spotted Mr. Gordon and Mr. Steel. Others were still falling, strewn about the darkness.

Lucifer sat himself up. The wound on his back throbbed. His hair, once golden, was now jet-black, and his blood too, dried black along his hairline and down his face. Those who had already fallen began to move, their bodies emerging slowly from the ashes, sludging like zombies toward him.

Mr. Graves hobbled over, leaving a slug-like path in his wake. His face, smeared black with ash, made his eyes look very white. He was followed by Mr. Gordon, whose face was black except for his big teeth, which accentuated them even more. He was *all* teeth now.

"This worked out well," Graves said.

It brought a smile to Lucifer's face, despite the gloom.

"Now what?" Mr. Gordon said.

Lucifer shrugged.

"I don't know."

Mr. Graves turned and faced Lucifer head on.

"It's you who must lead us."

At that moment Lucifer knew his stance at the guillotine had cemented his leadership. Mr. Graves inflated his chest.

"You are to be called Satan," he said. "The great and mighty Satan. It means 'adversary'. If that's what God wants, then that's what he'll get."

"Satan."

"Yes."

"I like it."

All the others were standing, waiting. Then, without hesitation, Satan brushed the ash from off his shoulders, slicked his hair back then climbed to the top of a small mound.

"We are home," he said. "And I promise you, from this day forward things will be better. What we have before us is an undiscovered country and all the time in the world."

⁂

The train pushed on.

"You all took it pretty well," Hemingway said.

"It was a hasty coronation," Satan said, ignoring him. "But it was imperative that we organized ourselves quickly."

"Kings have been crowned everywhere," Hemingway said.

"We moved away from the mountains and found the river and constructed a settlement along it," Satan said. "With Eden's opening it was not long before Mr. Graves realized the plan, and that we were to be excluded."

☙

"Look at this place," Mr. Graves said. He motioned toward the row of scantily constructed mud huts they'd built along the river. "Is this the best we will be?"

Satan shrugged.

Mr. Graves picked up a hard piece of earth and tossed it into the river.

"Is this what you really want? To live in squalor—like dogs—in this heat?"

"Of course not."

"We deserve our share."

"He does not share," Satan said.

"Then we take it," Graves said. "Otherwise, this is as far as we go."

Satan peered across the row of mud huts. His hands were dirtied.

"Take what? What is there to take?"

"There is plenty," Graves said.

Satan crossed his arms. He was energized by Mr. Graves' anger, how his face reddened, how the yellow of his teeth showed.

"You are talking about a war."

"No," Graves said. "We can't win a war—not yet." He allowed himself a moment to calm down before he spoke again. Satan admired this in him. Since the guillotine, Mr. Graves had become a thinker, and more importantly, a calculated one. "Do you know why we were sent to Eden?"

"Surveying," Satan said. "Collecting samples. Data."

"But what for?" Graves said. "Do you not know?"

Satan shrugged.

Mr. Graves grinned.

"In Eden a new creature will live, born free, to its own decisions, its own temptations." He placed his hands on Satan's shoulders. "It's time we put your name to work."

"Wait a minute," Hemingway said. "You mean to tell me you didn't know about Adam and Eve?"

"You are forgetting, Ernest, I never questioned anything. I was obedient, as every good dog is to its master. It had never occurred to me to question anything, not until my first visit to Eden, when I picked that first flower. That was when I acquired it."

"Free thought," Hemingway said.

Satan nodded.

"The most powerful weapon I could attain."

"The nuke of all nukes," Hemingway said. He grinned. "*Lead us not into temptation.*"

"Yes," Satan said. "And yet nobody wanted to do it. And just as it was at the guillotine, I stepped forward once again."

"You can never undo bravery," Hemingway said. "Once you face the biggest bull, they expect it of you every time you step into the ring."

She stood naked, eyeing the fruit hanging from the tree. Her hair was soft and brown and flowed down her back. Her shoulders were lightly freckled, her breasts small and firm, nipples erect, and her skin, pink and cool, was covered in goosebumps. A snake slithered among the branches, its green scales camouflaged within the leaves. When it came into her view, she took a step back.

"Oh, hello," she said. Her voice was as pure as air.

Satan flickered his tongue. An apple dangled beside him. He slithered around it and snapped it from the branch.

"For you," he said.

The apple looked extra red in the green of the snake's scales coiled around it.

She took another step back.

Satan balanced the apple on the flatness of his head then slithered down the trunk and propped himself up by the length of his body, coiled behind him, so that he was face-to-face with her.

"A bite," he said. "Surely a bite will do no harm."

"It won't kill me?"

Satan grinned.

"My child, it will do the opposite. It will open your eyes. You will be like God. Do you want to be like God?"

She was still staring at the apple. Saliva gathered inside her mouth.

"Of course, you do," Satan said.

She cupped her hands, her breasts pressing together, a small, soft cleavage.

"You've had one?" she asked.

"Many," Satan said.

"And do you feel like God?"

Satan grinned again.

"I do."

She licked the edge of her lip.

"How does it taste?"

"Sweet and crisp."

He slithered closer.

She ran the tip of her tongue along her upper lip, and then she withdrew, sheepishly, turning so that her body was sideways. She peered over her shoulder at the apple again. Satan moved closer. She withdrew again, but just enough to invite him to move closer still. Then, to Satan's surprise, she snatched the apple from off his head and studied it, turning it in her hand.

She placed her lips to the apple, settling them on it, testing the smoothness of its skin. Then, opening her mouth a bit wider, she sank her teeth into it. The crunch of the bite surprised her, how the crispness tore the piece away. She closed her eyes as she chewed, the sweetness of the juice filling her mouth. She took another bite, and another, until only the core remained. She pulled and plucked another apple from the tree. Then she paused. The snake was gone. And suddenly she felt very alone. She glanced down at her nakedness, aware of it now—ashamed of it—then she crossed her arms to cover her breasts, then her loins, and, standing there all by herself, she blushed.

Hemingway was frowning.

"That's it?"

Satan puffed on his cigar.

"It was forbidden, Ernest. He does not respond well to disobedience."

"There was a colonel in Italy like that," Hemingway said. "I remember we were driving our ambulance past troops marching along the Piave and one of the soldiers stopped to tie his boot. Orders were given that there was no stopping under any circumstances. The poor fellow, he was unlucky: at the very moment he knelt, the colonel was passing on horseback. The colonel took out his revolver and shot him in the back of the head, and the body flopped down the riverbank and splashed into the water. The colonel didn't flinch, nor did his horse."

"Arrogance is weakness," Satan said. "Had God accepted our flowers we would have remained in Heaven and been happy, and I would not have become who I am today."

"A royal pain in the ass," Hemingway said.

Satan grinned. And then he started coughing; a deep, dry cough which made his eyes water. Once it had passed, the tightness in his chest began to ache. It was a dull, flat ache, and he stared into the fire, his eyes glossy.

"It was not long until our population began to grow. We took advantage of our workforce, of our natural resources, mining, construction, finance. An economy emerged. Our once pitiful settlement along the river grew to a village, then a village to a town, a town to a city, until the flow of souls was so great that some migrated to their own corners of Hell and built their own settlements which grew into cities—under my rule, of course—until you have what Hell is today."

Hemingway was looking out the train window.

"You did alright, in the end," he said. "What with Capital City and the Boulevard, what it's done for everyone. I can't imagine life here without that light. Don't know how anyone lives outside Capital City in this black ass gloom."

"But what did he expect of us?" Satan said. "It was a long while in complete darkness. We made several requests for light, but none was given."

Hemingway frowned.

"Then how'd you do it?"

"Persistence," Satan said. "We closed the Gates and caused a crippling backlog in Purgatory. Then finally we were given it, not sunlight, but *some* light, the gloom you see out the window now. For a while it was a welcomed relief; anything was better than darkness."

All that could be seen out the train window were the silhouettes of lichen-covered rocks that littered the barren landscape. Every now and then the distant lights of another city appeared as the train sped past. Satan endured the ache and tightness in his chest, but he soon developed a chill. Not long after that, his whole body began to ache. He sent for Mr. Gregory to get a blanket. And there he sat, wrapped in the blanket, smoking his cigar, in front of the glow of the fire.

"We worked fiercely to recapture Heaven's light, to rid ourselves of the gloom. We attempted to grow flowers, but it was impossible. God surely had a hand in that. And so, we had them made from iron and copper, and painted, as we still do today."

"They don't look so bad," Hemingway said.

Satan raised a finger.

"They are merely decorative. They do nothing in terms of illumination." He coughed again. "But I knew I was onto something. I knew art was the answer."

"Art lights the world," Hemingway said. "And everyone in it."

The train swayed, the darkness whizzing by.

Satan flicked the last of his cigar into the fire, grunted and tucked his chin under the blanket.

"I commissioned every artist I could find. They painted murals, mosaics, tapestries."

"A fine accomplishment," Hemingway said.

Satan raised a finger again.

"But insufficient still. Nothing could replicate Heaven's light." He shivered under the blanket. The ache in his chest had grown into a sharp pain that caused him shortness of breath. He coughed a little, in the hopes of loosening it.

"How you feeling?" Hemingway asked.

The fire snapped and sizzled. Satan's face was flushed and extra gaunt in the glow of the firelight, his sunken cheeks like crevices, shadowed, his eyes like holes, empty and black.

"I am fine."

"You look like shit," Hemingway said. He held out a glass of scotch. "Sip it a little at a time, let it settle on the tip of your tongue and roll it along the length of it before you swallow. That way you taste it thoroughly, the way it's meant to be tasted."

Satan sipped slowly, just as Hemingway had told him.

"Lovely."

Hemingway grinned.

"Isn't it? Fitzgerald taught me that. He always said it's not what you drink but how you drink it. I was just a kid back then and I gulped down damn near everything I could get my hands on without ever tasting it. The war had taught me that. I was stinking drunk the entire time. We all were. It was the only way." He sipped his scotch. "You gulp when you are afraid; when you must face the fire. But Scott showed me how to enjoy a drink truly, that you sip when you want to enjoy it, which is the best way, unless, of course, you need to gulp. And trust me, there will always come a time when you need to gulp." He sipped again. "Even you."

Satan grinned.

"Even you," Hemingway said again.

Satan swirled the glass, watching the ice rolling in the scotch.

"Many blame me for alcohol."

Hemingway lifted his glass.

"And I thank you."

"It changes a man; transforms him into someone else," Satan said. "There is no greater sin."

"Being a coward," Hemingway said. "That's worse. I knew a matador in Seville who was a coward. His work was vulgar, and he was a disgrace to his family. He should've killed himself but he didn't even have the balls for that." He sipped his scotch. "Though being a coward, he'd died a thousand deaths already."

Satan rolled the ice cubes in the glass.

"Those flowers, their colours had burned themselves into me. It was all I thought of. I began to think of a grand project for Capital City, something that had never been done before."

"The Boulevard," Hemingway said.

"Yes," Satan said. "But would I dare do it? That was the question."

"The hard part about art isn't in the doing it," Hemingway said. "It's in the putting it out there."

"I am no match for his wrath," Satan said. "If he ever found out it would be the end of us. And for that it has been our greatest secret."

"You live or die by your audience," Hemingway said. "But piss on it. Piss on it all. The only obligation an artist has is to make people think. It's not to make them happy or sad or satisfied. And the worst sin an artist can commit, besides trying to please his audience, is not making them think at all. That's what the critics don't get. Besides, what's the point of getting into the ring if you can't take a punch?"

Satan grinned.

"But Ernest, you despised your critics."

"I said *take* a punch," Hemingway said. "You don't have to like it. Nobody likes it. It's about taking it and staying on your feet."

"I cannot take this punch," Satan said.

"You won't know till it comes," Hemingway said. "You're already in the ring. Now it's time to find out if you've got what it takes. But by the sound of things you've already thrown in the towel."

"I am not proud of this," Satan said.

Hemingway adjusted himself in the chair once again.

"Let's not talk of this rot anymore," he said. "The Boulevard. How'd you do it?"

"I needed to find an artist," Satan said. "Not just any artist. Someone special. Centuries passed before I found one."

<h1 style="text-align:center">6</h1>

She crossed the square with such grace that it appeared as though she hovered inches above the cobblestones, too perfect to touch the ground. Her hair tickled her shoulders as she moved, her shapely hips rolling, her lips pressed, upturned at one side of her mouth, ever so slightly, as though holding a secret only she knew.

She approached a thin old man sitting on a wooden stool sketching a dog, his long stringy beard down to his chest. He was dressed in attire better suited for a much younger man: a burgundy robe over a short green tunic. The sky was bright and he sat in the shade under the stone arches of the entrance to the monastery where he lived.

"Your beauty brightens even the sun," Leonardo said, focused on his sketch.

The woman, whose name was Lisa, smirked.

"Do you speak of me or the dog?"

The old man smiled.

"You have come for your portrait? If so, it is not yet finished."

"It has been four years," Lisa said. "Do not worry, my husband has forgotten it." She paused, waiting for a reaction, but none came. "What is it that attracts you to it so?"

Leonardo smiled again.

"It is not yet finished." He faced the dog still, studying the lines of the snout, the curve of the ears, how the skin wrapped itself around the muscles in the shoulders and the legs, and how each curve represented a different muscle working in a different way. In this case the dog was sitting on its hind legs, the front legs supporting the upper body. Leonardo leaned forward, into the sunlight, patting the dog with his wrinkly hand. "How obedient you are."

The dog wagged its tail.

"I have come to see it," Lisa said. "If it does not trouble you."

"But of course not," Leonardo said.

He led her inside and upstairs to his studio located on the upper level of the monastery, into the octagonal room with its exposed beams and frescoes of birds in a variety of poses, pecking, perching, and in flight. High arched windows let in the sunlight from all sides. The room was littered with canvases and sketchbooks, paints and brushes, tables filled with models of flying machines and war machines, the envy of every boy in town when Leonardo brought them into the square. He was to them the greatest toymaker in all the land.

Lisa stepped over to a table, and as cautious as one who sees a strange creature for the first time, she grinned girlishly at a gadget, of what appeared to be a boat of some kind, but with a flattened hull and horizontal circular sails.

"Signore, what is this?"

Leonardo picked it up.

"A creation—nothing more."

"What does it do?"

"It flies."

"Like a bird?"

"More like a butterfly," Leonardo said. "It does not glide. It flutters."

Lisa laughed.

"You cannot be serious!"

"But I am, signoria," Leonardo said. He held the gadget up so that it was in front of her face. "These," he said, twirling the sails. "They spin and push the air downward so that it lifts off the ground. As a sail catches the wind upon the sea, so too does this."

Lisa was smiling.

"You have a spirited imagination. 'Tis little wonder the children call you Magic Man."

"I pray that is not true," Leonardo said. He was smiling too. "Lest I find myself swinging from the gallows for sorcery." Then he became serious. "Though the eyes may see magic, 'tis but simple mechanics."

Lisa lost interest as quickly as she'd attained it, and she spotted her portrait which was perched on its easel, small and unassuming. She stepped around the table and approached it. Leonardo watched her, how she stood without speaking.

"It becomes lovelier each time I lay my eyes upon it," he said.

"An impression, for certain," Lisa said. "But that smile…"

Leonardo frowned

"It troubles you, signoria?"

Lisa paused.

"I cannot recall it." She paused a moment more. "In truth, there are entire sittings I do not recall. Entire periods of time in this room have vanished from memory, as if dust in the wind."

"You sat right there," Leonardo said, pointing to a small bench along the wall. "Surely you remember smiling. I said to you *Signoria, your smile—hold it please, if only for a moment more.* You said: *Like this?* And you made a comical face and then laughed and apologized." He frowned, remembering it. "You have forgotten that?"

"I do not recall any of it," Lisa said. Then came that smile. "What magic did you work on me? Indeed, the gallows may await you yet."

"Well holy shit," Hemingway said. "That was you?"

Satan grinned.

"Truly, I thought Leonardo was the one. I could not help but smile."

"Explain that to me," Hemingway said. "Possession—always wondered about that."

Satan grinned again. Then his chest tightened and he sat himself up straight and coughed, trying to loosen it, but it only made him cough more, and the tightness remained.

"It was not possession, Ernest. It was only temporary—like being hypnotized, and as easy as opening a door and stepping through." He sighed. "Possession is far too much work."

"So how do you do it?" Hemingway asked. "How do you step through that door? You just snap your fingers and voila?"

Satan smiled.

"I do not think of it, Ernest."

Hemingway leaned forward to stoke the fire, poking at one of the logs Mr. Gregory had placed, until the coals sparked and the log caught fire again.

"I was just curious," he said. When he sat back he saw himself sitting in Satan's chair, and he jumped. "Jesus Christ!"

"It ain't hard," Satan said in Hemingway's voice. "Not one goddam bit."

Hemingway laughed loud and fell back into the chair.

"That's pretty damned good," he said, laughing still. "Do I really sound like that?"

"What in Christ else would I sound like?" Satan said. "What other goddam son-of-a-bitch would I sound like?"

Hemingway was curled over laughing, and then, after a minute, once he caught his breath and looked up, Satan was back, and he was smiling.

"I must admit, Ernest, that was somewhat liberating."

"That's a hell of a party trick," Hemingway said. He chuckled, emptying the last bits of humour from his belly.

"Leonardo had a charwoman named Maria," Satan said, serious now. "She was a simple woman who did not understand her societal position and did not care, openly commenting on anything, including Leonardo's work. But it was for this reason, her candor—her simple and honest nature—that Leonardo quite enjoyed her company, and there, before me, another door opened."

She was short and squarely built, and she hobbled like a woman who was short and squarely built. She was permitted to enter the studio as freely as any room in Leonardo's apartment to perform her duties of sweeping, dusting, cleaning the floors, and wiping down the crockery. She was under careful instruction not to touch anything on his work desk and not to rearrange anything in the room and she did her job very well.

Ever since Lisa's visit the week before, Leonardo had taken a keen interest in the portrait again. He'd agonized for years over its completion. Had he done enough? Was it perfect? He sighed, fighting it, daring to deny the inevitable realization that it would never be perfect. Maria was a few feet behind him, on her knees scrubbing the floor, when she lifted her heavy-set frame with a grunt and a huff.

"What is it you wish to say?" Leonardo asked. He was not cross, but curious, and his tone, albeit direct, was still friendly.

"I do not know," Satan said.

"Ah, 'tis something worthwhile," Leonardo said. "Your eyes speak."

Satan hobbled back a step.

"Well?" Leonardo said.

"I am in no position—"

"Oh, be damned with that!" Leonardo said. "I have no concern other than your opinion."

Satan stepped forward and narrowed his eyes.

"Pardon my saying so, but…"

"Out with it, woman," a smiling Leonardo said.

"Well…" Satan said. "Is it not bleak?"

Leonardo frowned. His hair was long and stringy, as was his beard, and when he frowned his eyebrows scrunched together and looked like a fuzzy caterpillar wriggling its way across his forehead.

"'Tis indeed dark," he said. "But in nature all is dark that has not been exposed to light."

"Perhaps then, expose her?" Satan said. He said this too quickly, he knew, and he lowered Maria's head.

Leonardo stared at the portrait and caressed his beard.

"'Tis not in her nature."

Satan kept Maria's head low, counted to ten and was surprised Leonardo was still waiting for a response. He lifted her head slowly.

"Is it not in all our natures to have a light inside?"

Leonardo grinned.

"I supposed it is." He rocked back and forth, caressing his beard, pinching it between his fingers. A beam of sunlight made a bright patch on the floor in front of him. Specks of dust floated in the light.

The next day Satan came into the studio and saw that Leonardo had lightened Lisa's forehead, cheekbones, and chest. But it was lacking. It did not light the room, not even the space around it; the pigments simply weren't vibrant enough. Perhaps it was its size; it was a small portrait, and he should not expect it to emanate much light. Or should he? He tried to convince himself of this, but he knew, quite simply, that Leonardo couldn't give him what he sought.

"There, old woman," Leonardo said. He was sitting at his workbench, fidgeting with a gadget. "Does it satisfy you now?"

"Indeed, signore," Satan said, offering a warm, sympathetic smile. "*Grazie*."

"But Leonardo wasn't the one," Hemingway said.

"No," Satan said. "But you must understand, Ernest, I was looking for the sun and he could not give it to me. I had no choice but to look elsewhere." He sipped his scotch. "It would not be long before another candidate emerged."

Hemingway leaned forward and poked the logs with the stoker. The sparks flickered. He prodded the top log, turning it so that it was perched against the flat log, creating a space between the coals. He leaned closer and blew softly into the coals until their glow brightened and a blue flame appeared and ignited the perched log. He sat back in the chair and stared into the fire. Then suddenly he perked up.

"Michelangelo."

He'd been at work on the dreaded ceiling of the Pope's chapel for over two years and was still only halfway finished. He was thirty-five years old but looked like he was fifty. His muscles ached constantly. He worked high up, on the top level of the curved scaffolding, the supports arching with the ceiling, creaking and cracking, his neck bent back, his face tilted up, like a giraffe eating leaves from a tree. His arms were upstretched to the ceiling, his huge peasant-like hands gripping the brush, cramping, bit by bit, stroke by stroke, the details unrecognizable from so close but somehow perfect from the floor, nearly sixty feet below, where an assistant mixed sand and lime to make the plaster.

The assistant, whose name was Paulo, often stared at the ceiling, awestruck. From where he stood, he could see the glorious first half of the completed frescoes. He particularly liked the scene of Noah with his family. It was the first section completed in his presence, and for this reason it was his favourite. The other half of the ceiling was of a blue night sky with gold stars, painted years before by Piero Matteo d'Amelia, and though Paulo would never tell Michelangelo, a small piece of him was saddened it was slowly being buried forever, right in front of his eyes.

He'd just finished mixing another batch of plaster when Michelangelo hollered down to him.

"Our friend has returned," he said, his voice echoing throughout the empty chapel.

Paulo squinted and saw, near to where Michelangelo was, a hummingbird fluttering near the ceiling, the same bird they'd seen the day before.

"How it focuses," Michelangelo said. "But not on the ceiling, but the woodwork, the scaffolding."

"Perhaps it smells the wood," Paulo said.

Michelangelo rubbed the stiffness of the back of his neck.

"'Tis perhaps the only one who appreciates the pain of this." He tilted his head again to the ceiling, just as a drip of plaster fell and splattered on the bridge of his nose and into both his eyes. "Paulo," he said. "Your assistance, *per favore*."

Paulo was still squinting up at the bird and could not see Michelangelo on the other side of the scaffolding.

"I am not yet finished with this batch, signore."

"I have plaster in my eyes."

"Are you injured, signore?"

"I AM BLIND, YOU FOOL!"

Paulo started up the long wooden ladder then climbed onto the upper scaffolding and found Michelangelo sitting, rubbing his eyes with a dirty cloth.

Michelangelo heard Paulo behind him. His eyes were closed, his arms extended. Paulo crawled across the planks and took Michelangelo's arm and led him slowly to the wall where he guided his hand to the ladder. Michelangelo, his face cringing, eyes tightly shut, twisted his body around and found his footing on the rungs and descended. Paulo followed him.

Once on the floor, Michelangelo rinsed his eyes with Paulo's cup, dipping it into a bucket of water and pouring it over his face, struggling to keep his eyes open with the flush of the water.

"I swear it, that hummingbird is cursed," he said. He opened his eyes, and they were bloodshot.

The hummingbird was still fluttering up near the ceiling.

Michelangelo dried his face with a cloth.

"Yesterday it startled me, and I very nearly stepped off the plank. And now this." He sat, picking the plaster out of his fingernails. "I swear it, lest I fall to my death, this chapel will make me a cripple—mark my words." He dipped the cup again into the bucket and took a long drink. "Would Julius sacrifice thus for a war? I think not." He sighed. "'Tis no different."

Paulo didn't know what to say. He did not want to say anything against the Pope, especially here, in his chapel.

Michelangelo wiped his eyes again with the cloth.

"Evil lurks in that bird, I tell you."

7

"Why not Michelangelo?" Hemingway said. "He had it all."

"Indeed, he did," Satan said. "And it was plain to see, once the chapel was completed, just how magnificent it was. There was nothing like it. But Michelangelo was not a painter, not in his heart. He was a sculptor. Marble was his canvas. Even if I had lured him here, he never would have painted the Boulevard. I needed someone with passion for paint." He coughed, lightly, muffling it with his hand. "But he was correct in his observations. I was indeed studying the scaffolding. I knew it would be useful." He coughed again, but hard, and he buckled forward, and when he sat up there was a trickle of blood on his lip and he licked it away before Hemingway saw it. "There was no other talent like that of Leonardo or Michelangelo, not until Rembrandt, but with him there was only darkness." He took another sip of scotch. "After Vermeer painted his milkmaid, I was hopeful, but he never moved into more colourful work."

Suddenly a woman stumbled into the car and tripped over her own feet, revealing Mr. Gregory behind her.

"I'm sorry sir, but I couldn't stop her."

It was Jean Rhys. She wore a slim-fitting sparkling evening gown and high heels and she was very pretty, with black hair cropped short, flawless olive skin, high cheekbones and piercing Creole eyes as clear and as green as the Caribbean Sea. She lay on the floor, holding her drink—a martini—and she let out an exaggerated laugh. "Ha! Never spilled a drop!"

Mr. Gregory stepped over her.

"She's a mess, sir."

Hemingway stood up.

"That's my mess, I'm afraid."

Jean Rhys glared up at Hemingway and scowled.

"What the hell kind of man brings a woman on such a god-damned trip as this and then leaves her alone to rot?"

Hemingway glanced back at Satan.

"Clerical error," he said, with a smirk.

He took her by the arm and lifted her to her feet, then escorted her out of the car. "Come now, Jean, let's get you to bed."

Once they were gone the tightness gripped Satan hard in the chest and he grabbed the armrest, cringing, holding on until it loosened, and he breathed, relieved. Mr. Gregory, now standing beside Satan, handed him a cellphone.

"Sir, it's Mr. Graves."

Satan grunted and reached for the phone.

❧

Mr. Steel crossed the street and into a six-floor walk-up in the Latino quarter, in the heart of Capital City. The apartment door was open, and he let himself in. The apartment smelled of refried beans and candle smoke. He found the man on his patio garden at the back. It was a cramped patio garden with painted flowers in pots lining the small space along the cement floor and hanging on hooks from a crossbeam covered in vines. The flat colours of the painted flowers—roses, irises, daffodils, and dahlias—gave a cartoonish impression, some roughly painted and coarse, a pocket of fabricated paradise found in such places as Wonderland or Oz, but because of the small space it looked more like background props for a children's play, built by a caring but amateur hand. Mr. Steel stepped onto the small patio.

Carlos Castro, his back turned, was sitting on a milk crate, hunched over, painting a rose made of iron. He was heavy-set, the fat of his back rolled into his t-shirt under his arms. He had a shaved head, and his neck was shiny with sweat, and the collar of his t-shirt was yellowed. He turned and saw Mr. Steel's horns.

"Senior Castro?" Mr. Steel said.

"Si."

"Senior Castro of the Hernandez drug cartel?"

Castro turned back to painting the rose.

"What do you want?"

Mr. Steel pulled a folder from inside his blazer.

"You've quite a resume. Started as a mule at the age of fifteen—"

Castro sighed.

"That is not me."

"—smuggling shipments of cocaine into the US," Mr. Steel continued. "Then earning the rank of courier for top cartel communications, eventually joining the inner circle until, at the age of thirty you were made Security Chief for cartel leader Juan Andres Hernandez."

"Another life," Castro said. "Another man."

Mr. Steel was nodding as he read, eyebrows raised.

"You were so proficient not only did you protect your boss from competing cartels and the DEA, your name was never known to any agency; you were simply referred to as *El Fantasma*. The Ghost."

Castro focused on the rose.

"I am a florist now. I run a small shop. Nothing more."

"*El Fantasma*," Mr. Steel said.

Castro stopped, cleaned his brush and motioned for Mr. Steel to hand him the tin of paint at his feet. Mr. Steel knelt and passed it to him. Castro opened the tin, dipped the brush into it and continued on the rose.

"You have a most impressive garden," Mr. Steel said. "It must take a lot of work."

"I enjoy it," Castro said, concentrating. Flints of red paint speckled his fingers. "The first ones I made looked like bricks, but these ones I am particularly fond of. But they smell of iron and paint, nothing more."

Mr. Steel closed his eyes and breathed exaggeratingly through his nose.

"Ah yes," he said. "Even an old demon like myself enjoys the smell of fresh flowers."

Castro stopped painting.

"What do you want?" he asked again.

Mr. Steel stepped a little closer and knelt and tapped the folder.

"I don't care what's in here—I really don't. But what it tells me is that you're a man of great efficiency. You get things done. I need a man like that."

Castro rubbed the back of his neck.

"What for?"

Mr. Steel told him of the email.

"He's coming here?"

"Yes."

"And what do you require of me?"

"You will be in charge of securing the Boulevard," Mr. Steel said. "While it is being dismantled, and during his entrance—a parade."

Castro frowned.

"What you are asking is no small task."

"I pay handsomely," Mr. Steel said.

"I do not want your money," Castro said. "My people depend on the Boulevard's light."

Mr. Steel grinned.

"*Please*," he said. "You protected a man responsible for hundreds, if not thousands of deaths of *your people*."

Castro rubbed the paint from off his fingertips.

"No," he said. "That was another life. That was not me."

Mr. Steel pursed his lips, still grinning.

"You know as well as I do this is no place for redemption."

Castro continued rubbing the paint from his fingers.

Mr. Steel looked around the small garden.

"Your flower shop does well?"

"Well enough."

"You make lovely flowers," Mr. Steel said. "This part of the city has more flowers than any other. Much credit to you."

Castro turned.

"Gracias."

Mr. Steel pulled an envelope from the folder.

"Put that away," Castro said. "I have already said it is not about money."

Mr. Steel grinned again.

"What is it that you want?"

Castro thought a moment.

"A dahlia."

Mr. Steel looked around the small garden.

"You have many already."

"You know what I speak of," Castro said.

Mr. Steel smiled.

"A real flower?"

"Yes," Castro said.

"But it would die quickly."

"I do not care."

"One flower?"

"Not just any flower," Castro said. "A dahlia. Mexico's national flower. Can you do it?"

"I can do anything," Mr. Steel said. "But it would only be for you. For your private garden here."

"I understand."

"It won't survive," Mr. Steel said. "You know that."

Castro picked up his brush then turned back to his rose.

"Let me worry about that."

Mr. Steel ran his fingers over the envelope. There was the faint smell of turpentine and the copper-red smell of the paint in the open tin.

"I'm offering you a lot of money."

"Do not insult me," Castro said.

Mr. Steel frowned.

"One dahlia?"

"One dahlia," Castro said.

Mr. Steel took another moment.

"Alright," he said.

Castro turned, shook Mr. Steel's hand, then went back to work on the rose.

⁂

Hemingway returned to Satan's car. Mr. Gregory had added two more logs to the fire.

"How is Ms. Rhys?" Satan asked.

Hemingway poured himself a glass of scotch and sat, snug in the chair.

"She's a little hot. I put her to bed. She'll sleep it off."

"She has spunk," Satan said.

Hemingway smiled.

"When she's sober, she's a fine and pleasant woman. But when she drinks, she turns into that." He sipped his scotch and watched the fire burning for a moment before sipping again. "So, no Rembrandt," he said. "And no Vermeer."

"I had a dreadful time of it," Satan said, happy to be telling his story again. "Centuries passed."

"But why Vincent?" Hemingway asked. "Why him above everyone else?"

Satan shrugged.

"Naturally, after Leonardo and Michelangelo, other candidates emerged. But I learned it was not only the artist I required, but the level of the craft itself, and that did not come until the Nineteenth Century, wherein three things changed the art world: organic chemistry, a good eye, and tubes."

"Right," Hemingway said. "I know about the tubes. Painters used to crush their own pigments; made their own colours."

"That is correct," Satan said.

Hemingway's chest inflated.

"Then came the screw-on, squeezable metal tubes, and artists were able to buy their colours pre-made."

"Correct again," Satan said.

Hemingway grinned.

"Writing and painting are the same once you peel away the gloss. When I write of a writer or a painter, they're both the same character. They've got x-rays now to see how a painting was made; to see under the surface; its construct, its errors and corrections; its DNA. If you could do that with a novel you'd find the same things."

Satan nodded.

"It was around this time, Ernest, that organic chemistry brought about new colours never seen on canvas before. Pigments more vibrant than anything up to that point. And with that, a decade earlier, the concept of complimentary colours."

Hemingway grinned again.

"Word placement."

"And so with new colours and new ways to use and store them," Satan said. "Artists now had all the tools necessary to produce the work I was searching for."

"You still haven't answered my question," Hemingway said. "Why Vincent? You mean to tell me Monet didn't have it? I have a hard time believing that."

Satan stared into the fire.

"Monet was the master of them all. He had an energy; all of the young painters did; an energy that separated them from the establishment."

"The greatest misconception of youth is that they're lazy," Hemingway said. "But the next generation always has more energy. It's what gets them to their feet before they charge and break the line."

"The Salon was the line in those days," Satan said. "If it was not in the Salon, it was not considered art. Indeed, the line seemed unbreakable." He paused, lost in thought. Then he blinked. "Nobody could do with colour what Monet could do."

"So, what was wrong with him?" Hemingway asked.

Satan shrugged, then smiled, almost sadly.

"He was *too* good."

8

December 1868.

Claude Monet was 29 years old and lived with his girlfriend Camille and their new-born son, Jean, in Étretat, Normandy. Monet had taken a keen interest in the effects of light on snow, and one cold morning, after wandering the countryside, he'd found his scene, and as he stood in front of his easel, wearing three heavy coats, his toes frozen in the snow, Satan visited him for the first time.

Monet was painting a snow-covered wattle fence, and the house and trees behind it. There had been a fresh snowfall the night before and the snow was thick and fluffy and the shadows from the fence were blue.

Satan, in the form of a squirrel, climbed a tree behind Monet and sat on a low branch to see what he could see. His first impression of Monet was that he was extremely patient; he simply observed everything before he began, but once he was ready, he worked quickly, and on all parts of the canvas at once. Then he would look again and find more colours; the blues in the long shadows of the wattle fence. He did not paint the sky blue, or the snow white, but used various stained whites for the sky, and blues for the snow, and Satan marveled at what was happening: Monet was seeing colours everywhere, and not only was he seeing them, he was applying them to his canvas and it brought a vibrancy to the painting that felt more realistic than anything Satan had seen before. Monet carried on, his toes and fingers numb, his nose red and running, his breath white in the frozen air.

Next, Satan took the form of a trapper trekking through the deep snow, emerging from the treeline and the road behind Monet. His face was heavily bearded, with ice in his beard and his thick eyebrows. His eyes and nose were red and runny. He wore a rough fur coat and had two dead rabbits flung over his shoulder.

"Bonjour," Satan said. "Ah, un peintre!"

Monet turned.

Satan, taking heavy steps in the fresh fallen snow, looked beyond Monet to see the painting up close.

"Ah, c'est beau! Vraiment!"

Monet nodded.

"Merci."

"La neige, c'est bleu?"

Monet nodded again.

"Snow is blue, yes," he said.

"Vraiment?"

Monet seemed irritated that this stranger was interrupting his work. He removed his gloves and rubbed his hands together and then cupped them and blew on them. The warmth of his breath brought some feeling to his fingers.

"Snow is a reflection of the sky, and if you look long enough you will see more blue than white."

"More everything," Satan said, looking at the painting. "Yellow and red too?"

"Light brings all colours to everything," Monet said. He blew on his hands again.

"Vous allez à Paris?" Satan asked.

"I will show it in Paris, mais oui," Monet said.

"At the Salon?" Satan asked.

Monet looked a bit puzzled; how did this rough trapper know of the Salon? He smiled, amused.

"That is my plan."

Satan smiled, and around his thick dark moustache and the straggly ends of his long stringy beard, bits of ice flaked away and he wiped them with his sleeve.

"Does your work sell in Paris?"

Monet chuckled.

"Not as well as I wish."

He nodded to the rabbits over Satan's shoulder.

"Et toi? Combien pour un de tes lapins?"

Satan flopped the rabbits onto the snow, untied the string from one—which were knotted around the hind legs—and handed it to Monet.

"Rien," he said. "C'est pour vous."

"I cannot take it for free," Monet said.

"I insist," Satan said. "It has been a good day for me." He peered over Monet's shoulder to the canvas again. "And for you as well."

Monet lifted one of his coats to dig into the pocket of the coat underneath it. Satan reached out and pulled Monet's hand from the pocket.

"I insist," he said again, peering down at the rabbit, whose soft brown coat rested in the trampled snow.

"Your hands," Monet said, feeling the coarse, weathered hands of the trapper. "How are they so warm? And without gloves?"

Satan shrugged.

"It is in my blood. Trapper's blood."

Monet shivered, then grinned.

"Perhaps I'm in the wrong profession."

"I don't believe so, monsieur," Satan said, and he bowed. "Very well then, au revoir." He gathered up the other rabbit, flung it over his shoulder and headed down the road, keeping inside a set of wagon tracks in the snow. Once he was out of sight, he returned, this time as a bird—a magpie—and he perched himself on the fence's gate.

Monet, seeing the black of the bird on the gate, muttered "La belle pie." And then, in a few quick strokes, the magpie appeared.

❧

Satan leaned toward the fire.

"The Salon jury rejected *The Magpie*, citing its rough brush-strokes and sloppy edges."

"Goddamned establishment," Hemingway said. "It's the same with anything; once it has determined the bar, it's finished."

"*The Magpie* is a lovely piece," Satan said.

"I know it well," Hemingway said. He took a long squeeze from his wineskin.

"Monet knew it was worthy of the Salon, and his frustrations grew," Satan said. "But from his frustrations came determination. Five years later, he and a few of his friends, having tired of the Salon's rejections, decided to hold an exhibit of their own, to coincide with the Salon."

❦

Satan, in the form of a wealthy French importer named Pierre Gagnon, stood in front of a painting just as a man stepped next to him. The man was chuckling to himself and writing in a notepad.

"Would you just look at this, heh?" the man said. He chuckled again and scoffed and shook his head. "It is the work of a child."

Satan kept his eyes on the painting, at the bright orange sun in the haze over a harbour.

The man leaned in to read the card beside it.

"*Impression, soleil,*" he sneered, as he wrote it into his notepad. "By Monsieur Monet, but of course! Ha!" He was still writing in his notepad. "But what kind of impression does he seek?" He turned to Satan.

Satan shrugged.

"Not a good one," the man said. "Mais vraiment, c'est un embarrass."

Satan crossed his arms and held his stare with the painting.

"Regarde toute la salle," the man said, his arms out, his body twisting around to the four corners of the big room. "Just look at this…this spectacle! These rejects with their unfinished work—these unpolished canvasses—the blotches and there—" He pointed to a painting three away from the Monet they stood in front of. "Those black tongue-lickings there at the bottom!"

"They are people," Satan said. "Surely you can see that."

The man turned sharply.

"I can see it," he said. "And I can also see blotches." He wrote something else in his notepad, and whatever it was, it amused him, and he chuckled again as he wrote.

"You are a journalist?" Satan asked.

The man nodded and kept writing and chuckling. When he was finished, he pinched the pencil into the notebook and held out his hand.

"Louis Leroy," the man said, and he shook Satan's hand.

"Pierre Gagnon," Satan said.

Louis Leroy huffed.

"Well, Monsieur Gagnon, I am tasked with reviewing this spectacle."

Satan looked around the room.

"I quite like it."

Louis Leroy scoffed.

"You can't be serious!"

"But I am," Satan said. "And I am safe to assume your article won't be?"

"Mais donc," Louis Leroy said loudly. "Je ne comprends pas—" he said, looking around again. "I don't understand how any of this can be taken seriously."

"I had no expectations," Satan said.

"But surely you didn't expect this," Louis Leroy said. He stepped sideways, to another painting. "Look at this, for example. Pierre Renoir. He makes good use of colours but he doesn't bother to draw. Look at the dancer's legs! Where do they begin and end? Where are the edges?"

"You are mistaking visibility over vision," Satan said.

"Vien ici," Louis Leroy said, taking Satan by the arm and walking him to another painting, this one by Pissarro.

"Look at this."

"I quite like it," Satan said.

"It's nothing but palette-scrapings and mud-splashes!" Louis Leroy said. He flipped open his notepad and wrote the words *palette-scrapings* and *mud-splashes*.

"Breathe," Satan said. "You could give yourself a stroke."

Louis Leroy laughed. Then he paused to look around the room again.

"They have no interest in detail," he said. "These are but car-icatures."

"They are impressions," Satan said.

"Then they are no longer artists, but impressionists—ha!" Louis Leroy said, and he wrote this down as well. And then he wrote *The exhibition of the impressionists*. He bowed to Satan. "I can't take this much longer. A good day to you, Monsieur Gag-non."

Satan bowed, and Louis Leroy made his way through the few small groups of people and engaged someone else. Satan could hear him laughing from across the room.

"So why not Monet?" Hemingway asked again.

Satan looked at Hemingway, who grinned.

"Short version."

"I was a gardener at Giverny and I saw him every day," Satan said. "His farmhouse provided him with two acres of land. A small orchard and an array of wildflowers, a walled garden, a pond, and a river to walk to. He planted flowers everywhere and let them grow as they pleased, and herbs and vegetables, and for him it was paradise. By this time, the Impressionists had prevailed and their work had gained respect and sold well."

"They broke the line," Hemingway said.

Satan nodded.

"Monet was living comfortably enough to hire workers and I was one of them. I was certain he was the one. There was no one better. What he could do with colour and light, no one could match him. And just as I began to think of a plan, it all came to an end."

An elderly man named Bernard Leclerc sat in the sunlit door-way of a shed on the property, resting at the end of the day, his clothes dirtied from the day's work. Monet had been in the house cooking dinner. He loved to cook, to use the vegetables and herbs from his gardens. Leclerc did not see Monet until he was upon him, and he sat up. Monet was holding a small plate and fork.

"Pour vous," Monet said.

"Ah, merci," Satan said, taking the plate and fork. "*Pâté?*"

Monet nodded and sat down beside him.

"Try it."

Satan picked a sliver of the *pâté* and ate it.

"Délicieux."

Monet smiled warmly.

"I thought you might like it."

"C'est quoi?" Satan asked. "I can taste the bacon, and onion." He paused and chewed. "And brandy, too. Oui?"

He ate another sliver.

"Is that all?" Monet said, looking down at the plate. "It is my own recipe. You really don't know what it is? That is surprising."

"Pheasant?" Satan said.

Monet paused, waiting a moment before he spoke.

"C'est lapin," he said. "Rabbit."

"Ah, mais oui," Satan said. He finished the last sliver and placed the empty plate at his feet.

For a minute, neither of them spoke. They simply sat, the low, early-evening sun on their faces.

"Most people rest in the cool of the shade," Monet finally said. "Mais pas vous. "

"J'aime le soleil," Satan said.

Monet continued. "And most of my workers drink water. Lots of water on a hot day like this. But not you. In fact, I've not seen you drink any water. Not ever. You are truly unique to these elements. It reminds me of a trapper I once met, years ago, in the dead of winter, gloveless, but with warm hands—as though he'd held them to a fire." He shuffled his feet in the dust of the doorway. "Can you imagine that? Vraiment unique." He let a quiet moment pass between them. "Perhaps it is time you leave me alone. I don't know what it is you seek, but you will not get it from me."

    JERROD EDSON

Satan huffed. He picked at the dirt under his nails. "Monsieur—"

Monet turned sharply and looked him straight in the eye.

"By the grace of God, leave me be, or I shall go into town tomorrow and bring back as many clergy as I can find and let them deal with you." He gathered the plate and fork from the ground, stood up, and went back into the house. Once inside, he stood over the sink, breathing fast, his body trembling.

❧

The train pushed on.

"I greatly underestimated him," Satan said. He smiled, in admiration. "Monet's genius was his ability to see what nobody else saw, and I was careless." He shrugged. "Most people took no notice of such insignificant things."

"Claude Monet's not most people," Hemingway said.

Satan nodded and smiled again.

"We used to tell the Krauts by their eyes," Hemingway said. "There was always something that separated them from the others—a coldness that made them more silver than blue, how ice turns blue water white. If you put ten men in a line, all wearing the same clothes, the same colour hair, I could pick out the Kraut. I mightn't be able to tell you why, but nine times out of ten I could pick him out." He laughed. "You a Kraut?"

Satan grinned.

"I left Giverny that evening," he said. "I went to Paris, disheartened and prepared once again to wait another century—or forever—when I met the least likely of the lot; a young, inexperienced painter from Holland, with hair the colour of carrots."

9

THE FIRST TIME SATAN EVER HEARD THE NAME *VINCENT VAN Gogh* was from the artist's brother, Theo, who worked at the Boussod & Valadon Gallery in Montmartre. The Impressionists, with their bold colours and wildly worked canvases, had a friend in Theo van Gogh, who supported them, and because of this, many of them often frequented the gallery.

Satan went under the guise of Pierre Gagnon, a wealthy businessman whose interest in art and artists, along with his pocketbook, earned him considerable respect at the gallery. He went so often he got to know Theo, and many of the painters talked to him whenever they saw him, eager for the attention of a potential buyer.

One day, Theo was talking about his brother with Claude Monet, who had come in from Giverny. Theo showed him some of Vincent's sketches. Monet was wearing a black beret and a black overcoat and matching cravat. He had a long and tangled dark beard with scrapes of grey along his moustache that gave him a look of eccentric sophistication.

"What training has he had?"

Theo shrugged. He was thin and well-kept; hair cropped short and a neatly trimmed thick moustache. His tie was always straight, and he stood straight and stiff, and as he shrugged there was a slight hop in his stiffness.

"Not much. He has been working some with our uncle, but he is mostly self-taught."

"He needs artists," Monet said. "He needs Paris."

Theo grinned.

"I love him dearly, but my brother is, how should I put it? —*off-centre.*"

"Then certainly, yes," Monet said. "He is an artist."

Satan poked his head between them.

"Ils sont tous fous ! They're all crazy!"

Monet laughed. "Très bien, Monsieur Gagnon." Then he caught eyes with Satan, and for a moment he paused. Then he turned to Theo. "Invite him to come. It will be good for him."

Theo smiled. He knew his brother in a way only brothers know each other, and he knew Vincent had a strangeness that went beyond simply being an artist. He would not fit in with this group. They would not out-paint him, Theo knew, but Vincent was of a different breed. Indeed, *off-centre*.

"Claude, for you I will ask him and see what he says."

But he hesitated with the invite.

❧

Two weeks later, Monet was in Paris again, and at the gallery again, this time with Pierre Renoir.

"Show Pierre the sketches from your brother," Monet said. Theo went to a back room and returned with the portfolio Vincent had sent him.

Renoir had a narrow, skeletal face with high cheekbones and stringy patches of facial hair in an apparent attempt at a beard, and, like his beard, he was carefree, and to those who knew him, it suited him perfectly. He studied the sketches for a few minutes without speaking. There was a gleam in Monet's eyes as he peered over Renoir's shoulder.

"He needs more colour," Renoir finally said. "Mais, oui, c'est merveilleux."

Monet turned to Theo.

"Has he responded to your invitation?"

"I have yet to write him," Theo said.

Monet's mouth dropped a little.

"Do as you wish. But if you believe in his work, you're doing him a disservice by not inviting him."

"May I see them again?" Satan asked, nodding to the portfolio. Renoir handed it to him, and he flipped through it. "I prefer more colour too," he said after a moment, and both Monet and Renoir nodded in agreement. Though Monet was distant from Satan, and Satan knew it.

"Il a besoin de Paris," Monet said.

"Bien sûr," Renoir said.

Theo brought Renoir into the back, discussing one of Renoir's recent works, and Monet and Satan were left alone for a few minutes.

"Theo's brother shows promise," Monet said.

"Mais, oui," Satan said.

Monet leaned in and whispered:

"Perhaps you should leave him alone."

Satan frowned, but Monet was not phased.

"Run along, little rabbit."

Theo and Renoir returned from the back room laughing about something, and Theo turned to Monet.

"I will write to my brother," he said. "I give you my word."

And because Theo was a reasonable man, and because he respected Monet, and Renoir too, especially when it came to art, finally, he wrote to Vincent, suggesting he should come to Paris. To his surprise, Vincent replied, saying he would be there in June.

Hemingway finished his scotch, dropped a few ice cubes into the glass and refilled it.

"I had a hell of a good time in Paris. Hadley was so lovely, and little Bumby was as happy as could be. He spoke only French and he'd look up at me with his full cheeks and say *La vie est belle, Papa*. We didn't have any money, but it didn't matter. I was hungry all the time and thirsty all the time and I worked all the time and it was the happiest time in my life."

"It was similar for Vincent in the beginning," Satan said.

Hemingway took his first sip of his next glass of scotch. He loved the first sip of any new glass and with the smooth, sharp liquid on his tongue he swirled the ice in the glass and squinted and looked through it to the blurred flicker of the flames.

"No better place to be a young artist just starting out."

Satan nodded.

"Vincent lived with Theo in his small apartment at 25 rue Laval. I had begun to form a friendship with Theo. I bought a few works from him, and we discussed art and artists often."

"What about Monet?" Hemingway asked.

"I never saw him again," Satan said. "He went back to Giverny and I remained in Paris."

"And that was that?" Hemingway asked.

Satan nodded.

"Monet was no longer my focus."

"It was Vincent."

"Not yet," Satan said. "Though he was on my radar, and so I decided to stay in Paris a while longer."

❧

"Just look at that, Pierre," Theo said one afternoon at the gallery. He pointed to a Monet on the wall. "Look at the colours, the vibrancy. You cannot tell me there is anything better in contemporary art."

"I couldn't agree more," Satan said. "And what about your brother? How is he settling in?"

"He's doing well, actually," Theo said. "He is practicing at the Cormon and meeting many artists."

"He must be happy."

"If you knew Vincent as I do, Pierre, you would know that's not possible."

Then the front door swung open and in walked a scrawny, fair-skinned figure with stringy orange hair.

"Well, here he is now!" Theo said, arms extended to greet him. "Vincent, this is Pierre Gagnon. We were just talking about you. Pierre was asking about you, and…" he smiled and winked. "Mr. Gagnon is quite interested in what we're doing around here."

Vincent perked up a little and shook Satan's hand and offered a courteous smile.

"Bonjour, Monsieur Gagnon."

Satan was surprised at how soft-spoken Vincent was. He had fierce, sharp eyes, a solid jawline, a prominent nose, and a red, straw-like beard that accentuated the sharpness of his chin. Satan hadn't expected such humility in the voice that came from such a face.

"Your brother speaks highly of your work. Il est très fier de vous. What are you working on now?"

"Self-portraits," Vincent said. His fingernails were dirtied with flecks of dried paint. "It is cheapest that way."

"And those," Satan said, peering down to the two canvases tucked under Vincent's arm. "May I see them?"

Vincent laid the two small canvasses on the counter, both self-portraits, and although they were nicely done, they were dark.

"Lovely indeed," Satan said, without letting on his disappointment. "You've got skill."

"But?" Vincent said.

"Nothing," Satan said. "They're quite dark—morose even—is that what you're trying to achieve?"

Vincent didn't blink.

"No," he said, then: "Yes—maybe—I don't know."

"You've come all the way to Paris," Satan said. "Art here is about colour, about vibrancy."

Vincent clasped his hands and lowered his head, like a boy being scolded.

"Forgive me," Satan said. "It is not my place to criticize your work."

"No," Vincent said. "You are right. I have brought the Hague with me, and for what? I'm here to learn. Everyone has told me the same thing: colour, colour, and more colour! Henri showed me some Japanese prints just today and they are alive with colours." He then offered Satan the kind of smile that comes when a burden has been lifted; a warm, genuine smile. "Thank you, Monsieur Gagnon."

"You helped him along?" Hemingway said.

"That was the extent of my influence," Satan said. "Although he was eccentric in his ways, so too was every other artist in Paris. He did not need me. It was a small community; it was inevitable that he would meet others of the same ilk who would push him also."

"But you still helped him along," Hemingway said.

"He worked within his own free will," Satan said.

Hemingway chuckled.

"Sure, sure."

"I never broke any rules, Ernest."

"Anyone who says that usually has."

Satan grinned a little.

"More bent than broken, Ernest."

Hemingway chuckled again and sipped his scotch.

The line of cabaret dancers moved across the stage, kicking their legs, their hands on their hips, stiffly, as if made of wood, like marionettes. The air was thick with tobacco smoke and there was the smell of sweat and liqueur and the varnish of the hardwood floor, stained with spilled liquor.

"Les belles marionettes! I can see your strings!" Henri de Toulouse-Lautrec shouted, his voice lost amongst the crowd who sang and laughed and drank. He waved his cane in the air like a sword, swinging it wildly about.

Paul Gauguin leaned in close to Vincent.

"He had brittle bones as a child. That's why he's the way he is."

Vincent watched as Lautrec, all of four feet eight inches tall, danced on his chair.

"When he was fourteen, he broke both his legs," Gauguin continued. "The bones stopped growing after that."

"What's that you say of me?" Lautrec said, peering across the table at them.

They both straightened up.

"Nothing," Gauguin said. "I'm just explaining to Vincent your condition. He was too polite to ask."

Lautrec grinned.

"Paul is full of shit!" he said, then he looked at Vincent. "I was *thirteen*." He swung his cane again toward the dancers. "Mes belles marionettes! Let me slice your strings and set you free!"

The whole room was spinning, colours swirling. Gauguin stood up and swayed for a moment before sitting down again. He had a thick head of dark hair, prominent nose and deep-set eyes, which were drunkenly fixed upon Vincent. He flopped his arm around Vincent and pointed over to the bar.

"Can you see how Manet captured it?"

The barmaid was pouring drinks, the huge mirror behind her showing all the room.

"I would have done better," Gauguin said, and he winked.

"But it was *his* vision," Vincent said, winking back. "Not yours. Anyone can paint a bar, or a woman, or a flower."

"Not anyone," Gauguin said.

"Anyone," Vincent said. "What separates it is how *you* see it, and how you paint it as you see it."

"I'm too drunk to talk of such complications," Gauguin said. "But another time, I'm sure you and I will discuss much."

"I hope so," Vincent said.

Lautrec danced on his chair.

"You talk rot," he said to Gauguin. "This is no jungle. This is Manet's world. Not yours." He danced on the chair and waved his cane and yelled over to the bar for more drinks.

"I've no more money," Vincent said.

Gauguin nodded toward Lautrec.

"His family is rich. And he has no children to support—or none that he knows of."

"Yes!" Lautrec said and laughed wildly. "And none to abandon!"

Gauguin swiped at Lautrec's legs and Lautrec waved his

arms out, like a tightrope walker, trying not to fall.

"Here, here," Gauguin said. "Sit down and have a drink."

Lautrec regained his balance, perched his cane against the table and sat in the chair and grabbed the first glass he saw—which was half full of red wine—and drank it down.

"I didn't abandon my children," Gauguin said to Vincent. "They are better off with their mother. What was I to do? Drag them off to this? They wouldn't have survived."

"It's not my business," Vincent said.

Gauguin swiped at Lautrec again.

"Do you see? Vincent is a gentleman. You would do well to learn from him."

Lautrec stared at one of the dancers.

"I should like to have her tonight," he said, his tongue rimming his lips. "We will invite them to our table after the show."

Then a man with curly hair and a thick, curly beard appeared as if out of thin air, pulled up a chair and helped himself to the champagne. He was dressed in a brown suit and brown cravat.

"Well, the hermit appears!" Gauguin said.

"You should do well to keep quiet," the man said.

Gauguin turned to Vincent.

"He is better than all of us," he said. "But keep it quiet. It is a rumor I've started."

"It's true," the man said.

"Vincent," Gauguin said. "Meet Georges Seurat."

Vincent and Seurat shook hands.

"I know your work," Vincent said. "Admirable."

Seurat nodded in appreciation.

"He paints with dots," Lautrec said.

Vincent smiled.

"Yes, I know."

"As children do," Lautrec said. He lifted his cane, held it across the table as a fencer with his foil, and thrusted, dabbing with each word. "Dot, dot, dot!"

"Changing the art world one dot at a time," Gauguin said.

"You dab the paint," Vincent said. "In points, not dots. No

dragging of the brush. It's quite remarkable."

Once again, Seurat nodded and smiled.

"Ok, Vincent, you've made your *point*," Lautrec said, and he and Gauguin laughed.

Seurat rolled his eyes.

"That joke gets worse every time they tell it."

"Point taken," Lautrec said, and they laughed again.

Vincent's eyes were fixed upon Seurat.

"But it must take an eternity."

"Oh, but it does," Seurat said.

"Especially with the size of his canvas," Gauguin added. "Bigger than any of ours."

"Dot, dot, dot!" Lautrec said, his cane knocking over a wine glass.

"Vincent is Theo's brother," Gauguin said, gathering the spilled glass.

"A fine man," Seurat said.

"Vincent is also a painter," Gauguin said.

Vincent blushed.

"I figured that," Seurat said. "Why else would you be sitting here with these fools?"

"I'm at Cormon," Vincent said. "I met Henri there."

"A reputable school," Seurat said. "Good for you. I'm not too sure about Henri, though."

Lautrec waved his cane in Seurat's direction.

"Dot, dot, dot!"

The barmaid appeared with a bottle of champagne, popped the cork and filled everyone's glass, then curtseyed. Lautrec dropped his cane on the table, lifted his glass and drank.

"You are a thing of beauty," he said to the barmaid. "I would not hide you behind the bar as Manet did."

The barmaid had chestnut hair and beautiful full lips and innocent round eyes. Vincent turned to Lautrec.

"Oh, it is she," Lautrec said. "This is the Folies Bergère, is it not? And I should say it again: Manet did you a disservice by hiding you such. I should like to take you home with me tonight and paint you in the nude, revealing all for the world to see. What shall you say?"

The barmaid did not know what to say, and so she simply smiled and returned to the bar.

"That was her?" Vincent said. "Manet's barmaid? Truly?"

Gauguin rolled his eyes.

"Henri thinks every barmaid here is Manet's."

"She will be my barmaid tonight," Lautrec said, reaching across the table for more champagne. "Mark my words."

Vincent turned to Seurat.

"I am interested to see more of your work."

Seurat watched as Lautrec poured the champagne until it spilled over the glass.

"You are welcome to visit any time."

"Ah, the mighty attic!" Lautrec said. "Beware the guard dog—she bites!"

"Ha!" Gauguin howled, catching himself from falling off his chair.

Vincent didn't understand the joke.

"I live with my mother," Seurat said. "And I choose to ignore these buffoons."

"A wise choice," Vincent said, though he could not help but smile.

10

"Paris was everything Theo had promised Vincent it would be," Satan said. "A tightly-knit community of artists who worked and lived and laughed together, and for the few fortunate ones, sold together. At first Vincent struggled to rid his work of the darkness of his Holland days versus his Paris colleagues and their use of vibrant colours. But he had come to Paris for change,

and so he eventually forced upon himself the discomfort of starting anew."

"I went through the same thing in Paris," Hemingway said.
"It took all my being to cleanse myself of Sherwood Anderson."

"Vincent began using brighter colours, daring himself to
omit any blacks, browns, and greys," Satan said. "And what he
found surprised him: the use of colour to emit good feelings. No
darkness, but only light. And something opened inside him, like a
flower blooming, bursting, so much that his brain could not begin
to organize all the possibilities Paris offered."

"Creative overload," Hemingway said.

"He could not begin to categorize all he wanted to do," Satan
said. "His mind swirled, trying to decipher what it was he was
seeing and feeling, and the meticulous calculations on how to
translate it all onto canvas. It was an exciting time."

⁂

"Now all he talks about are Japanese prints," Theo said one morning at the gallery. "You've lit a fire in him, Pierre. He is *catching*
it now."

"Catching what?" Satan asked.

"What everyone else around here is trying to catch—" Theo
said. "*Light*. But he not only catches it, he releases it—even, dare
I say, he *creates* it." He hopped slightly in his excitement now that
he'd said it. "He creates his own light."

Satan shared Theo's excitement but did not show it.

"How is that possible?"

Theo shrugged.

"Perhaps, so new to his craft, he has very little to unlearn, and
so he is doing it without reserve, without hesitation, and because
of that there's a rawness to the work, an inexperience that's not a
weakness but a strength." He halted and snapped his finger. "Give
me a minute." He skipped to the back of the gallery and returned
with an unframed canvas and perched it up upon the counter.
"He brought this to me yesterday. It's a portrait of our friend,

Julien Tanguy. Look at the colours, the thickness of the paint, the rough, bold brushstrokes—the audacity! And yet somehow, it's more alive than anything I've seen. It's quite remarkable, wouldn't you say?"

Satan could not take his eyes off the portrait. The colours, they actually glowed. It was a simple portrait made quite intricately. The man was sitting, hunched a little, his hands in his lap, but he came off the page, as though he were about to sit up, reach out, and touch him.

&

The train moved steadily along. The fire burned bright. Satan tightened the blanket around him. Hemingway poured himself another drink.

"You found your man."

Satan nodded.

"But he was only just beginning; a mere seed in the ground."

Hemingway sipped his scotch.

"So, what'd you do?"

"I released him," Satan said. "And left him alone and watched him grow."

"As the farmer watches his crops," Hemingway said.

Satan smiled.

"Waiting, of course, until they are ready for harvest."

&

It was a warm evening, the stark of the Paris night, the dull shine of the cobblestones in the moonlight. Vincent and Theo had closed the gallery and were walking home through the city. They'd since moved to a bigger apartment, in Montmartre, overlooking Paris, at 54 rue Lepic. Vincent stopped, packed his pipe, struck a match, and lit it. The smoke curled around him.

"I cannot focus, Theo. I am too excited with too many things. Paris is so different than the Hague. Where the Hague offered truth, Paris offers hope. How I've been colourblind! Now I see colours I'd never imagined. I may just abandon my charcoals altogether, even for composition. You must attack it with colour!" He allowed himself a quick breath before he continued. "I've been given a new set of eyes, Theo. Everything is alive and so vivid it screams. Is there any better gift a painter can receive than the gift of sight?"

They took no notice of the light-footed black cat skipping in and out of the shadows, keeping pace. Theo put his arm over his brother's shoulder.

"I'm glad to see this energy. I've not seen you like this in years."

"I am reborn, brother," Vincent said. He turned to a garden of lilacs and stopped, as if ready to bow down and worship them. "Look at these. How can I ever focus enough to get it all down— all the beauty of the world—the way it is meant to be painted?" He pointed to a windowsill, to a potted plant, grey in the moonlight. "It's not just a flowerpot, but a mastery of greens and blues and yellows, and more greens again. Can you see it, Theo? Can you see all of those colours as I do? Am I painting? Are they painting? Look what they do with light and colour! Look what they dare to do! I've had it all wrong. *We* have all had it wrong— every painter who has come before! I tell you, Theo, this is a revolution! Is this not the best time to be alive?"

Theo chuckled.

"It is, brother. And I know how you feel; Paris does that to everyone. Once your mind settles, you will focus. When you focus, you will work. It's that simple."

"It's anything but simple," Vincent said.

"Then organize it," Theo said. "So that even if you fail to settle, you'll at least have a foundation for which to begin, a starting point."

"With no finish line in sight!" Vincent laughed.

"Time and chance will provide you with a finish line," Theo said.

Satan stared into the fire. The wood sizzled. His early memories of Vincent had re-energized him. He slipped his feet out from the bottom of the blanket and stretched his toes to the fire. His toes were long and wrinkly and well-groomed.

"Truly, after I first laid eyes on that portrait of Julien Tanguy, he dazzled me daily. His work before Paris was muted, but here, now, it began to sing."

Hemingway nodded in agreement.

"Paintings can do that. Andrea del Sarto's *Portrait of a Woman* did it for me. It's in the Prado; people think I went to Madrid for the bullfights, but I really went to see her." He gulped the last of the scotch, quite unlike how he had instructed Satan to drink it, then poured another glass.

Satan raised a hand for Mr. Gregory, who was quick to his side.

"Fetch me my medicine."

Mr. Gregory left the car then returned a few minutes later with a small wooden cigar box, which he placed in Satan's lap. Satan opened the box, revealing a dozen perfectly rolled joints. He plucked one from the box.

"What have you got there?" Hemingway asked.

"My medicine," Satan said. "Would you care for some?"

Hemingway held up his glass of scotch.

"I'm too loyal to betray this friendship."

Satan placed the joint to his lips and, like clockwork, Mr. Gregory flicked a lighter and lit it. Satan sat back and exhaled a smooth blue stream of smoke that hovered along the ceiling. He sat in silence and smoked, and it relaxed him, relieving his aching body, his face softening a little. But after a few minutes the tightness struck him like a cramp, sharp and severe in his lungs, and he began to cough and hack, and he curled forward, his whole face cringed red.

Hemingway turned to Mr. Gregory, who was standing at the other end of the car.

"You got a doctor on this train?"

Mr. Gregory scuttled off to find a doctor and returned a short while later with an old man with a kind and sad face. He and Hemingway helped Satan to his sleeping quarters and into bed.

"He should rest," the doctor said.

Satan shook his head defiantly.

"You don't look good," Hemingway said. He turned to the doctor. "He got an ulcer, does he?"

"No. It's coming from his side, under the ribs."

"Maybe a bad bit of food?"

The doctor rubbed the top of his head in thought.

"I don't think so."

"Then what is it?"

The doctor motioned for Hemingway to follow him into the corridor. Hemingway squeezed himself against the wall and the window of the narrow space, the bulk of his shoulders squished in discomfort as the train rocked along.

The doctor was a small man and in the narrow passage he still had room to move.

"The smoking hasn't helped his lungs. But the truth is, I just don't know—I've never seen this before. He's a demon, *the* demon in fact. Demons don't get sick. Not like this."

Dawn cast a low grey light over the land as the train moved along. Satan lay in bed. He could hear a tapping sound from the main car, and it was only once he stepped into the corridor that he realized it was the tapping of a typewriter. He smelled weed smoke, mixed with the smoke of a newly lit fire. Hemingway had pulled a small table over to the fireplace and had lifted a chair and had placed it on the table. On the chair was his typewriter, his *Royal Quiet Deluxe*, chest high, and he stood in front of it, tapping away, a pair of round spectacles sitting low on his nose. Satan flopped into his chair and wrapped the blanket around himself.

"I heard you coughing during the night," Hemingway said.

His eyes were bloodshot. "A shot of whiskey would've taken care of that."

Satan sighed, winded by the short walk to the end of the car. He noticed his cigar box, open, at Hemingway's feet.

"I helped myself," Hemingway said. "Never tried it before. Been going hard at it all night. Stuff opens the senses. Hope you don't mind."

"Not at all," Satan said. "I am surprised you have never tried it before."

Hemingway shrugged.

"I had plenty of morphine in Italy when I busted up my knee as a kid but never liked it much. With morphine everything goes numb, the sharpness dulls." He peered down at the cigar box. "But with that stuff it's different. You're still here, and everything is more present than it is, sharper than it is. If I'd had that instead of morphine, I might've written instead of following my pecker and wasting my time lovesick over a damn nurse." He paused. "But I got a good book out of it."

"A fine book," Satan said.

"All I'm saying is that I could've written more, should've written more," Hemingway said. "That's the torment of this place —you're able to look back and when you do there's regret, and guilt, which I suspect is eating you a bit too."

Satan said nothing.

"I figured it out last night," Hemingway said. "You needed Van Gogh to be a suicide."

Satan managed a grin.

"There are some rules even I must follow, Ernest."

Hemingway lifted the chair and typewriter off the table, slid the table aside, and sat in the chair and adjusted himself, his body snug between the armrests.

"That's why you're going to see him, isn't it? Don't tell me you've got a conscience."

Satan said nothing.

Hemingway huffed.

"Well, I'll be damned." He took a squeeze from the wineskin.

"So, what about me?"

Satan shook his head then curled under the blanket and coughed deeply, painfully. When he emerged, his eyes were watery.

"That was all you, Ernest."

Hemingway was silent.

"I am sorry to disappoint you," Satan said.

"Ah hell, it's on me," Hemingway said. "No regrets." He thought about it, then shrugged. "Well, maybe a few. The lack of work. Leaving the party early. But ask any suicide and he'll tell you the same thing." He paused, his eyes glazed over, and Satan knew that in his mind he was elsewhere. "I remember everything about that morning," Hemingway said. "The house smelled of summer, of the timber beams and the pine forest. Out the big window the sky was pink and then the sun appeared over the mountains. The mountains reminded me of Spain, especially in the early morning, and it saddened and frightened me knowing I'd never see them again. The valley was dark and cool and the dew on the trees was sparkling, not brightly, but subtly, in the grey morning light. I'd written of such a scene many times before and I watched as the sun rose clear of the mountains and just the flint of pink remained, nestled lightly on the mountaintops. High overhead the sky was clear and cold and blue, as it only is in the morning. I rubbed the sleep from my eyes and stood looking out the window and my chest rumbled with it, with the Black Ass."

Satan listened intently. It was soothing, how Hemingway spoke.

"Mary was asleep upstairs. The house was still. I listened to the house creak. I wished I'd written of that, of the solitude of the creaking of the house, and of the quiet too, and of how I'd felt so small and so big within it all. I opened the closet and pulled the shotgun and loaded both barrels and clicked them shut. It was loud, the clicking, in the quiet of the house. Then I stepped away from the window, to the left, and crouched down onto my knees. One of my favourite cats, Big Boy Peterson, was there, bright-eyed, back arched and tail up. I patted him roughly on the scruff of the neck, right where he liked it, and he purred loud, like lion cubs purr on the Serengeti when they wrestle and play with each other to prepare for adulthood, when they must kill to survive. But they're just playing and they're happy as when children play, and they caw and growl and purr so loud you can hear them from a distance. Big Boy Peterson was purring like that, and I shooed him away; I didn't want him to talk me out of it. I placed the stock against the floor and leaned my forehead to the barrels and worked my hands down the gun until I found both triggers. Then, thinking of the mountains again and how sharp and lovely the blue of the sky, the Black Ass rumbled, and I closed my eyes and pressed firmly down and that was that."

Satan stared into the fire.

"It was a fine death, Ernest."

There was a long silence between them, just the crack and snap of the last bits of burnt kindling and the sounds of the train as it moved steadily along. Satan coughed, fighting it, smothering it with the blanket.

"This business of being ill, it is rather unpleasant."

"It stinks," Hemingway said.

Morning had arrived. Endless fields stretched the length of the horizon, grey as ash as the gloom settled over the land.

Hemingway glanced down at the cigar box.

"I only smoked one and then started with one true sentence and haven't stopped since."

"And Ms. Rhys?" Satan said. "How is she?"

"She got off at Cabo San Vito last night."

"I was asleep," Satan said.

"Can't believe you didn't hear her," Hemingway said. "She was cursing me up and down. All I could do was laugh. I tried not to, but the stuff was in me and I couldn't stop laughing. The more she cursed the more I laughed."

Satan grinned.

"You were medicated, Ernest."

"I guess I was. She'll get over it. I gave her the name of a good gin joint that'll keep her busy till I get there." He turned and gently placed two logs over the burnt kindling, which collapsed the kindling onto the coals. He knelt low and blew on the coals and the smoke curled and the logs ignited. "Tell me more about Van Gogh."

"Where did we end last night?"

"Paris," Hemingway said.

"Yes, yes," Satan said, but he took to coughing again. He pulled out his handkerchief from under the blanket and hawked and spit into it.

Hemingway leaned over.

"You want me to get the doc?"

Satan shook his head and took a moment, waiting it out. When it passed, he sighed, relieved.

"Not long after the portrait of Julien Tanguy, Vincent did a study of a sunflower. He had just begun the first of thirty floral works he would do that summer. Theo had convinced him to do these, saying perhaps he could sell them easier than his portraits. Tanguy ran an art supplies shop and often took paintings as payment from artists who could not otherwise afford supplies. He had recently placed one of Vincent's paintings in his shop window and this had given Vincent an instant boost, which was followed by an urgency in which he set about to explore colours further." He coughed into the rag then wiped his lips. "Vincent was not exceptionally talented, no more than any of his contemporaries, and in some instances, less. But it was the rawness of his energy, the purity of his vision, which drove him forward in his work. And now he was part of the Paris scene, part of a group, and he was the hardest worker of them all."

"Art isn't just about talent," Hemingway said. "It's about how much you can bleed."

"Vincent bled, to be certain," Satan said. He leaned forward, his palms open to the fire, feeling the heat as the logs began to burn. "And for a time, he was, perhaps, happy, whether he realized it or not. Particularly when Julien Tanguy decided to exhibit their work."

11

Julien Tanguy had acquired a small collection from Vincent and his friends and one day he offered to host a street-side exhibit outside his shop at 14 rue Clauzel. In all, there were about thirty canvases, each one propped up outside his shop along the curb and on easels. He'd also set up chairs and a table with wine and cheese. Vincent and his friends spied from a café across the street, eagerly watching as passersby stopped to look.

"There!" Vincent said, wide-eyed. "That fellow seems interested." Nobody spoke, not until the man turned to another painting, and Vincent did his best to mask his disappointment. "Oh look, now he is considering yours, Paul. I think he likes it. Look at how he tilts his head. Très bien!"

The youngest of the group, a teenager, Émile Bernard, took a gulp of wine.

"Émile," Vincent said. "And yours too. It pleases the eye to be sure."

"I'd rather it pleased the wallet," Émile said.

Vincent spotted Pierre Gagnon strolling toward them, and he sat up and waved him over.

"Bonjour, Pierre. We have an exhibit at Julien's."

"How wonderful," Satan said.

"We've sold nothing," Seurat said flatly.

Satan hauled a chair over to their table and sat.

"Vincent," Lautrec said, tugging at his shirt. "That large fellow has been standing in front of one of yours for some time now."

"He's talking to Julien about it," Gauguin added.

The man they were watching was none other than Mr. Graves, whom Satan had sent to stand for a period of time and appear interested in Vincent's work, only to turn to look at another.

Satan still held his open palms to the fire.

"I wanted to provide him with the proverbial nibble, to push him further in his determination."

"You put the first bait around the shank of the hook," Hemingway said. "Something small, like sardines. A big marlin will nibble the bait before he takes the main bait, which is always bigger than the sardines; the head of a tuna that covers the entire hook. After the sardines are eaten the marlin is ready to take the tuna and he'll swallow the hook and then you let him run until the hook is well in his belly and you've got him."

"It was too early for that," Satan said. "But yes, the bait was in the water."

"The small bait," Hemingway said. "The sardines."

Satan sighed.

"Vincent was not a fish, Ernest."

"But you were fishing nonetheless," Hemingway said. "You were out there with your line, ready to take your prize."

"Vincent was a prize, yes," Satan said. "I will give you that."

"And you baited him," Hemingway said.

Satan sighed again.

"Yes."

Hemingway poked at the logs so that the flames grew, and the coals glowed.

"Then he's a fish," he said. His eyes were still glossy. He poked at the logs again. "It's a damned fine analogy."

Later in the evening, after Tanguy's exhibit, Vincent and Theo went to the Restaurant du Chalet on the Avenue de Clichy. The server had brought them wine and they were waiting for their food.

"I don't understand it," Vincent said. "How does nothing sell? Even but for a few francs; surely my work is worth that." He took a sip of wine. "Perhaps an exhibit in a restaurant like this or a café would generate more interest. Émile thought it a brilliant idea."

"Émile Bernard?" Theo said.

"Yes."

"He's so young."

"Not yet twenty," Vincent said. "But what confidence! And it is a true confidence, not naivety, I am sure of it. He looks up to me, yes, but Theo, I learn much from him too."

"That's rare in one so young," Theo said, nodding.

"He is contagious," Vincent said. "When he talks, I listen."

"And he likes the restaurant idea?"

"Very much. He likes all my ideas. And I like his. He is bold in his expression; unapologetic. I wish I was the same." He paused. "But the restaurant idea—it could work. Patrons could sit and eat and not be forced to look at the work, but be surrounded by it, so that they can see the paintings as they're meant to be seen. *Seen*, not studied and picked apart."

Theo looked around the restaurant.

"Why not do it here?"

Vincent looked around now too.

"This could work."

"You should talk to Etienne," Theo said. "I'm sure he would let you do it."

"If not," Vincent said. "Then maybe Chez Bataille?"

"Talk to Etienne," Theo said.

Vincent sighed heavily.

"Maybe it's a foolish idea."

Theo sipped his wine, then looked his brother in the eye. "No idea to promote your work is foolish. Keep at it, Vincent. Your time will come."

Vincent sighed again.

"Not in my *life*time."

"Then you'll have to settle for immortality. Your paintings will be around long after you, Vincent."

Vincent smiled.

"Not if nobody buys them."

"They will hang somewhere," Theo said. "In someone's home somewhere. It may not be the Louvre, but they will find a wall to call home, and someone will look at them and love them. Think of my shelf of books at the flat. There are unknown authors who occupy space next to Hugo and Shakespeare. And they will be there forever. It makes no difference if the whole world never knows who you are, Vincent, but somebody will, and you only need one to endure, to live on forever. Immortality is not determined by the number of those who remember you."

Vincent lowered his head, as if ashamed.

"Why are you so good to me, Theo?"

Theo saw the server coming with their food and he slid his wine glass aside as their plates were placed in front of them—mutton and potatoes and green beans. He waited for the server to leave before he spoke.

"I believe in you, Vincent. I believe in your work. And if I can't believe in my own brother then who can I believe in? You paint for you. Lose yourself in your work. Nothing else matters." He looked down at his plate, at the potatoes steaming, and his mouth watered, and he smiled. "Except for this—at the moment this meal is all I care about; I'm starving."

⁂

Vincent painted and sketched all day and every day. When he painted, he no longer used black or brown or grey which had dominated his Holland days. Now he used variations of the boldest colours: bright shades of green, blue, yellow, and red. His brushstrokes became more spontaneous, more alive, and he slapped the paint on, layering it thick so that it popped from the canvas.

Within a month he'd completed several floral studies, and one day he lined them up, one by one, perched against the wall, to see how his palette had evolved. Theo had come into the flat. He'd often referred to these studies as Vincent's *finger exercises*.

"Look from left to right," Vincent said. "Can you see it?"

Theo crossed his arms and smiled.

"It's like watching a sunrise."

"Yes indeed!" Vincent said.

A spider crawled across the ceiling and settled directly over them, seeing too how each canvas was brighter than the next, and how even the room on the side with the more recent works was brighter than the other side of the room, and how this very light would one day brighten Capital City.

Theo grabbed one of the canvasses.

"It has real weight to it. How much paint did you use?"

"Too much and not enough," Vincent said.

"Monticelli would be proud," Theo said.

Vincent was nodding, his eyes on the canvas.

"I sometimes think I am continuing him."

"Every artist is but a continuation of those who came before," Theo said.

❧

"No man is an island," Hemingway said.

"Touché," Satan grinned. "And you, Ernest? Whom did you follow?"

"No one," Hemingway said. "I should've said *not many men are islands.* There's me, Shakespeare, Mark Twain, and that other fellow, the rough one. Bukowski."

"You have met him?"

"I know him well," Hemingway said. "I like him. There's no bullshit. I like that in a man. And he likes me. We get along well. We box. He's got a heavy left hook but he's slow and clumsy as an ape. But he can write." He squeezed a mouthful of wine. "Every artist starts with the same thing. Painters have paint. Writers have the alphabet. What separates the good from the bad is talent, or lack of it."

"What about bleeding?" Satan asked. There was a slight smirk at the corners of his mouth.

"Anyone can bleed a bit," Hemingway said.

"Vincent had much talent," Satan said.

"Yes, he did."

"The point is," Satan said. "Vincent had begun his time in Paris on a high." The stitch in his side had returned and he was unable to get comfortable in his chair, shifting about, unable to sit still for more than a few seconds at a time. "But after two years it had consumed him like it consumed you."

"There's no place like it," Hemingway said. He placed a third log on the fire, on top of the two burning logs, which were now half burnt, their undersides glowing in the coals. "She took my heart and she never gave it back."

Satan grunted and shifted in his chair.

"You are mistaken, Ernest. Paris does not take your heart. She gives you a piece of hers and you are left with two."

The music hall was alive. A *demimondaine* with blonde hair and big blue eyes sat on Lautrec's lap, her am on his shoulder, holding a glass of champagne. She towered over him, and every now and then Lautrec would turn and press his face into her bosom and she would laugh and slap him playfully.

"Are you all painters?" the girl asked.

"Some of us," Vincent said.

Lautrec took a drink straight from the bottle of champagne, then pointed at Vincent.

"He is a master."

"A master?" the girl said. She held her champagne glass up, as if to balance it, level with her chest.

"His name is *Monsieur Sérieux*," Lautrec grinned.

The girl perked up.

"Vraiment?"

Lautrec nodded.

The girl giggled.

"Non!"

"Ask him," Lautrec said. "What's the trouble, Vincent? Why

the sad face?"

"No reason," Vincent said.

"He disapproves of you," Gauguin said, and Vincent shot him a look.

Lautrec peered across the table.

"Is it true?"

"Of course it is," Seurat said.

Lautrec leaned forward and the girl hopped off his lap. He reached across the table with his cane and tapped at Vincent's arm.

"You've been drunk for three days," Vincent said.

"And what business is that of yours?"

"It is all our business," Vincent said. "When one of us falters we all falter."

Lautrec's jaw dropped. His eyes were swimming.

"I've faltered? How?"

"You haven't worked all week," Vincent said. "We promised Julien a new collection to show by month's end."

Lautrec sat back in his chair and laughed.

"Have a drink, Vincent."

"I've had enough tonight, thank you."

Lautrec slammed the champagne bottle down and it bubbled over onto the table.

"Have a drink," he said, then slid the bottle toward him. Vincent caught it before it slid off the table. Gauguin snatched the bottle from Vincent's grip and gulped down the champagne. Seurat turned to Vincent.

"It does not concern you, Vincent."

"But it does," Vincent said. "We are a collective, are we not?"

"Indeed, we are," Seurat said. "But we are all equal. Lautrec is not to be governed by anyone but himself."

"But his work—"

"Not your concern, Vincent."

The girl who had sat on Lautrec's lap now danced beside the table. Gauguin stood and took her in his arms and twirled her around, then they fell backwards, over Vincent's legs and onto the floor where they remained, on their backs, she on top of him, laughing. Lautrec crawled under the table and emerged, then hollered toward the bar. "More champagne!"

"Now that would make a fine painting," Seurat said, peering down at Vincent's feet, at Gauguin and Lautrec and the girl, her hair soaked with champagne.

Vincent did not laugh.

"Oh, lighten up!" Lautrec said. He snatched the bottle from Gauguin, got to his feet and, like a child, sat upon Vincent's lap, his feet dangling. "Please, Vincent, for our friendship, a drink."

Vincent sighed and took a swig from the bottle. Lautrec slapped him hard but lovingly on the back, then, cane in hand, he hobbled over to a woman at a nearby table and struck up a conversation. Vincent watched as they talked and laughed and drank until a sharply-dressed gentleman in a top hat approached the table and stood over Lautrec, who began a strained conversation—Vincent didn't know of what—that appeared to anger the man, and he took Lautrec by the shirt and lifted him off the ground. Lautrec, his legs flapping about, hit the man twice in the side of his face with his cane, the top hat tumbling off his head, and he dropped Lautrec, who straightened his tie and made his way back over to Vincent's table, where he sat, winded, and drank down a glass of champagne.

Gauguin had a big grin.

"What was that all about?"

They watched as the man gathered himself at his table, a welt already forming above his eye, and sat opposite the woman who hadn't moved, frozen, not quite knowing what had just happened.

"I asked him how much it would cost to take his lady friend home tonight," Lautrec said, laughing. "He said it was his wife. To which I said: 'Wonderful, a cheaper fare, I presume?'"

Vincent's face flushed with embarrassment.

Seurat worked his fingers through his beard.

"A fine spectacle," he said.

"A spectacle, yes," Vincent said. "But there is nothing fine about it."

The following day was cold and grey.

"They are pitiful," Vincent said to Theo. They were on their way home, strolling through Montmartre, at the base of the Stone Quarry with the windmill on the hill, which Vincent had painted. He now felt he'd painted everything in Paris. Theo had a brown paper bag with a baguette and a block of cheese. Vincent carried two bottles of cheap red wine, one in each hand. The park wound through a meadow of crab-apple trees. The trees were black and bare and the crookedness of their branches had caught Vincent's eye, how their sharpness made the sky behind them more blue than grey, but to change it, to brighten it entirely, like Monet, the grey-blue to violet, the branches layered thick to give dimension, to give them life. He paused, imagining it. Theo was patient. It was not unusual for Vincent to lose himself in a thought and Theo knew it was best to give him a moment and he would be back, which he did, and Vincent was. "They struggle to sell and so they go out and drink and take women in the night, then rise and work then do it all over again. It's shameful."

"Now Vincent," Theo said. "You've been with them on such nights. You've drunk and taken women too."

"I'm not talking about that," Vincent quickly said. "It's what comes from it. The work suffers. There is no focus. Lautrec takes a different woman every night. He could be Rembrandt if only he could control his *brush*."

Theo laughed, his breath puffing into the cold air.

"Your focus is admirable, brother, and no doubt it will get you further than most, but you can't change them. It's just their way. They love many things. There's nothing wrong with that." He shivered and quickened his pace, paying no attention to the blackbird that flew alongside them, tree to tree.

Vincent had seen it, how different the tree looked when the blackbird settled on a branch, and how the whole tree had changed with the bird in it, the focus no longer the tree, but the bird, and how the tree protected it, mothered it on her branch, which became an arm and hands, and her trunk her body, strong and curvy and beautiful.

"It is not possible to have love and art at once," he said. "Real love makes one disgusted with art. You must dedicate yourself entirely to either art or love, not both."

"What about Agostina?" Theo said, mentioning a woman Vincent had recently been involved with.

Vincent grinned.

"My dear Theo, that's not love."

"Don't you think you're getting a little carried away?" Theo said.

"Not in the least."

"Then it's their work that suffers—not yours," Theo said. "Worry only about yourself. You've got too big a heart, Vincent. You need to be more selfish."

"I am plenty selfish," Vincent said, raising his voice. "I don't care for any of them. Not anymore."

Theo stopped and turned and faced him.

"Calm down, Vincent. These are your friends. They may not have your focus but they're still artists, just like you."

"They are nothing like me."

Theo offered a sympathetic smile.

"Think at what you've accomplished here, at how your work has evolved. You've an unrecognizable palette now! Paris has treated you well, and so have your friends."

"I'm done with Paris," Vincent said. "I'm leaving."

"To go where?" Theo said. "Surely not back to Holland. You might as well tuck your paints away for good."

"Not Holland," Vincent said. "*Arles.*"

12

The three logs burned as one bright flame; the two in the coals had collapsed and settled under the weight of the third log, its underside glowing orange now too. Hemingway unbuttoned his shirt at the top, his chest moist with sweat.

"Two hearts, you say."

"Two hearts beating in his chest now as one," Satan said.

"That's one too many for any man."

"Indeed."

"A moveable feast with heartburn," Hemingway said.

Satan chuckled and then coughed until his eyes watered. Mr. Gregory stepped between them, holding the cellphone. Satan shooed him with his hand.

"What is it now?"

Mr. Gregory offered the phone.

"Mr. Graves again, sir."

✤

Mr. Gordon and Ms. Victoria made their way through a crowded corner of Capital City's Little Italy, near the river's edge; the rotten smell of the water, the pungent sulfuric steam from the manholes, the humidity, thick in the air, and the sour stench of sweat and filth of those who moved about, without expression.

"There," Mr. Gordon said, pointing to an unassuming pizzeria squeezed between a rundown copper flower shop and a dusty pawnbroker. They skipped across the street.

Behind the counter stood a greasy, ogre-like man chewing on an unlit cigar. He had a flabby round face and a double chin that sagged to his shirt collar—a tight, grease-stained t-shirt underneath a yellowed apron smeared with tomato sauce. His eyes scanned the length of Ms. Victoria and he grinned, showing a missing front tooth, and licked his lips without shame.

"Capone," Mr. Gordon said.

The man walked to the back then returned a moment later.

"This way."

They stepped behind the counter, slipped past the heat of the ovens that smelled of pepperoni and onions, and down the narrow staircase to the basement and into a musty room lit by a single lightbulb hanging from the low ceiling.

Alphonse Capone sat at a round table with six other men, each holding their hand of cards. Capone had thinning black hair and big cheeks and blank, wide-open eyes. He was dressed in a three-piece pinstripe suit which accentuated the dinginess of the room. His jacket had been flung over the chair behind him. His vest bulged from his bulk. The table was filled with poker chips, overfilled ashtrays, beer bottles, half-drunk tumblers and dirtied paper plates with remnants of pizza slices. Piles of unassembled pizza boxes were stacked along the walls.

Capone placed his cards face-down on the table, cut a cigar, and lit it.

"Good day," Mr. Gordon said. His huge teeth made him look like he was grinning, which annoyed Capone.

Capone sucked on his cigar.

"What do ya want?"

"I think you know," Mr. Gordon said.

Capone sniggered.

"A bit nervous for the royal visit, is he?" He sucked on his cigar and, making sure he was noticed, he ran his eyes slowly up and down Ms. Victoria. "Ladies first."

Ms. Victoria straightened her shoulders, inflating her chest, which made Capone smirk. From his cigar, a cloud of brown smoke hovered just above him, which, in the light of the hanging bulb, gave him a halo.

"I need fire," she said.

"Fire?"

"Yes," she said. She crossed her arms, squishing her cleavage together, and waited until Capone looked her in the eye. "Lava and fire."

"How much fire?"

"Enough to blacken the air," she said. "Controlled fires placed about the city, lit at specific times and burning as long as he's here."

"And the lava?"

"Truckloads," she said. "In the river, ongoing and discreet. I want the river to boil." She uncrossed her arms, revealing her cleavage again. "Can you do it?"

"Darlin," Capone said, scanning her body again, "I can do whatever I want." He thought a moment. "A pipeline would be better than trucks."

Mr. Gordon grunted.

Capone sighed. "And you?"

"Halt all trash collection," Mr. Gordon said. "Let it pile up. Let it stink."

"Why don't I burn it too?" Capone said. "It'll smoke good, and smell like shit."

Mr. Gordon turned to Ms. Victoria, nodded, then back to Capone.

"That would work."

Capone sucked on his cigar.

"What else?" he said. "You didn't come all this way to ask me about fires and trash."

Mr. Gordon cleared his throat a little to make way for the words that were to come.

"Capital City has to be stripped of all colours. Anything vibrant must go."

"The Boulevard?"

Mr. Gordon clasped his hands and paused.

"What'd I tell ya?" Capone said, turning to a thin, rather sickly-looking man beside him.

He turned back to Mr. Gordon.

"Spit it out."

Mr. Gordon paused, searching for the best way to say it,

and in doing so, inadvertently brought more attention to it. He cleared his throat again.

"Destroy it," he finally said.

Capone plucked the cigar from his mouth and shot forward, his halo whooshing away.

"Say that again?"

"You heard me," Mr. Gordon said, his voice cracking.

"Say it again," Capone said.

"Scrape it bare."

Capone's lips puckered.

"That'd be like burning the Sistine Chapel," he said. "You prance in here with your little horns and your shiny shoes thinking we ain't cultured. You ever been to Italy?"

"I don't presume anything," Mr. Gordon said. "And yes, I have."

"Then you should know we're the most cultured people who ever lived."

"You shan't discount the Greeks," Ms. Victoria said.

"Fuck the Greeks," Capone said. He glared at Mr. Gordon. "You demons think you're so special, don't you? You and Miss Titties here. Yet you have no problem asking me to do something like that." He took a moment to think it over. All he could see were Mr. Gordon's teeth. "Yeah, you keep grinnin," he said. "This ain't gonna be cheap."

"I assure you," Mr. Gordon said, doing his best to close his lips over his teeth. "You will be compensated accordingly."

Capone sucked on his cigar, his eyes shifting about. Then, finally, almost reluctantly, he nodded in agreement.

"Good," Mr. Gordon said. "I'll have a contract drawn up straight away."

Capone puffed out his chest and crossed his arms.

"I want this district."

Mr. Gordon frowned.

"But it's already yours."

"I run it, sure," Capone said. "I wanna *own* it."

"That's impossible."

"Like I said, it ain't gonna be cheap."

Ms. Victoria stepped in, and Capone turned to her.

"Please," she said.

"Darlin, no offence, but this is between me and Mr. Teeth."

"You know we don't work that way," Mr. Gordon said.

"I don't give a shit," Capone said. "Let me tell you how I work: You come in here with your panties in a knot, asking me to do something like that. You have no idea the ramifications of this, how the city will look at me once I'm done. This ain't no regular job, and regular compensation ain't gonna cut it. You don't like it then go back and tell your boss I'm out. And you know as well as I do, I can shut this city down if I want."

Ms. Victoria crossed her arms again.

"I'll make a call."

"You do that," Capone said, a new halo of smoke around his head. "And tell that old prick Graves I said hello."

⁂

"What do you mean, *own it?*" Satan said into the phone. He sighed. "Tell Mr. Gordon to give him half—his borough to the East End. Nothing more." His chest suddenly tightened, and he dropped the phone and burst into a coughing fit. Mr. Gregory sat him upright and wiped the blood from off his lip. After it had passed, Satan attempted a grin for Hemingway.

"Forgive me, Ernest. I have not been a very gracious host. Are you hungry?"

"I could eat a fuckin horse," Hemingway said. He leaned forward and poked the fire, breaking the burnt logs so the top log crumbled onto the burning coals.

Satan glanced down at the cigar box.

"It entices the appetite."

Hemingway's stomach grumbled.

"Entices? Ha! More like launches an all-out assault."

It wasn't long before the dining table was filled with an assortment of eggs, bacon, sausage, beans, toast, and fruit.

Hemingway's mouth watered at the sight and smell of the food. He made his way over to the table and sat. There was a dish with scrambled eggs and he scooped a pile onto his plate, and then a big spoonful of beans, the syrup mixing a little into the eggs. Then, using his fingers, he picked a few sausages, a few strips of bacon, and two pieces of toast.

It was morning now, and a grey gloom had settled in. Hemingway peered out the train window as he ate. It was as though a varnish had been painted over everything, a dimness that blurred the vastness of the barren landscape. The only indication that the land stretched as far as it did was the faint line of the horizon, arcing over the darkness, the land and sky nearly indiscernible. Then there was a break in the land, a divide, and the train rattled as it passed over a bridge that crossed a huge gorge. Hemingway stood and looked down into the gorge; a black void, where, far below, snaked a thin orange river of lava. The window fogged from the rising steam and he wiped it with his hand.

"That's gotta be what, six hundred feet down?"

Satan moved slowly across the car to the table. He grunted when he sat, then grunted again as he reached for a piece of toast.

"Seven hundred twenty, to be precise."

Hemingway returned to his seat once the train had cleared the gorge and they were on solid ground again. He poured a cup of coffee and nodded toward the window.

"Boy, you feel it, eh? That black ass gloom gets into your bones just by looking at it."

"Indeed," Satan said. He took a moment, relieved to be sitting again. "It is unavoidable."

Hemingway leaned low over his plate and shoved the food into his mouth. He talked with his mouth full.

"That's one thing I miss: the sunrise. I used to love the morning. I'd get up early no matter what, no matter the madness of the night before." He took a quick sip of coffee. "There was always something new if you woke up early enough, before everyone else, in the quiet of the early morning; something fresh and hopeful." He nodded to the window again. "But that out there? It's the opposite." He slurped a forkful of beans into his mouth, the syrup catching the hairs of his upper lip. Then he tapped the side of his plate with his fork. "Damned good breakfast."

Satan adjusted himself in the chair. He took a nibble of his toast and chewed slowly.

"I am curious to hear your view on what is happening to me."

Hemingway put down his fork.

"To be honest, I don't know what to make of it. You were fine yesterday?"

"I have been fine forever," Satan said. "Now I feel as though I have stepped out of my usual self and into a heavier, hollow version."

Hemingway shrugged.

"Could be anything. You say you're cramping? Could be dysentery."

"A human condition," Satan said.

"I don't know any demon diseases," Hemingway said. "You have kidneys, don't you? What about kidney stones? I had them once. Feels like you're pissing a cactus."

Satan took another nibble of toast, chewed, and cringed as he swallowed. He did this until the toast was gone, and then he sat back, watching Hemingway eat another plateful of food and drink two more cups of coffee. Satan struggled to stand, gripping hard the edge of the table to pull himself to his feet, then made his way over to the fire and dropped into his chair.

"Whatever you've got, it isn't good," Hemingway said. "Something's got itself into you."

Satan sighed heavily, glad to be in front of the fire again. Hemingway squirted a quick drink from the wineskin to rinse his mouth from the coffee. The fire sparked and cracked and spit, and they sat, watching it.

"Where were we?" Satan asked.

"Arles," Hemingway said.

"Ah yes, Arles." He straightened up a little. "Vincent arrived in February. The sky was grey. The trees were bare. The ground was covered in dirty snow. It was not an ideal introduction for a man who had been mesmerized by colour and had gone there to explore it further."

13

VINCENT TOOK A ROOM IN THE HOTEL RESTAURANT CARREL at 30 rue de la Cavalerie. He went on daily walks to scout the town and its outskirts, but it was cold and windy and without any colour and it affected him more and more with each passing day. The first week he rose with vigour at dawn, when the air was crisp and the mud crunched under his feet, his eyes wide and hopeful. He sketched often, but in the beginning painted less and less; there seemed to be no colour in anything. And every day that followed he slept in a little longer, that by the end of the first month he did not rise until late in the morning, when the sun was high in the sky, and soon he became less cheerful, less hopeful, and there was no skip in his step as there'd been that first week.

But spring soon arrived, and as Arles awoke from its slumber, so too did Vincent. He became cheerful again. He rose early and marched through the town, easel and canvas strapped to his back, paints and brushes in hand, his face hidden under his straw hat, the pipe jutting out. The locals quietly chuckled as he strode by, calling him the little Dutch soldier, for he marched like he was off to war.

Arles soon began living up to its promise; everything Vincent saw was instantly a work of art. One day while walking down a cypress-lined dirt road of fields and farmhouses he stopped to look at a brick shed, a rotted tree, and the sky. The red of the brick next to the black of the branches against the pure open blue of the sky was all so beautifully simple and completely and perfectly balanced, indeed, already framed for a canvas. He made a quick charcoal sketch and carried on. He saw everything this way now. It was the same with the people he saw. He was especially attracted to those closest to the land—peasants and labourers and everyday workers. And he sketched and painted as many as he could. But then one day someone caught his eye more than any other.

There was a café next to the hotel. It was a clean, well-lighted café and Vincent sat at a table near to the window, close to the entrance, and looked out onto the north end of the square. He ordered a half carafe of wine and a bowl of fish soup, known as *bouillabaisse*. He ate the soup and drank his wine quickly and was feeling tingly, and with the food in his belly he felt hopeful about the day, and just then the café door opened and in walked a huge, heavily bearded man. How robust! That fierce brown beard, like a fat Dostoevsky, he thought. And his beautiful blue uniform, trimmed in gold. Vincent felt the weight of the man's footsteps as he made his way across the room to the proprietor behind the counter. The man placed a parcel on the counter and spoke loud enough for Vincent to hear him clearly. "Good day to you!" he said and marched back outside. Vincent kept his eye on him, how he strode, the thickness of his chest, the broadness of his shoulders setting him apart from everyone else in the square. He was as big and as bright as the sun.

"Who was that?" he asked the server.

"That's the postman, Joseph Roulin," the server said.

"I would like to meet him," Vincent said.

"He will be back tomorrow," the server said.

Vincent came the next day and sat at the same table by the window. He waited, sipping a glass of wine until the postman marched in with a parcel for the proprietor. As he made his way back toward the entrance, Vincent stood and stepped into his path. Joseph stopped.

"Pardon me," he said, his voice exaggeratingly polite.

Vincent motioned toward his table. "My name is Vincent. Can I offer you a drink?"

Joseph massaged the corners of his beard and saw the carafe

of wine and the two glasses on the table.

"I suppose I've got a minute."

He plopped down into the wooden chair which creaked under the sudden weight, its legs buckling a little but holding. Feet firmly planted on the floor, Joseph pushed himself back a bit so that his belly did not press against the edge of the table, the chair shrieking as the stressed legs scraped loudly, wood on wood. Before Vincent sat, Joseph poured himself a glass and gulped it down then smacked it onto the table as if taking a shot of whiskey, the tiny amount at the bottom of the glass spilling out onto the tablecloth. He was like a giant in a doll's house and he did not seem to care about anything except Vincent, whom he smiled at, a huge, brimming grin, the bits of wine darkening the hair of his upper lip.

"What can I do for you?"

Vincent poured himself a glass of wine then refilled Joseph's glass.

"Would you sit for me?"

Joseph peered down at his feet and around the floor as if he'd dropped something.

"I'm sitting now."

"But privately," Vincent said. "So I can paint you."

"Paint me? What for?"

"It is what I do," Vincent said. "Forgive me, but you're a rather striking figure, what with your beard and your uniform."

Joseph placed his hands on his chest, his thick fingers gripping his lapels, and he laughed.

"Ha! You want to paint me? Wait till Augustine hears this!"

"You will do it?"

Joseph gulped down the wine.

"Come to my place tomorrow for soup," he said. "You can meet my family. They'll be tickled to watch you paint their papa!" He stood up and smiled so that his whole beard lifted with his face. Then he bowed and was out the door before Vincent could say another word.

"But I don't know where you live," Vincent muttered, and chuckled to himself.

It wasn't difficult to find the house. Everyone in town knew Joseph Roulin. He lived just down the street from the hotel Vincent was staying, near the railroad tracks.

Joseph greeted him with open arms and gave him a big hug.

"Come in, come in!" he said, moving inside the narrow entranceway. "Augustine! The painter fellow is here!"

It was a small, cramped house for such a large man, and it was warm and humid and smelled of boiled cabbage. A plump, squarely-built woman stepped into the hall. Her hair was pulled back in a bun, revealing the fullness of her face, which was plain, with stern, thin lips, and the tired eyes of a peasant. She held a sleeping baby in her arms.

"My wife, Augustine," Joseph said proudly.

Augustine, lips pursed, offered a cautious smile. Behind her, a head peeked out.

"Come here, boy!" Joseph said. The boy stepped from behind his mother. He was ten years old, his mouth agape, looking up at the strange, red-haired man in his doorway. "This is my son, Camille," Joseph said. "Camille, say hello to…" His face suddenly went blank, and he broke into a boisterous laugh. "I've forgotten your name! My apologies!"

Vincent smiled.

"Vincent."

"Ah yes, Vincent the painter," Joseph said. He turned to the boy. "He is going to paint Papa today."

The boy looked up at Vincent again.

"It's true," Vincent said. He could feel the busyness of the house, the clutter, the hard work that went into this family, and most of all, the love, despite Augustine, who stood stiffly, holding her baby tight.

"Very well then," Joseph said. "Let's get started." He led Vincent into the small parlour. "Is here good?"

"It's fine," Vincent said.

"You don't look so certain," Joseph said.

"No, the room is perfect," Vincent said. "But your uniform. Could you put it on?"

Joseph peered down at his plain clothes, the grubbiness of his buttoned shirt.

"Of course," he said. "Augustine, some wine!" He winked. "It's not too early for a drink, is it?"

"Never," Vincent said.

Joseph laughed loudly.

"I like you," he said. "Vincent the painter."

"You have a lovely family," Vincent said.

"I have another son, Armand. He works as a blacksmith's apprentice."

"You are a lucky man," Vincent said. "Truly."

Augustine, still holding the baby, brought a bottle of wine, and two glasses pinched between her fingers. Joseph poured a glass for Vincent and one for himself. He gulped his down and went out of the room then returned a few minutes later in his uniform. He'd combed his beard and it fell to his chest in a sea of curls. His hat, with POSTES stitched across the front, accentuated the size of his head. He sat up straight, with a serious face.

"Like this?" he said.

Vincent sat at the table and placed a couple of pages upon it, then began to sketch with an ink pen.

"Yes, wonderful," he said.

"Do I look okay?" Joseph asked, still sitting upright.

"You have the head of Socrates," Vincent said. "It is perfect."

He sketched quickly, doing two sketches in the same sitting.

"Do you enjoy your work?" Vincent asked, making small talk as he sketched. "Delivering the mail?"

"I don't deliver it much," Joseph said. "This week the regular carrier is ill. I normally sort the mail at the train station."

"I shouldn't be thankful for an illness," Vincent said. "But I may never have met you."

"I have seen you around," admitted Joseph.

Vincent looked up at Joseph.

"Truly?"

Joseph nodded.

"I didn't know you were a painter."

Vincent smiled.

"I look okay?" Joseph asked again.

"This is going to make a wonderful painting," Vincent said.

Joseph nodded slightly at the sketch.

"You draw it first?"

"Not all the time," Vincent said.

"So, I won't see the painting today?"

"I will paint you today," Vincent said. "Don't worry."

Joseph relaxed a little, and he chuckled.

"The kids are going to get a laugh seeing their Papa in a painting."

"Perhaps I can paint them too," Vincent said. "With your permission, of course."

"Oh, they'd love that!"

⚜

"He and Joseph quickly became good friends," Satan said. "Vincent sent many paintings to Theo in Paris and since Joseph was the postman, they saw each other often. The Roulin family would prove to be invaluable to him. He painted all of them, several times. But none more than Joseph, whom he was quite fond of."

"I suppose he was a man hard to miss," Hemingway said. "The big, burly boisterous type."

Satan peered over at Hemingway.

"I'm big and burly, sure," Hemingway said. "But not boisterous." He took a squeeze from the wineskin. "Ah shit, I don't know." He flopped back into the chair.

Satan looked out the window, the grey gloom passing as the train moved along.

"Vincent was progressing quickly in Arles, especially once he settled into more permanent lodgings."

The yellow house was an affordable, two-storey, four-room flat at 2 Place Lamartine. It was a pleasant little abode with red tiled floors and white walls. Vincent hung some of his paintings throughout the house, along with his favourite Japanese prints he'd brought from Paris.

By the time summer arrived, flowers bloomed everywhere, bursting with colours. Wheat grew golden in the fields across the countryside where the peasants worked and the trees swayed in greens and blues against the gold, all in the white of the summer breeze.

For a time, Vincent averaged a painting per day and he couldn't have been happier. Many were studies, which he sent to Theo. He rarely ate, preferring to spend his daily budget of five francs on supplies, wine, and absinthe. He drew and painted everything, florals and landscapes and portraits, and the more he worked the more he saw—colours became more apparent, more obvious, and sometimes after a good day of work he'd quietly chuckle to himself at how unaware he'd been, how blind he'd been before coming here, and each evening he would write to Theo and tell him of his day.

Satan followed Vincent everywhere. He was a child pulling a wagon, a passing peasant on the road, a snake behind him in the grass, a crow, a cat, an ox, watching in amazement the canvasses Vincent created, always part of the background of daily life in Arles. One afternoon he was an old farmer stopping to chat with the eccentric foreigner who'd set up his easel along the road, at the edge of an orchard.

"It is a beautiful time of year to paint," Satan said.

Vincent was standing close to his canvas and hadn't seen the old man approach.

"It's lovely when it's in bloom," Vincent said.

"May I see it?"

Vincent stepped back.

Satan's heart fluttered. Here was the orchard before him,

tones of whites and yellows and greens so thickly layered that he felt as though he could put out his hand and touch it. It was as real as the actual orchard. He took a breath to calm himself before speaking.

"Are those the plum trees?"

"They are," Vincent said. "They're actually a yellowish white. If you focus on the black of the branches you can see the true colour of the blossoms."

"Being a painter must open your eyes to many colours," Satan said.

"Most days," Vincent said.

Satan stepped back from the canvas.

"Such colours. Remarkable." He patted Vincent on the shoulder and continued on his way down the road.

"How does it make you feel?" Vincent asked.

Satan turned.

"How do you mean?"

"Art brings Heaven to Earth," Vincent said. "It makes anything possible, don't you think?"

Satan smiled.

"I'd like to think so. But I'm a simple farmer. What do I know?"

"You know only your opinion," Vincent said. "And that is enough to make you an expert."

Satan took a step in Vincent's direction and examined the canvas again.

"It has a life of its own—a *light* of its own."

Vincent grinned.

"There, do you see? You are an expert." He turned to his canvas and went back to work.

14

THE TRAIN PUSHED ON. SATAN STARED INTO THE FIRE.

"Later in the summer, Vincent received a letter from Theo informing him that their uncle had died and had named Theo as heir. Vincent would be receiving some extra money, for which he was guiltily elated."

"Money in any form is good money," Hemingway said. "My second wife Pauline got plenty from her uncle Gus. He financed a safari that cost a pretty penny and I never once felt guilty."

"Vincent wanted to convert the yellow house into more than just a studio for himself," Satan said. "But to make it a sanctuary for his Paris friends who wanted to—*needed* to—get out of the temptations of the big city in order to focus on their work. He would call it the *Studio of the South*. With his money he bought another bed and a dresser and a chair. He also hired a charwoman for one franc a day." He paused. "And it was all too easy. She was the same woman Leonardo had: sturdily built, with big shoulders and wide hips."

"A brick shithouse," Hemingway said.

"Yes, and an honest but ignorant way about her; a proud peasant, which, to Vincent, suited him just fine."

The warm morning sun shone on Vincent as he sat at his desk writing a letter to Gauguin. Satan, on his hands and knees scrubbing the floor, sat upright and sighed, wiping the sweat from his brow.

"Poor woman, you work too hard for only a franc a day," Vincent said. "I wish I had more money to offer."

"You are going to paint sunflowers?" Satan asked, nodding

to a series of sketches Vincent had pinned to the wall. The walls of the house had begun to fill with Vincent's work. Canvasses hung in the kitchen, the hallway, the bedrooms; paintings Satan marvelled over.

Vincent, pleasantly surprised at the woman's interest in his work, smiled.

"But these," Satan said, nodding to the black and white sketches. "What colours will you use?"

"Only the brightest I can find," Vincent said.

"And you write your letters with such vigor. Do you paint the same way?"

"Always," Vincent said. "I am writing to a friend, inviting him to come stay with me."

"Here?" Satan said. "In this house?"

"Yes."

"Is he a painter too?"

"He is."

"Won't he interfere with your work?"

"Quite the opposite," Vincent said. "We will learn from one another."

"I wish you luck, monsieur."

Vincent painted his first *Sunflowers* that same afternoon as Satan cleaned the house, peeking in from time to time. When Satan returned two days later it was on the small kitchen table, perched against the wall. The three flowers were reddish orange, like grapefruit, and painted so thickly that the sunlight shone in different places and in different ways, casting tiny shadows where it was so thick it bulged from the canvas and gave it an entirely alternate dimension. The sunflowers themselves were in a green vase on a deep brown bottom which contrasted the turquoise background, bringing the petals even more to the forefront. Satan wanted to touch them, to smell them.

Vincent came into the kitchen and saw his charwoman staring at it.

"It's a series," he said. "I've done another if you'd like to see it."

He led Satan into the studio, where a second version sat on

the floor against the wall. It was darker than the first; browns and blacks mixed in with yellows and oranges, and for a moment there was a tinge of disappointment. Vincent saw it in the charwoman's eyes.

"You don't like it?"

"I do," Satan said.

"But?"

"It's not as bright as the other. Flowers are meant to illuminate, not to darken."

"You like the brightness?"

"Very much," Satan said.

Vincent crossed his arms and examined the painting. Then he went into the next room. Satan could hear him setting up his easel and mixing paint on the palette, and the shuffle of the chair as he brought it forward to begin.

When Satan returned to the yellow house three days later, Vincent had completed two more *Sunflowers*, and both were much brighter than the previous two. There were more sunflowers in these two versions, and no browns at all, but light blues and more yellows. In fact, one of them was completely yellow, in all different shades. Thick yellow brushstrokes burst from the canvas. Oh, the yellow! How vibrant it was, producing, miraculously, its own light. It was exactly what Satan had been searching for, and now, finally, he'd found it, and he was awestruck.

"You like that one?" Vincent asked.

Satan simply nodded.

"I intend to use it decorate my friend's room, should he choose to come," Vincent said. "The flowers have a richness to them the longer you look at them."

"This one," Satan said. "It is perfect."

Satan stared into the fire.

"It *was* perfect," he said. "I lose myself when I think of it now. What Vincent had discovered was art of the purest form: yellow on yellow, light on light, beauty on beauty. It was his best work."

"According to who?" Hemingway said. "Him or the critics?"

Satan managed a grin.

"To me, Ernest. He was unknown. There were no critics."

"He's lucky for that," Hemingway said. "Those leeches can ruin a man. They ruined Fitzgerald. They tried to ruin me."

"But they did not succeed," Satan said.

Hemingway scoffed.

"They got their shots, but they never knocked me down. But Fitzgerald, he wounded easily, and after that he was vulnerable because he'd forgotten how to swing without worry, like when he was the champ. And there's nothing sadder than seeing the champ hit the canvas."

Satan could see that Hemingway had become agitated, how his words had quickened, chest inflated.

"Yes, well, you are still the undisputed champion, Ernest."

Hemingway exhaled. The fire hissed and popped.

"It was time to make a move," Satan said "But one does not launch a siege without first trying to negotiate a peaceful settlement."

In August, Vincent started painting at night. He'd recently begun a canvas in the main room of the Café de la Gare, located a few blocks away from the yellow house at 30 Place Lamartine. He'd set up his easel in the corner of the smoke-filled room. This was the third night in a row that he'd come. Satan, as a vagrant, half-asleep in the middle of the night, sat at one of the small tables to the side, beside the billiards table that occupied the middle of the room. Satan stumbled over to Vincent and stood behind him, peering over his shoulder at the canvas.

"It is very good."

Vincent smirked.

"It's one of the ugliest paintings I've ever done."

"But this place is ugly," Satan said. "And so, you've done your job."

"It's very ugly," Vincent said. "An empty, dreary room painted blood-red. Everywhere there's a clash of colours."

Satan motioned to the billiards table.

"A game?" he asked. "To celebrate?"

Vincent frowned.

"Celebrate what?"

"Your painting," Satan said. "It's finished, isn't it?"

Vincent took a moment, then shrugged and stepped toward the billiards table.

"I am really quite terrible at this game."

"All the better for me," Satan said. He racked the balls and placed the cue ball at the other end. Then he lined up the ball, took aim, and struck it with such force that the balls gave a sudden crack that awoke the few derelicts slumped at the tables. He studied the scattered balls. "I've seen you in here the last three nights."

"Colours are richer and more alive at night than during the day," Vincent said.

Satan peered toward the canvas.

"Am I in it?"

"Go see for yourself," Vincent said.

The barman came through the curtained doorway at the back of the room. Satan raised his hand then dug into his pocket.

"Absinthe—for my friend and I."

Vincent lit his pipe. Satan stepped over to the canvas and saw, in the painting, his figure sitting along the wall, to the right, slumped over the table.

"There I am," he smiled. "Indeed, it is an ugly painting." He laughed and took up his cue. Then he leaned over the table, took aim, and fired a ball into the corner pocket. "Tell me, what would it mean to you to sell it?"

Vincent puffed on his pipe, the tobacco glowing then cooling with a plume of smoke, then glowing again, then more smoke, until it was sufficiently lit and it smoked on its own. He peered over at Satan.

"You want to buy it?"

Satan shook his head.

"I have no money. I'm only asking."

"Truthfully," Vincent said. "It would mean everything to me."

"Have you sold anything?"

"Nothing of importance. A few ink drawings to my uncle. That is all."

Satan looked down at Vincent's worn shoes.

"It would be something to sell a painting, no?"

"Yes, it would," Vincent said.

"A man cannot put a price on such a thing, I suppose," Satan said.

Vincent glanced at the painting.

"Fifty francs."

"I mean to sell your work in general," Satan said. "To have people lining up to buy your work. To have them spend their hard-earned money on your art."

"Ah, yes," Vincent said. "That would be nice."

"You said it would mean everything to you," Satan said.

"Everything," Vincent said.

"What about your soul?"

"What about it?"

"Is it worth that much?" Satan asked.

Vincent chuckled.

"It's only a painting. And like I said, an ugly one at that."

"What about all your work together?" Satan said. "Sold before the paint dries. Is it worth your soul?"

"You're drunk," Vincent said.

"Forgive me. I'm only making conversation."

Vincent puffed on his pipe, and shook his head.

"It isn't a pretty conversation."

Satan twisted in a graceful pirouette before leaning over the table, taking aim, and sinking another ball, this time in the side pocket.

"Which is why we have this place. For such conversations. Indulge me...Would you do it?"

"Sell my soul?"

"Yes," Satan said. "To become the greatest artist who ever lived. What if I told you I could give you that?"

He took aim again, focusing down his nose, over the cue, then banked a near impossible shot between two balls and into the corner pocket.

Vincent cleared his throat.

"I would say it again: you're drunk."

"But would you do it?"

Vincent looked over the table, and puffed his pipe.

"Am I going to get a turn?"

"Not until you answer my question," Satan said.

"No," Vincent said.

"No?"

"My soul? It's too much to give."

"But you said it was everything to you."

"Then I was wrong," Vincent said.

The barman appeared with their drinks and set them on the edge of the billiards table. Satan perched the cue against the table, took up his glass and glanced over toward the canvas.

"It's too bad I haven't any money," he said, taking a sip. "I do like it."

15

"So, no deal," Hemingway said.

"Correct," Satan said. "Had he agreed, he could have signed a contract, and I would have left him alone for the rest of his days. And who knows what may have become of him, what masterpieces he would have created had he lived ten, twenty, thirty years more." He turned to Hemingway. "I could say the same about you."

"I did my work," Hemingway said. "And I'm still working. Got a new one coming out next month. Sure it's here, and not up there, but I work with what I've got." He adjusted himself a little in the tightness of the chair. "When did Gauguin show up?"

"October," Satan said. "When Vincent got news that Gauguin was coming, he got the yellow house ready. He sketched more in order to save money for canvasses which he knew would be in greater demand once Gauguin arrived."

Hemingway leaned forward and threw another log on the fire. The bark on the new log smoked then ignited and crackled and burned quickly.

"What was your plan?"

"A siege, naturally," Satan said. He coughed into the rag again. "Vincent had become pathological in his work. He saw colour in everything. His happiness depended on it. His sanity depended on it. I knew that was the way. That was my plan. And I took my time." He paused, pressed the rag to his lips, but did not cough. "Vincent did not have any friends in Arles other than Joseph Roulin. But Vincent could not discuss his work with him. He could not express himself about his work, as he did with Theo, and so he was lonely. He counted the days for Gauguin's arrival." He coughed again into the rag.

Hemingway fetched a serviette from the table. Satan took it and nodded appreciatively.

"And so, when Gauguin arrived it was a joyous time." He took a moment, lifting the serviette to his mouth, waiting for it to pass.

Mr. Gregory came with a clean rag and a glass of water. Satan took a sip to wet his throat. He shivered. Then he coughed into the rag, violently, his whole body bent forward. Once it passed, he straightened his legs and placed his toes on the bricks of the hearth.

"You get any closer you'll burn them off," Hemingway said.

Satan grunted and wiggled them a little closer to the flames.

"You're probably running a fever," Hemingway said. He turned to Mr. Gregory who was standing behind the chair. "Go fetch the doctor."

Satan grew annoyed.

"I have never been ill. It is a miserable lot."

"Try not to think of it," Hemingway said.

Satan grunted again.

"Impossible."

"Tell me about Gauguin," Hemingway said.

Satan breathed heavily against the weight in his chest. Even talking was becoming strenuous now.

"Gauguin…"

⁂

Vincent met Gauguin at the train station, and they lugged his trunk back to the yellow house. Vincent had filled the house with paintings, placing his favourites close to the front entrance so that those were the ones Gauguin would see first.

"You've been busy, Vincent."

"Arles is an easy place to work," Vincent said. "You will see." They left the trunk on the main floor for now, and Vincent escorted Gauguin up the narrow staircase to the bedroom he'd prepared for him. "It isn't much. We have gaslight and running water. There's no toilet, just the hotel next door."

The four sunflowers canvases were on the bedroom walls. Gauguin's eyes settled on the yellow-on-yellow version Vincent had put up over the bed. Gauguin was silent for a good while before he spoke.

"C'est remarquable." He turned to Vincent. "It belongs to you, the sunflower. You've made it your own. Nobody but you has it now."

It could not have been a better validation for Vincent, and he was tickled with joy. His insides glowed with hope. All his preparation had paid off. The yellow house was perfect, and here was his friend, standing next to him, in Arles.

They did not paint at all on that first day. Instead, Vincent took him to the café where they ate and drank into the night. Later, they went to a brothel, and after that they fell asleep in a field and awoke at sunrise. Vincent, who was still drunk, laughed.

"We've spent all of our money for the week in the first night. *Mais Paul, c'est belle, la vie—n'est-ce pas?* Life is good, Paul, isn't it?"

Gauguin, giddy from fatigue and drink, agreed. It seemed they had found their own piece of paradise. They walked home to the yellow house where Vincent gave him a canvas and paints and they left again, walking for some time, outside the town to a Roman necropolis with a long lane of poplars where the morning sunlight cast a mess of shadows onto the ground.

"*Les Alyscamps,*" Vincent said, setting up his easel and lighting his pipe. "But I should tell you, the vision I have comes from a drawing Émile sent me."

"Émile is a visionary, to be sure," Gauguin said.

"How is he?"

"He paints like a madman," Gauguin said. "He is all over the place."

Vincent smiled.

"That's why I like him."

"He is young," Gauguin said. "Too young to have any control, and without control he is yet to find himself."

"I trust that he will," Vincent said.

"We shall see," Gauguin said.

Gauguin studied the lines of the lane, the high poplars, visualizing how he would centre them on the canvas. Vincent was already mixing his paints.

"Come now, Paul. Let us work."

"I'm already working," Gauguin said.

Vincent raised an eyebrow.

"You can't work without a brush."

"Most of the work is done here—" Gauguin said, tapping the side of his head.

Vincent puffed on his pipe. The brown scent of pipe tobacco hung heavily in the air around him. The paint was thick on his palette and he hastily dipped his brush and began.

"It gets done here," he said, nodding to his canvas.

Gauguin was frowning.

"When did you stop sketching?"

"I sketch all the time," Vincent said.

"You're not sketching now."

Vincent smiled.

"Perhaps not all the time."

"And you think that is better practise?"

"You must attack it with the paint in order to capture it," Vincent said. He held four brushes in his hand at once, between his fingers, while cupping the palette. "If not, you will lose it." With each turn from palette to canvas he increased his speed and the amount of paint on each brushstroke, just to make his point, slapping it on until he settled into a rhythm, colours over colours, mixing and swirling and laying it on thick. "Have you never thought of that, Paul?"

"Never."

"Well, today I am capturing it," Vincent said. "I've sketched it enough times that perhaps it is already lost."

"It's a queer philosophy," Gauguin said.

"What's queer is that no other artist has figured it out yet."

Gauguin closed his eyes. His easel lay folded at his feet.

"What are you doing?" Vincent asked.

"Concentrating."

Vincent chuckled and smoked his pipe.

"Then you've already lost it, Paul."

"Please," Gauguin said. He breathed deeply to sharpen his focus, to block Vincent's slapping of the paint, the gooey slopping against the canvas.

Vincent shrugged and carried on. Ten minutes passed before Gauguin set up his easel and began. Neither of them took any notice of the butterfly that fluttered around them. Satan had followed Vincent to the poplars earlier in the summer too, but now that it was fall the foliage mixed with the sunlight and there was a whole new landscape, one Satan hadn't seen before, and now he understood why Vincent had waited until now to paint it.

By the time Vincent was nearly finished, Gauguin had barely just begun, taking his time, setting up his easel with a calmness that aggravated Vincent and made him slap the paint in a self-imposed, exaggerated anguish, hoping to spur on Gauguin. But Gauguin's calm equalled Vincent's fury, dabbing the canvas carefully, meticulously, and paying him no attention.

The butterfly fluttered around Vincent and perched on the edge of his easel. Then, as Vincent stepped back to look at his finished work, his eyes rolled back and his legs gave way and he dropped to the ground and his body began to shake. Gauguin rushed to his side and wrapped his arms around Vincent's head to keep it from slamming against the ground. He held Vincent tight, fighting the spasms until Vincent's breathing slowed, and he was back. His eyes were wild with confusion.

"You've had a seizure," Gauguin said. "Take it easy. Breathe. That's it."

Vincent remained on the ground for several minutes, and once his breathing calmed, so too did his eyes.

"It was so strange," he said. "Like a nightmare—no colour in anything—everything grey, then it all came back, bursts of colours flooding into my brain, then blackness."

"Try to relax," Gauguin said. "Absinthe all night will do that. Try to focus on something."

Vincent looked toward the sky. The poplars swayed, the leaves rustled, and it was as peaceful and as calming as in a dream, and he remained there a good while as Gauguin painted, until he was well enough to stand on his own.

"You drank a lot last night," Gauguin said.

"You drank more than me," Vincent said.

Gauguin smiled.

"I'm French. I can handle it. Your Dutch blood is too thin."

The next morning, Vincent remained in bed. Gauguin was careful not to disturb him. He took a long walk, to see more of the town and the countryside. When he returned later in the afternoon,

Vincent was still in bed. Gauguin knocked softly on the bedroom door and peeked into the room.

"Are you awake?"

Vincent was on his side, facing the wall.

"No."

"I bought some bread and cheese," Gauguin said. "I thought you might be hungry."

Vincent said nothing.

"Very well then," Gauguin said. He stepped into the bedroom and put a plate with two pieces of sliced bread and a small block of cheese on the washing station table next to the window. "It's here, should you decide to eat."

The following morning, Gauguin peeked his head into the bedroom again. He saw that the bread and cheese hadn't been touched.

"Vincent, should I send for a doctor?"

Vincent didn't reply.

"I'm going to find one," Gauguin said.

"No," Vincent said.

"Are you alright?"

"I'm fine."

"You've been asleep for two days."

Vincent rolled over and sighed heavily.

"It has taken a lot out of me."

"The seizure."

"Yes."

"Then perhaps we should have a doctor see to you," Gauguin said.

"I've been through this before," Vincent said. "I'm fine."

Gauguin frowned.

"Seizures?"

"No," Vincent said. "This. *La tristesse.*"

Gauguin was still frowning.

"La *tristesse?*"

"It will pass," Vincent said.

The next day, Gauguin left the house without looking in on

Vincent. He returned with a bale of jute and carried it into the first-floor studio and was pleasantly surprised to discover Vincent had gotten out of bed.

"Bonjour!" Gauguin said, plopping the bale at his feet.

"Bonjour, Paul."

"You're well?"

"Well enough," Vincent said. "I'm sorry. I—"

"Don't be sorry."

Vincent smiled.

"Thank you, Paul." He peered down at the jute. "Is that what I think it is?"

"It is," Gauguin said. "It should last us a good while."

"Cheap canvases," Vincent said.

"*Economical* canvases," Gauguin said. "God bless your brother; one painting each month for two hundred and fifty francs. It's not a lot but it works." He patted the bale as one pats a horse. "It's coarse," he said. "I thought it would work nicely with how you slop your paint in gobs."

"Okay then," Vincent said.

"How are you feeling?" Gauguin asked, still patting the bale.

"My mother has epilepsy," Vincent said. "It would be of no coincidence if I suffer the same fate."

"I have a cousin with epilepsy," Gauguin said. "He lives a normal life."

"We are artists," Vincent said. He managed a slight, but noticeable grin. "Our lives are anything but normal."

16

THE TRAIN PUSHED UP A LOW BUT STEADY INCLINE, THE THRUST of the engines pulling the weight of the cars once the hill began to outlast the train's momentum.

"It wasn't epilepsy," Hemingway said. "Was it?"

"It was not," Satan said.

Hemingway nodded.

"The siege had begun."

Satan nodded back.

"I quickly realized depriving him of colour triggered an after-effect that would put him in such a depressed state it would take days, sometimes weeks, to recover from. And in that time, he was most vulnerable to his own darkness, his *tristesse*, which, if all went as planned, would inevitably overtake him in the end."

"You encouraged nature to run its course."

"Precisely."

"A nudge."

"Yes," Satan said. "No rules broken, Ernest. It was an experiment, of course, and like any experiment, success depends a great deal on trial and error."

Hemingway leaned forward and stoked the fire.

"You overdosed him, eh?"

Satan shifted in his chair. His joints ached and he grunted.

"Depriving him of colour was simple. Giving it back would prove to be a more delicate matter."

※

A week after the seizure, in the evening, Augustine Roulin came to the yellow house to sit for both Vincent and Gauguin. Vincent met her at the front door and he immediately saw the apprehension in her face, and so he did his best to make her comfortable.

"Madame Roulin, thank you so very much for coming. You look lovely. Right this way, if you please." He escorted her into the studio, where Gauguin greeted her, and she smiled back, without worry, which Vincent had noticed. Their easels were set up side by side.

"Where would you like me?" Augustine asked Gauguin.

Gauguin motioned to a chair in the corner of the room,

where she sat, facing him. Vincent's easel was to her right, the yellowish gaslight on his side, lighting her face in such a way that her skin looked earthy.

They began mixing their paints. Augustine sat, her elbows on the armrests, her face plain and serious. She kept her eyes on Gauguin.

"And how are things, Madame?" Gauguin asked. "I trust all is well. And your children, how are they?"

Augustine smiled, her body stiff, only her mouth moving.

"They are well, merci."

"And your husband?" Gauguin said. "I assume he remains a gentleman despite his friendship with this fool—" His eyes rolled exaggeratingly toward Vincent.

Augustine smiled again, but nervously.

"What wonderful cheekbones," Gauguin said, realizing he'd made her uncomfortable.

Vincent splashed the paint on, flecks of paint flying about. They worked without speaking, without looking at the other's canvas, before Gauguin broke the silence.

"Don't be so careless, Vincent. Slow down."

Vincent tried to keep the agitation out of his voice.

"How else can you capture her if you don't work quickly?"

"She's not going anywhere," Gauguin said. "There's nothing to capture."

Vincent sighed.

"It must be painted in the moment or it is lost, much as a fisherman works his net."

Gauguin chuckled.

"We're not catching fish, Vincent."

Vincent rubbed his eyes in frustration.

"What is it then? What makes yours better than mine?"

"Yours is harsh, too deliberate," Gauguin said. "The colours are true but it's messy. This isn't what impasto is meant to accomplish."

"All of life is messy," Vincent said. "I'm not going to close my eyes and try to imagine someone who's right in front of me." He pointed to Gauguin's incomplete canvas. "Yours is but a dream!"

"You use too much yellow," Gauguin said.

"And you too much green," Vincent said.

"Not blue?" Gauguin said.

"Blue, green, whatever. You use too much of it."

Gauguin offered Augustine a warm smile.

"Forgive us, Madame."

"Perhaps I could come back another time?" Augustine replied, the stiffness in her voice matching her posture.

"I'm nearly finished," Vincent said. "You'd be coming back here for a month before Paul is finished."

Gauguin bowed.

"Thank you, Madame. I can finish on my own. It's nearly complete."

Augustine lifted herself from the chair, her legs stiff. She hobbled out of the room, escorted by Gauguin. When he came back, Vincent's face was red. Gauguin put his arm over his shoulder and spoke warmly.

"Enough of this. Let's go get a drink, shall we?"

Vincent pushed him forcefully away.

Gauguin pushed him back.

"They duked it out?" Hemingway said.

"It ended as quickly as it had begun," Satan said.

"Painters," Hemingway said. "Reminds me of the time in Madrid this kid brushed up against the lady I was with, a beautiful Spanish girl with olive skin and legs..." He fell away in his thoughts, grinning. "Legs as long and as smooth as the Spanish earth. Hips that rolled like the hills. A work of art and not half my age, but because she'd read a few of my books she'd inserted herself into our little group touring with the bullfights and damned if it didn't give me a boost. All Spanish women had that effect on me." He was nodding to himself. "Anyway, the kid had done it on purpose, brushing the back of his hand across her shoulder. I watched him as he took his seat a few tables away. The bar was opened to the street and we were sitting at one of the big patio tables in the shade. *Do you know who that is?* she asked. *No,* I said. *And I don't care.* She said: *That's Juan Mirez. He's a student of Picasso's.* It annoyed me that his little scheme had gotten her attention. *He's a little shit,* I said. We were drinking martinis that were as cool and refreshing as the shade and made the sun that much brighter and that much hotter, which made the shade cooler and lovelier and only made us drink more. I'd had five or six and was feeling good, and so the little prick didn't stand a chance when he came back and brushed up against her again. I said: *Hey, boy, watch what you're doing there.* He turned with a cocky grin and said: Quién eres, viejo, su padre? *Who are you, old man—her father?* I stood up, and when he realized who I was, his face sank and I socked him in the nose. He crumpled to the floor and wailed as if he'd been shot. It was embarrassing. I bloodied him pretty good but it was only a jab. Nothing of any damage. But he kept crying. I helped him to his feet and told the waiter I'd pay his bill, which I knew only humiliated him more. I told Pablo when I saw him later that summer. He wasn't impressed. Said the kid wasn't a good painter anyway." He laughed, remembering it. "At least Vincent and Gauguin could paint. But fight? No painter I know could ever fight like a man. Not even for a pair of legs like that."

"What they lacked in steel they made up for in stubbornness," Satan said. "Each digging his heels deeper than the previous day, equally cemented in their opposing views, but they were more eccentric than dangerous."

"Eccentricity is dangerous enough," Hemingway said. "Those are the unpredictable ones, and they scare the bejesus out of anyone with half an ounce of normalcy."

"One could label you eccentric," Satan said.

"Me? Hell no! Why, because I'm a writer?"

"No," Satan said. "Because you are you."

"I'm meat and potatoes," Hemingway said. "With a splash of gravy."

"It is the gravy I am speaking of."

"What's that supposed to mean?"

"I kid with you, Ernest."

Mr. Gregory appeared and stepped between the two wing-back chairs. He was holding the cellphone. Satan's arm emerged from under the blanket.

"Excuse me, Ernest."

The phone felt cold against his ear.

Crews now filled the Boulevard. Hundreds of workers assembled scaffolding and moved about like a colony of ants, each with a purpose, carrying, lugging, attaching, building up and up along the length of the Boulevard. High-powered hoses were coiled and stacked along the route, where teams of scrapers awaited orders. Carlos Castro directed workers installing a fence to keep protesters out, but a few had snuck in and were yelling at the workers and Castro and his team moved swiftly to arrest them. He glanced over to the huge cement barriers being positioned by bulldozers along a section of sidewalk, and then made a note of the barriers already in place, the distance of the sidewalk to the street, how packed with onlookers it would be, how more barriers were needed, and more security, more everything, and how little time he had. Then Mr. Steel approached.

"You have enough men?"

"Yes," Castro said. "They are working well. It will be done."

"Good," Mr. Steel said. "The workers who are not yours are Capone's. Treat them with respect." He turned and continued down the Boulevard for three blocks before stepping into a run-down tavern called the Lighthouse, a seedy watering hole that attracted the most miserable souls Capital City had to offer.

A large, ornate bar stretched the length of the wall, its surface stained and worn. Behind it was a huge, cracked mirror and shelves lined with various bottles of liquor. Mixed and matched tables and chairs were spread out along the walls. Thick blinds dimmed the Boulevard's light, and there was the sour smell of sweat and urine. Mr. Steel remained in the doorway before spotting the man at the bar. He made his way across the room and sat in the stool next to the man and ordered a beer. The Boulevard's light shone through the slits in the blinds, slicing the darkness like lasers.

"Nothing like a cold beer," Mr. Steel said.

The man didn't flinch.

"Are you alright there, friend?"

"I am not your friend," the man said. He had a long nose and a pointed face, like an arrow, and his hair was thin and slicked flat to his head.

Mr. Steel took a drink of beer.

"Sorry. You look like you could use a friend."

"This is no place to make friends."

"Indeed," Mr. Steel said. "But it helps pass the time."

The man took a drink.

"Eternity is a long time."

"It's long enough," Mr. Steel said, nodding.

"If you don't mind," the man said, looking straight ahead. "I do not wish to make any friends today."

Suddenly a table flipped over in a darkened corner of the room. A greasy-haired man with a big nose and pockmarked face held a broken beer bottle and snarled at another man who stood, cornered, nose bloodied. The pockmarked man had bowlegs and his long, ape-like arms swiped the broken bottle in the man's direction.

"Come on, you son-of-a-bitch! Fight you goddam coward! Pick up a bottle. COME ON!"

Mr. Steel watched the showdown.

"Is that who I think it is?"

The bartender slapped his towel on the bar.

"Bukowski, get outta here!"

Bukowski turned toward the bartender, nostrils flaring.

"You want some of this, Rodney, huh? You got the balls? Come on, you miserable prick!"

The bartender sighed again.

"Go home, Hank."

"You're fuckin gutless, Rodney. You know that?"

"Go on," the bartender said.

Bukowski breathed loudly. Nobody in the bar moved.

"Go on now," the bartender said, louder this time, waving the towel as though shooing away a stray dog.

Bukowski dropped the bottle and stumbled over to the door, never taking his eyes off the bartender, whose towel was flipped over his shoulder again.

"We'll see you tomorrow, Hank."

Bukowski took a long look around the bar, then turned and stepped outside. The table was put back, and the man in the corner sat down again, holding his nose, and it was as though nothing had happened.

The man at the bar sipped his beer.

"What a character," Mr. Steel said.

"He is an asshole."

"That's why he's here," Mr. Steel said. "Do you know why he's here—what he did? He arrived at Heaven's Gate and when God greeted him, he told him to go fuck himself." He grinned. "I believe the term he used was *Get fucked*."

The man took another sip of his beer.

"He leaves me alone only because I am German."

"That you are, Colonel."

The man turned.

"Colonel Hess," Mr. Steel said. "Colonel Olaf Hess."

When the Colonel saw Mr. Steel's horns, he rolled his eyes and sighed.

"What do you want?"

Mr. Steel opened the folder.

"It isn't what I want, but what I have to offer."

"I assume this has something to do with the Boulevard?"

Mr. Steel flopped a folder onto the bar and pulled a piece of paper from it.

"Colonel Olaf Hess: Foot soldier in the First World War.

Survived the mud and the rats of Ypres and after the war found yourself in Berlin, where you worked in a top-secret munitions factory that produced high-powered cartridges for the German Fleet, it too a secret."

The colonel sighed.

"My life is not a secret anymore."

Mr. Steel continued reading.

"By the spring of 1935 you joined the SS and soon became one of only twelve personal bodyguards for Adolf Hitler, where the Fuhrer eventually befriended you and appointed you to the rank of Colonel, in charge of his personal security force. It was you who masterminded the plan to fake his death, and it was your plan that was followed when he boarded a submarine and crossed the Atlantic and smuggled into Argentina a week before the end of the war. You died in April 1945, by Russian shelling, on a street in Berlin."

"I have no contact with the Fuhrer anymore," Hess said. "He is a celebrity here. I have no use for him."

"I've not come for him," Mr. Steel said.

"What do you want then?"

"A man of your skillset is of value to me. And I pay handsomely."

"I do not want your money," Hess said.

"What is it with you people not wanting money?"

"I do not need it," Hess said.

"Ah, but you do," Mr. Steel said. "Why else would you be drinking the cheapest ale in the place?"

The Colonel rolled the mug of ale between his fingers.

"I like the taste."

Mr. Steel smirked.

"The taste of piss?"

Hess lifted his mug and drank, swallowing with a slight wince, which he tried to mask, unsuccessfully.

"Maybe I do."

Mr. Steel pulled an envelope from the folder and placed it in front of Hess, who took notice of its thickness.

"The visit," Mr. Steel said.

"What about it?"

"I want you to oversee the itinerary. Co-ordinate everything —where he stays, when he moves, where he goes and for how long. You will work alongside Mr. Castro, who is dealing with the Boulevard already."

The Colonel glanced down at the envelope again.

"That's only half," Mr. Steel said. "The other half comes when he's on his way home without incident." He slid a piece of paper over. "Mr. Castro's address."

Colonel Hess finished his mug of ale, sighed and shook his head slightly, as if agitated. Then, reluctantly, he reached for the envelope.

17

SATAN HANDED THE PHONE TO MR. GREGORY, tucked himself back under the blanket, and wiggled his toes close to the fire again. Out the train window the dark landscape gradually sloped as the train pushed on through the dimness.

"Forgive me, Ernest. Vincent and Gauguin…"

"They were at odds," Hemingway said.

"That is putting it delicately," Satan said.

"I hated most every other writer I knew," Hemingway said.

"Out of jealousy?"

Hemingway shrugged.

"I had nothing to be jealous of. Not from anyone. It was more from annoyance."

"They annoyed you?"

Hemingway grinned.

"They sure as hell did. Half of them couldn't write a true

sentence if you held a gun to their head. The other half didn't have the one tool every writer worth his salt must have—a built-in, shockproof shit detector. The great painters all have it. Vincent had it. Gauguin too. But I'm sure Vincent annoyed Gauguin, and vice versa, for the simple fact of each other's presence."

"Yes, to be sure," Satan said. "But I do not mean to say that Vincent and Gauguin did not always get along, nor that they did not learn from one another. Indeed, there were instances of true growth."

⁂

"You must paint the café, Paul," Vincent said, late one evening. "I have done it and I'm curious to see what you can do with it."

"I'm tired," Gauguin said. "I'm going to bed."

"Please," Vincent said. "Do this for me, just this one thing."

"I don't paint cafés," Gauguin said. "Especially that one."

"*Please.*"

"You're going to beg me?"

"Yes."

"Jesus. Okay. Just don't beg."

They grabbed their things and walked over to the café. Gauguin set up his easel by the end wall, not far from where Vincent had painted here. Gauguin stepped back.

"It's dungy. The colours are too coarse."

"Come now," Vincent said. "It's life, right in front of you, ready to be captured."

"I see nothing but prostitutes and drunks," Gauguin said.

"Life," Vincent said.

"I like you better when we argue," Gauguin said.

Vincent took him by the arm and placed him behind the easel.

"Bonsoir, Paul."

"Where are you going?"

"Home to bed," Vincent said. "It's late."

Gauguin looked over the scene and sighed.

"And don't come home until you've finished," Vincent said, and out he went.

Vincent woke up early the next morning. Gauguin's painting was perched against the wall by the front door. Vincent grabbed it and rushed into Gauguin's room.

"It's magnificent!"

Gauguin buried his head under his pillow.

"Leave me alone. I just got home."

"But you've captured it, Paul, the essence of it. Madame Ginoux in the foreground—look at her face—how she quietly protests those behind her, but how she takes their money!"

"It's me, you fool," Gauguin said. "I'm protesting *you.*"

"Oh, it's Marie, for certain," Vincent said. "And the drunk, asleep on the table, and the three whores, the green and the vermilion shawls with the red wallpaper, and the lines of smoke. You've done it, Paul!"

Gauguin rolled over and grunted.

"It is what it is. Now let me sleep."

Vincent left the yellow house in high spirits. In his pocket was the money from Theo that had arrived yesterday, and more importantly, perhaps now, finally, after weeks of fighting, he was getting through to Gauguin. He was whistling when he entered the small art shop owned by an old man and his wife. Their names were Henri and Jean-Lise.

Henri's old frame was hunched over as he watered a row of potted flowers that lined the shop's front window. Vincent enjoyed this old man who always smiled whenever he saw him. He wanted to paint him someday, the crookedness of his long body, the wrinkles on his face, and his humble, old man smile.

Jean-Lise was sitting on a stool behind the counter, cutting the stems from a bunch of flowers—local wildflowers that grew in the fields—when Vincent walked in. He loved how white her hair was, and how it brought out the colours of the flowers.

"Bonjour, Madame," he said, making his way over to the brushes he'd eyed a week before while waiting for Theo's money to arrive. He plucked six from the jar and approached the counter.

"Some beautiful yellows have just come in," Jean-Lise said. "I know how you love yellow."

Vincent perked up. He didn't need any more paint for now, as Theo had sent him a new order with the money, but he couldn't dare turn down a peek, especially yellow.

"May I see them?"

Jean-Lise placed the flowers on the counter and called to her thirteen-year-old niece.

"Jeanne! Bring out the three yellow containers I set aside for Monsieur Vincent." The girl came out, set them in front of Vincent, then returned to the back room.

"But those are grey," Vincent said.

The old woman opened one of the containers, clearly puzzled.

"Mais, c'est brilliant," she said. "It's as bright as the sun! You cannot get any more yellow than this!"

"My dear, Jean," Vincent said, "but this is the grey of fog. How do you see yellow?"

The old woman's frown intensified.

"Because it is, and only is and nothing else."

Vincent shook his head.

"Is this a joke?"

The old woman opened the second container.

"Here, the same as the first, although not quite as bright. Denser, I believe."

Vincent put his hand to his forehead.

"It's the same as the first! Grey! Have you gone mad, woman?"

Henri appeared in the doorway. Vincent snatched one of the containers from off the counter and rushed over to him.

"Monsieur Henri, do please tell me what colour you see."

"But yellow of course," the old man said.

Vincent rushed back over to the counter and grabbed another container.

"And this? You tell me this is yellow too? I don't like what you're doing, whether in jest or not. I've purchased all my brushes here but no more! Do you hear me? NO MORE!"

He hurried out of the shop and down the lane and through

town, not stopping until he came to one of the bridges at the edge of town. It was a medieval bridge and the stones of the bridge were warm on his palms as he looked out to the fields, to what he'd always known but was missing, the gold and yellow of the wheat, the burning blue of the sky. Below him, along the edge of the creek, sat a man in a sunhat, holding a fishing pole.

"Kind sir," Vincent said, leaning over the side of the bridge. "Can you tell me the colour of those fields?"

Satan lazily turned his head toward the fields, then up to Vincent.

"Gold," he said. "And yellow and orange." He cast his line downstream, under the bridge, and gently jerked it back and forth.

"And the sky?"

"Blue."

Vincent skipped down over the bank to the edge of the water, which flowed smooth and curled against the rocks under the bridge where it was shaded and where Satan's line cut into the water, taut against the current.

Vincent ripped a bunch of wildflowers from the bank.

"And these?" he said, shaking them.

"Purple."

"Yes?"

"And blue and yellow and white."

"And the stems green?"

"Yes, of course," Satan said.

Vincent clawed his way back up the bank to the road and headed home. When he arrived at the yellow house, he could hear Gauguin snoring in his bedroom. Vincent shook him awake and told him of the episode with Henri and Jean-Lise.

"We won't be buying from them anymore."

"Come now," Gauguin said. He sat up in bed, his thick hair matted on one side.

"I mean it," Vincent said. "From now on we get *everything* from Paris."

"It'll be more expensive," Gauguin said.

"I don't care," Vincent said. His pale, freckled skin was now blotched red, and his eyes, those intense eyes glared at nothing and at everything. "I don't trust anyone anymore."

Gauguin slipped into his trousers.

"Let's go for a walk."

"I'm going to bed," Vincent said.

Gauguin grabbed him by the arm.

"No, not again. I won't let you rot away in bed for the next week. We're going for a walk."

They stepped out into the street. Gauguin had slept a few hours and he was clearly glad to be out of the stuffiness of his room and into the fresh air. He was pleased to have worked well, despite his initial apprehension.

"I don't mind it as much, when I think of it," he said.

"Mind what?" Vincent said.

"The café piece."

"What is it called?"

"*Night Café*—" Gauguin said. "*At Arles.*"

"It's wonderful," Vincent said. He was calm again, to be talking of painting and remembering how hopeful he'd been about Gauguin when he'd set out in the morning. "It's all about the moment. Forget about memory. Memory makes it decorative and not realistic."

Gauguin smiled.

"My dear Vincent, all I'm saying is that I am pleased with it. My philosophy hasn't changed. I can't just turn it off."

"But you can," Vincent said. "Arles is about starting over. Together we can create something remarkable; a sanctuary for artists."

"For you to mould," Gauguin said.

"No," Vincent said. "For them to work as they should."

"You mean *in the moment.*"

"Yes," Vincent said.

"How *you* work."

"Yes," Vincent said again.

Gauguin stepped out in front of Vincent, stopping him.

"Your arrogance is astonishing!"

"I mean you no offence," Vincent said. "I am only trying to help."

"Help? With what?"

"With your work," Vincent said.

Gauguin's arms swung out then flopped against his sides.

"My work? *My* work? How many paintings have you sold? Can you tell me that?"

Vincent stepped around him and continued on.

"Not a single piece!" Gauguin said.

"And now *you're* insulting *me*," Vincent said.

"Good," Gauguin said. "YOU NEED IT!"

Vincent stopped.

"I did this—invited you here—because you needed to get away from Paris, from all of them."

"You must enjoy *life* too," Gauguin said. "Not only art. Your passion is your weakness, Vincent. Your intensity burns you."

"My work proves otherwise."

"I'm not talking about art," Gauguin said. "I'm talking about life."

"Life is art," Vincent said.

Gauguin flapped his arms again.

"Oh, to hell with that! Life is art. Art is life. Whatever! The point is, you're missing out."

"Missing out on what?" Vincent frowned. "Whores and drink?"

"No," Gauguin said. "You get plenty of that. I'm talking about happiness. Are you happy, Vincent?"

Vincent said nothing.

"You have a choice to be happy or not," Gauguin said.

"I disagree."

"But you do, Vincent. Though you cannot just decide to be happy you still make the decisions which lead to happiness. Or the ones that don't."

Again, Vincent was quiet.

"Do you even know what happiness is?" Gauguin said. He was calm now and his voice had become empathetic.

"Do *you?*" Vincent said.

"Yes," Gauguin said. "Everything I do contributes to my happiness." He paused. "Tell me, Vincent, how many friends have you here besides Joseph and myself?"

"What does that have to do with anything?" Vincent said. "I don't see the point in liking several people I barely know. I would rather put all my energy into loving the few people I know well."

"You put all your energy into your work, Vincent. Is there anything left for love? Have you ever been in love?"

"I suppose you have a choice in that too," Vincent said.

Gauguin smiled.

"Naturally, yes."

Vincent was quiet for a moment. He kicked at a pebble.

"I was in love, once. In Holland."

"And how did it feel?"

Vincent shrugged.

"At the time I thought I was happy."

"But you weren't?"

"Looking back now, no," Vincent said. "All we were doing was sharing the weight of our own misery. Painting is my happiness now."

"That's not enough, Vincent."

"Then what do I do?"

Gauguin shrugged.

"I don't know. I'm not a doctor. But painting can't be the only thing. You must find a way to be happy outside of your work; to go to bed happy, to dream well, then wake up and face the day with a smile."

"And you?" Vincent said. "Is that how you feel, Paul?"

"Sometimes," Gauguin said. "No one is happy all the time."

"Then I am fine," Vincent said. "I've made my choice. Some are rich, some are poor. Such is life. Who am I to complain? I am working better than ever. In that I am rich."

18

The train moved along through the dimness, swaying a little every now and then. Satan coughed into his rag.

"La *tristesse* was beginning to take hold of him, due in part to their eroding friendship. For weeks they battled. The yellow house was filled with tobacco smoke and smelled strongly of paint and turpentine. Soon paintings filled every available space on the walls and it was cramped for the two of them, each at the other's throat, criticizing, arguing and drinking. But all those paintings amid the dreariness of the house, how they lit it up, each a ray of sunshine, Gauguin's too, but Vincent's were far more vibrant."

Hemingway poked at the fire.

"I know what you're talking about. Gertie Stein's place was like that. You could smell the paintings. I always loved the smell of Stein's flat."

"But it was no paradise," Satan said. "Vincent drank heavily, and when he was drunk, he picked at Gauguin for hours on end, insisting he change."

Hemingway perched the poker against the hearth.

"He's lucky Gauguin didn't kill him."

"Vincent was stubborn like a mule," Satan said. "But there were times when he did actually listen to Gauguin."

After three straight days of rain, it felt like a miracle when the clouds finally dispersed and the sun came out and the sky was blue again. For Vincent and Gauguin, it was as though they'd been underwater and had now surfaced and could breathe, free of the cramped, smoke-filled house. They walked across town without speaking, until they stopped at a wine plantation where peasants worked the vines, bent over, with baskets at their sides.

"Tell me again why you invited me here," Gauguin said.

"I didn't," Vincent said. "It was you who suggested a walk."

"I mean here, to Arles."

Vincent walked a few feet ahead of Gauguin.

"Is this a trick? I haven't the energy to argue today."

"It's no trick," Gauguin said.

"To get away from Paris," Vincent said. "And to learn from you. To learn from each other."

"I'm pleased to hear you say that," Gauguin said. He surveyed the vineyard. "Today I want you to paint something for me."

Vincent frowned.

"From memory?"

"From memory," Gauguin said.

Vincent huffed.

"This *is* a trick."

"Please, Vincent."

"Forget it."

"I've tried your way with the café."

"And?" Vincent said.

"But you've conceded nothing!" Gauguin said. "You cannot argue, you cannot debate, Vincent. You give nothing, not one inch! You only see the way you see. You haven't considered one thing I've said." He then sighed heavily. "This isn't working, is it?"

"What?"

"This," Gauguin said. "Me and you, in Arles."

"Of course, it is," Vincent said.

"It's not working," Gauguin said.

"Don't blame Arles. It's not Arles. Arles is paradise."

"It's your paradise," Gauguin said. "Not mine."

"What are you trying to say, Paul?"

"I'm asking you—no, I'm telling you—that if you don't do as I ask then I'm going back to Paris."

Vincent shook his head, as if trying to flee the thought.

"You're not leaving. You can't."

"Then do as I ask."

"Fine," he said. "What do you want?"

"You choose," Gauguin said.

Vincent looked over to the vineyard, at the sun and the peasants bent over working the vines.

"This, here," he said, pointing.

"Good choice," Gauguin said.

"So that's it?"

"That's it."

"Nothing else?" Vincent said. "No acquired skill?"

"Put a blank canvas in your mind," Gauguin said. "Now see how you intend to paint it. Frame it, and consider each and every colour, how it balances within the frame. Think of colour as a means to creating the *feeling* of what you see. Go beyond the surface."

"I can't," Vincent said. "Your cheap jute is too coarse to penetrate."

Gauguin sighed.

"Focus. Please."

"I see the red of the vines," Vincent said. "And the yellow of the sun and the blue of the peasants' smocks interspersed in all the red."

"How do the colours feel?"

"Hot," Vincent said. "Sweaty and dusty and tired."

"Good," Gauguin said. "Now paint it in your mind. Take your time."

"This is silly," Vincent said. "I have it all. I can see it quite clearly."

"Are you sure?"

"Certainly, yes."

"Okay then," Gauguin said. "Let's go get a drink."

They drank all afternoon and into the evening. Before stumbling up to bed, Gauguin turned to Vincent on the staircase.

"Are you too drunk to paint?"

"I drank myself sober hours ago," Vincent said.

"Good," Gauguin said. "Now paint the vineyard."

Vincent scoffed.

"When?"

"Right now," Gauguin said.

"I am tired," Vincent said.

"Do it."

When Gauguin woke up the next morning, the painting was perched against the wall at the foot of the stairs. Vincent had heard him get up, and he stepped out of his bedroom and stood at the top of the stairs, looking down at him.

"What do you think?"

"The red works well with the yellow," Gauguin said. "And the peasants in blue—it's good." He smiled. "You might just sell a painting yet."

"It's called *The Red Vineyard*," Vincent said.

"It's excellent. Now let's see how good your memory really is. Do another one; one you *haven't* prepared for."

The pride in Vincent's face washed away in an instant.

"No," he said. "I did what you asked."

"You're not finished," Gauguin said. "Think of something else, something different from anything you've done before."

Vincent puckered his lips.

"You said do one painting. To which I did. And now another?"

"Yes," Gauguin said. "Think of something."

Vincent rubbed his forehead, rubbing away the annoyance. He sat on the top step.

"The bull games," he said. "I went in June."

"Perfect," Gauguin said. "Now get it done."

⁂

Vincent finished early that afternoon.

"I call it *Les Arènes*," he said, holding the canvas so Gauguin could see it. "It's a bit like a dream, how the crowd sweeps away."

Gauguin crossed his arms.

"Yes, it feels that way."

"It is more from imagination than memory," Vincent said.

"They are one and the same," Gauguin said.

Vincent frowned.

"Memory and imagination are two very different things."

"Not true, Vincent. Imagination is simply a mosaic of memories. Bits and pieces to make a whole. You took what you remembered of that day and any other day—the arena; any arena—the people; any people—and pieced them together."

Vincent perched the painting against the wall then stepped back.

"A mosaic of memories."

"Yes," Gauguin said.

Vincent smirked.

"Did you come up with that on your own?"

Gauguin returned the smirk.

"Literally just now."

They both chuckled, then Vincent turned to the painting again.

"Here is Madame Ginoux. She doesn't face it. She doesn't like it when the matador cuts off the bull's ear."

"Who would like that?" Gauguin said.

Vincent stepped back.

"Am I finished?"

"Yes," Gauguin said.

"Good."

"There, Vincent, now you see what can be accomplished from memory."

"Or imagination."

"Right," Gauguin said. "Whatever the case, you'll have it for a rainy day."

"What's wrong with painting the rain?" Vincent said.

"You're impossible," Gauguin said, unable to hide a grin.

There was a fleck of blue paint on Vincent's lip, and he licked it.

Gauguin tilted his head to look more closely.

"Do you eat your paint?"

Vincent licked his lip again and smiled.

"How does it taste?" Gauguin asked.

"Like paint," Vincent said. "It tastes good."

"Does it really?"

"No," Vincent said.

"It's a queer habit," Gauguin said.

Vincent looked out the window. He watched as a woman crossed the square.

"You aren't leaving, are you, Paul?"

"I don't know," Gauguin said. He was staring at the painting. "I don't know anything anymore, Vincent."

⁂

"Bullfighting is nothing like a dream," Hemingway said. "It's an art. It's life and death on display. I doubt Van Gogh considered that."

"I can assure you, Ernest, he thought about death all the time."

"Not when it came to bullfighting. Not in that painting. Miró is the only one to do it right."

"Do you know the painting?" Satan asked.

"I do," Hemingway said.

"Do you not like it?"

"I do like it," Hemingway said. "But I think he missed it. Missed the whole thing. He focuses on the crowd. It's like going to the theatre and turning your back to the stage."

"And you?" Satan said, the corners of his mouth lifted. "Have you ever missed any?"

"None," Hemingway said. "The leeches will say *Across the River and Into the Trees* but they've gotta pick something. Their reputations depend on it. That book is about what I knew, and it's truly written. Tennessee Williams knew it. He was about the only one who said anything good about it. Half the time the leeches don't know what the hell they're talking about." He sighed then paused before he spoke again. "It's a fine painting, but I know bullfighting. He doesn't."

"Nonetheless," Satan said. "He was working well and that is all that concerned me. Indeed, he and Gauguin worked well together for a few more weeks, but late in December it all came to an end."

"I know what happens next," Hemingway said.

Satan coughed into the rag.

"Everyone does, Ernest."

19

THEY STARTED DRINKING IN THE AFTERNOON OF DECEMBER 23 at the yellow house. They had each completed a small canvas in the morning, and now they sat in the kitchen and had just opened the second of two bottles of red wine Vincent had bought the day before.

Gauguin held up his glass, studying the wine in the light.

"C'est bon."

"It is," Vincent said, taking a gulp.

"Take your time, Vincent. You drink like you paint."

Vincent refilled his glass. His teeth were red from the wine.

"If I want wine, I drink it, Paul. You can keep the empty bottles for your memories."

Gauguin chuckled.

"Let's go to the café," he said.

Madame Ginoux sighed when they entered and stumbled past the billiards table and plopped at a table in the far corner. It wasn't the first time they'd arrived drunk before dinnertime. She made her way over to them with a bottle of absinthe, a small decanter of water, a spoon and two *pontparlier* glasses on a tray. The thickness of her frame cleared a path through the smoke of the room, a parting of the sea, a testament to the respect she commanded in her establishment. She knew all too well how things were going to go with these two; they were happy now, buzzy and jovial, but they'd argue and she'd tell them to keep it down, then they would drink more and she'd scold them and they would either obey or be told to leave.

"The two finest artists in all of France," she smiled, knowing it was best to keep them happy for as long as possible. She prepared two glasses at once.

Vincent watched her work, how she did it without effort, pouring the absinthe then scooping the sugar cubes and dabbing the water as the milky blend appeared, as if by magic, the perfect *louche*.

"You are the only true artist here," he said, his cheeks flushed.

Madame Ginoux grinned and slid the glasses toward them and then left them alone, leaving the room but not before slamming her hand down hard on a table to wake a drunk who'd fallen asleep.

Gauguin sipped his absinthe.

"Drink," he said.

"I will."

"What is it? Why so quiet all of a sudden?"

"It's nothing," Vincent said.

Gauguin grinned.

"My dear, Vincent, there is something on your mind. You do not hide it well."

"I received a letter from Theo yesterday. I've just thought of it again."

"And money?"

"Yes."

"But that's good," Gauguin said. "Was it not enough?"

"It was plenty."

"Then what is it?"

"He is getting married."

Gauguin perked up.

"Then let us celebrate tonight."

Vincent pushed out a smile.

"I am happy for him, truly. I am. But I'm worried, Paul."

"About what?"

"About me. About us," Vincent said. "He will start a family. He will not be able to support me." He finally reached for the absinthe and sipped. "I am awful for thinking it, I know. I mean it when I say I am happy for him, but I worry."

"Stop worrying and start drinking," Gauguin said. "I like you better when you're drunk."

Madame Ginoux came to their table often, fixing more absinthe for them until they asked for wine, and to her relief, they remained in good spirits. Vincent eventually livened up, putting his worries aside, and he and Gauguin laughed and joked and were pleasant until they left, stumbling out into the street.

"I'm nearly out of money," Gauguin said. His eyes were glossy, and then they widened a little. "But you're not."

"True," Vincent said.

Gauguin nodded toward a *Maison de Tolérance* a block away, and grinned. Vincent was already skipping toward it. Gauguin hurried to catch up.

"I want the redhead!"

Vincent laughed.

"I'll take that as a compliment!"

"What's her name?"

"Yvette," Vincent said.

"Mais oui—la belle Yvette!"

The doorkeeper was a skeletal old man propped up by a stiff white shirt and burgundy cravat, and his arm shook a little when he held open the door and they stepped past him and into the foyer. A teenage girl, sweeping the narrow foyer, bowed and stepped aside. The main room smelled heavily of tobacco smoke and was dimly-lit by angular candlelight, fluid and soft upon the walls and providing just enough intimacy in the darkness for the ladies who sat at the small round tables, grinning and sipping wine as the men ogled and drank and smiled and kissed their necks and whispered sweet drunken things into their ears before making their way upstairs.

Yvette was sitting in a lounge chair against the wall, dressed in a green corset, her bare shoulders showing. She looked no older than twenty but with tired eyes and lipstick smeared at the corners of her mouth, making her skin seem paler than it was, and her hair redder than it was. It was the smearing of her lipstick that Vincent noticed, and in his drunkenness his loins whirled.

Swaying, they stumbled over to her.

Vincent bowed.

"Bonjour, Mademoiselle Yvette."

Gauguin stepped in front of him.

"Bonjour, ma belle."

Vincent stepped around Gauguin, and Gauguin put out his arm, but Vincent shoved it away.

"I have the money," Vincent said. "My friend has none."

"You little shit!" Gauguin hissed. He turned to Yvette. "Please excuse my pupil. He's merely holding my money."

"*My* money," Vincent said.

"I have money," Gauguin said, digging into his pockets and pulling out a handful of francs.

"So you *do* have money," Vincent said. "How convenient."

Yvette's full red lips smeared into a grin.

"You can both have me if you like."

Gauguin turned lazily to Vincent and shrugged.

"It could work," he said. "You'd be finished before I begin."

A woman stepped out from behind a curtain. She was dressed in a corset, her black hair in a bun. Tiny ringlets fell over her ears. She was older than Yvette, and pretty, with a strong, confident face and beautiful eyes, blue and silver and sharp, like a wolf's.

"Gentlemen," she said. "There are many girls to choose from."

Vincent bowed again.

"Merci Madame. If you'd kindly find a girl for my friend, then Yvette and I can proceed."

Gauguin slapped Vincent in the face. Vincent stood stunned

for a second, before he lunged and they fell into a side table, a half-finished bottle of wine on the table tottering before the woman quickly secured it. They wrestled on the floor, rolling and swinging and grunting. The girl in the foyer stood dumbfounded with her broom, then the woman grabbed it from her and swatted them to a stop. Without speaking, she simply pointed to the door with the broom as the doorkeeper held it open. Vincent and Gauguin fell out into the street and settled on the curb. The worn stones of the road shone black in the moonlight.

"I am not your pupil," Vincent said.

"You invited me here so you can learn," Gauguin said. He stood up and stepped into the shadows and pissed against the side of a building. "You said so yourself."

"Do you honestly believe that?" Vincent said.

Gauguin peered over his shoulder.

"I do."

Vincent shook his head.

"Have you not learned anything from me?"

"Nothing," Gauguin said. He buttoned his trousers and started down the street. "Goodnight, Vincent."

Vincent got to his feet.

"You and your pathetic memory! You paint reflections, Paul. Reflections of reflections and nothing more!"

Gauguin stopped and turned.

"Goodnight," he said again.

Vincent dug into his pants pocket and pulled out a razor and held it out front of him, as one holds a candle.

Gauguin steadied himself the best he could.

"And now what? You're going to kill me?"

"I should," Vincent said. "It is likely you who's poisoning me."

"Do you not hear yourself? You're mad!"

Vincent's arms flung out from his sides.

"How else do you explain what's happening to me? All colour gone, shut off like a lantern only to come flooding back? Do you know how difficult that is? To see the world as it is, even but for a moment?"

Gauguin glanced at the razor.

"I don't know, Vincent."

"You're trying to kill me!"

"That's absurd and you know it," Gauguin said.

Vincent took a step toward Gauguin. Gauguin readied himself. Both were swaying.

"You haven't learned a thing from me?" Vincent said. "Not a thing? You are blind, Paul!"

The brothel's door opened, and the doorkeeper appeared. Yvette and another woman were in the window.

"Stop yelling," Gauguin said.

Vincent sighed, defeated.

"Have you done one spontaneous thing in all your life, Paul? Are you even capable of it?"

Gauguin relaxed his stance.

"I'm plenty spontaneous."

"Name one thing you've done."

"I came here."

Vincent spit onto the street.

"It took weeks to convince you," he said. "You don't understand, Paul—it's not in you to understand—to see what I see, to feel what I feel. I feel sorry for you."

"You're right," Gauguin said. "I don't understand. You can have your moment and your yellow house. It's all yours, Vincent. Goodbye." He started down the street again.

Gauguin knew, as he stumbled away, that he was done with Vincent, and done with Arles. He opted for a hotel instead of going back to the yellow house.

✤

Early the next morning, groggy, Gauguin entered Place Lamartine, his head low as he crossed the square. He didn't notice the small crowd that had gathered outside the yellow house until he was nearly upon it. Joseph Roulin, in his postal uniform, towered over them, a tree among weeds. Gauguin elbowed his way toward him.

"What's going on?"

Joseph shrugged.

"I just arrived. They're saying Vincent killed himself."

When Gauguin approached the front door, he was met by the local police inspector, Alphonse Robert. Gauguin knew who he was. He'd seen him before at the café whenever there was a melee. He would sometimes show up afterward and prance in as if to inspect the work of his officers, and he'd twist his long moustache and it gave him an air of arrogance. He was twisting his moustache now as he stood with two younger, uniformed gendarmes on both sides of him, like bookends, but with thinner moustaches.

"I live here," Gauguin said.

"There was a complaint," the inspector said.

"About what?"

"About the other man who lives here."

"Vincent?"

"Yes."

"What about him?"

"He was at the brothel last night."

Gauguin frowned.

"Yes? So? Is that a crime? Did he not pay?"

"There was an incident," the inspector said flatly.

Gauguin now noticed the dried blood on the door handle. Then he remembered Vincent and his razor, and his face went grey. He opened the door and looked inside.

"Vincent?"

The inspector and one of the gendarmes followed him in. A trail of blood led up the staircase. There was more blood smeared along the wall. They stepped into the bedroom and Gauguin stopped abruptly, gripping the doorframe. The room looked like a murder scene, with blood on the floor and the headboard and the wall. Vincent was lying in his bed. He was not moving. It looked as though his head had exploded. Clumps of blood mixed into his hair, matted and knotted and indiscernible from his face which was covered in blood, a deep and pure red. Gauguin remained in the doorway.

"Is he dead?"

The inspector leaned over Vincent's still body, stiffly, yet as casually as one leans when smelling flowers.

"It appears so."

The air was dry and stale and smelled of sweat and blood and paint. The young gendarme stretched over the small table and pressed his palms flat against the window-frames and pushed open the windows and a cool breeze whooshed into the room. Then, as the gendarme brought his arms down, Vincent moaned, which gave the gendarme a start and he jumped and bumped the table and knocked a jug of water onto the floor and it smashed and sent water everywhere. The inspector sighed, annoyed. Vincent moaned again, then turned his head and revealed the mangled flesh where his left earlobe had once been, the skin sheered, exposing the sliced cartilage, white in the red of the blood.

Gauguin's jaw dropped.

"Mon dieux, Vincent! What have you done?"

Unmoved, the inspector calmly pulled a notepad from inside his jacket.

"Your friend is very disturbed," he said, then looking down at the notepad he read: "Last night the doorman from la *Maison de Tolérance no 2* said Monsieur Van Gogh stormed into the establishment with a parcel. The doorman said there was a great amount of blood down his face and neck. He found a Mademoiselle Rachel—"

"Who?" Gauguin said, frowning.

"A mademoiselle in the foyer."

"You mean Gabrielle."

The inspector twisted his moustache.

"I was told her name is Rachel."

"Yes, well, she is called Gabrielle," Gauguin said. "I'm sure of it."

The inspector smirked.

"Forgive me, I'm not as familiar with this establishment's employees as you are." He peered down at his notepad again. "Monsieur Van Gogh handed her the package and told her to *guard it with her life—that it will be useful.* When the young woman opened it, she found what appeared to be a piece of flesh." He motioned toward Vincent. "His ear."

They stood for a moment without speaking, both looking over at Vincent, before the inspector turned back to Gauguin.

"He was ranting about you."

"I didn't do this," Gauguin said quickly.

The inspector peered down at his notepad again.

"The doorkeeper said that Monsieur Van Gogh entered the establishment mumbling about you, still holding the blade, then handed the bloody package to the prostitute."

"Gabrielle isn't a prostitute," Gauguin said. "She is a cleaning girl."

"I don't care what she is," the inspector said. "She received the ear."

Gauguin turned from the inspector to Vincent, then back to the inspector again.

"But why would he do such a thing?"

The inspector shrugged.

"He is your friend. You tell me. What were you arguing about?"

"We were drunk," Gauguin said. "We always argue."

"But what particular argument were you having last night? I was told it escalated into a physical altercation."

Gauguin shook his head.

"We pushed each other. We were drunk. It was nonsense. Like it always is."

The inspector rolled his eyes and twisted his moustache.

"There is no reason for doing what he did. Perhaps we will never know."

Gauguin shrugged.

"Earlier in the night he was upset about his brother getting married."

The inspector glanced over at Vincent, then back to Gauguin.

"And so, he does this?"

Gauguin said nothing.

The inspector twisted his moustache.

"Very disturbed," he said.

20

The train pushed on.

"It was not an act of madness," Satan said. "But that of a man trying desperately to prove a point he had grown tired of arguing."

"He wanted to show Gauguin how spontaneous he could be," Hemingway said, thinking aloud.

Satan managed a grin before coughing into the rag.

"Naturally, Gauguin did not see it that way. He returned to Paris the following day."

A moment later, Mr. Gregory arrived with the doctor who placed a thermometer under Satan's tongue, held it there for a moment, then plucked it from his mouth.

"Leave," Satan said.

The land sloped now, no flat fields anymore, but hills and protruding rocks. And it had grown steadily dimmer, into what can best be described as a light darkness; the varnish thicker. Hemingway backed his chair away from the fire before sitting down. Satan slithered a little deeper under his blanket and shivered again.

"Another log on the fire, Ernest, please."

Hemingway slid out of his chair and reached for a log and placed it on the burning logs. Satan coughed into the rag.

"Vincent was taken to the *Hôpital Arles*, where he was stitched and bandaged and woke up in a plain white room. Joseph Roulin was at his bedside."

"Loyal as a dog," Hemingway said.

"How you doing?" Joseph whispered. He was trying his best not to be loud in the quietness of the room, the stillness of it, and in that he became uncomfortable with his own voice, struggling to keep it to a whisper. "They patch you up alright?"

Vincent blinked, his eyes adjusting to the light and scanning the white room and its bare, chalky cleanliness. He became aware of the stiffness of the sheets, and how white the sun through the window made the wall look. So white it is blue, he whispered, his lips barely moving. So blue it's white. He suddenly became aware of the bandage, looping around his chin and over the top of his head, the pressure on his ear, where his ear had once been, up until now, whole.

"Go home," Vincent muttered. His throat was dry and his voice was croaky.

"Oh no," Joseph said. "No, I'm here, right here."

Vincent's eyes watered.

"Go home to your family, Joseph."

Joseph leaned in, as if ready to tell a secret.

"To be honest, I like it here. My house is never so quiet."

Vincent stared up at the ceiling.

"I'm sorry you have to see this. You are too good and too pure to be disturbed by the likes of me."

"Oh hush," Joseph said. He sat back in the wooden chair and gripped the lapels of his uniform, which seemed extravagant in the bareness of the room. The chair creaked under his bulk. "You sore?"

Vincent nodded a little.

"They got you all stitched up like Frankenstein," Joseph said.

Vincent's eyes opened a little wider.

"I read too," Joseph said. "I may not read the fancy stuff like you, but I read too. Madame Dupuis, do you know her? She is the one with the purple door."

"No," Vincent said. "But I know the door."

"She gives me books," Joseph said. "Her little house is filled with them. Stacks piled right up to the ceiling. I can bring some to you if you'd like. To help pass the time." He grinned again. "You don't need ears to read." He pulled a package from his pocket and placed it on the small table next to the bed. "Chocolates," he said. "Cherries in the centre. I picked them up from that place around the corner, the one with the cats in the doorway." He grinned, his voice getting louder the more he spoke. "I ate two of them on the walk over. I couldn't help myself." He placed another small package beside it. "And this," he said. "For you. For Christmas."

Vincent said nothing.

Just then, a young doctor in a white coat entered the room. His hair was cropped short, spiked at the bangs. A flawless goatee circled his chin, precisely where the jawbone separated from the chin, accentuating its sharpness, its prominence. This was a proud young man. He stood at the side of the bed with his papers.

"Bonjour, Monsieur Van Gogh," he said. "I am Doctor Felix Rey. How are you feeling?"

Vincent now realized the magnitude of what he'd done, the absurdity of it, and with this young doctor looking at him, holding his papers, he felt like an imbecile. The doctor and Joseph, despite their good intentions, would never—could never—understand what had happened, and Vincent felt sorry for them, especially for the young doctor, for how hopeful he looked; how horribly ignorant he was in his hopefulness.

"Are you in any discomfort?" Doctor Rey asked.

Vincent said nothing. A weight settled in his chest, with Joseph seeing him like this, the awful hollowness of *la tristesse* creeping in.

"Very well," Doctor Rey said. He made a quick note in his pad and left.

"He's just doing his job," Joseph said, more comfortable with his voice now, with how loud the doctor had spoken. "Maybe you ought to see what he wants. You want me to go get him?"

Vincent shook his head.

"You sure?"

Vincent nodded.

"Alright then," Joseph said. He sat back in the chair and twiddled his thumbs. "Can you hear alright with the bandages? You look like a mummy! Ha!"

When Vincent didn't respond, Joseph stood and placed his huge hand gently on Vincent's arm. "I've got to get back to work. You take care of yourself. Too bad you're here for Christmas. I'll be in to see you again."

Vincent's eyes watered again as soon as Joseph was gone. He was thinking of him and his family, who lived off 450 francs a month and so happy and their house so full of joy and love, and here he was, alone and bandaged like a fool, and so pathetic and so ashamed he did not even have the courtesy to say thank you or goodbye to Joseph who took time out of his morning, the day before Christmas, to come and be with him. How could it make him feel so miserable to have a friend like that? He peered over at the package and picked it from the table and tore it open. It was a red cravat, with a card that said *Joyeux Noel, cher Vincent. Ton ami, Joseph*. Tears fell down his face. It made no sense, the cruelty of the world.

The next morning was Christmas morning and Doctor Rey walked into the room whistling. Again, Vincent noticed the sharpness of his features, and how hopeful he looked in his ignorance.

"I am fine," Vincent said before the doctor could take his place at the foot of the bed.

"Joyeux Noel," Doctor Rey said. "You're talking today. That's good. Are you feeling better?"

Vincent said nothing.

Doctor Rey peered down at his papers.

"Do you know why you're here?"

Vincent nodded.

Doctor Rey gestured toward Vincent's ear.

"Do you know what you've done?"

Vincent nodded again.

Doctor Rey paused, thinking.

"Is it wrong that I know what I've done?" Vincent asked.

"No. But you are feeling better?" Doctor Rey said, a hint of hope in his posture.

"I just want to go home."

"I'm afraid that isn't possible at the moment," Doctor Rey said. "You'll have to stay a few days for observation."

"For my head or my ear?"

"There's something wrong with your head?"

"I did this to myself," Vincent said. "You tell me."

Doctor Rey did not look so hopeful anymore.

"It's unusual, the nature of your injury, to have inflicted this upon yourself. I've never heard of someone doing this."

"So, I'm mad, is that it?"

"Not necessarily," Doctor Rey said. "There could be a number of reasons for doing what you did."

Vincent eyed the whiteness of the walls. Out the window he could see a garden, bare shrubs and brown vines in the winter, and he imagined painting it, but not as it was now, but as it would be at the height of summer, lush and green.

Doctor Rey gestured to Vincent's ear again.

"Can I have a look?"

He carefully unravelled the bandage, worked the gauze and then leaned in and studied the wound.

"Yes, it looks good. It's clean. It has already begun to heal."

He rewrapped the bandage and stood at Vincent's side. A fly buzzed against the window then settled on the ceiling. A moment later, Vincent's eyes glared, and he shot straight up from the bed.

"Do you see that? The walls, the window! DO YOU SEE IT?"

Doctor Rey looked up to the ceiling.

"See what, monsieur? What do you see?"

"THERE!" Vincent screamed.

Suddenly he started convulsing, and Doctor Rey, quickly but

calmly, held him down, pressing firmly on his shoulders while managing to pluck a pencil from his breast pocket and place it across Vincent's mouth to prevent him from swallowing his tongue. Vincent bit down and snapped the pencil in two and Doctor Rey stuck his fingers in Vincent's mouth and retrieved the pieces, leaning hard still, pressing his weight against Vincent's body to keep him stable. Vincent's eyes rolled back in his head, his body shaking. A nurse sauntered into the room then quickly stiffened and held down Vincent's legs, and soon it was over, and Vincent lay limp and sweaty on the bed.

Doctor Rey was already thinking of possible epilepsy, but whatever Vincent had seen—or thought he'd seen—intrigued him. He stepped out of the room, and waited for the nurse.

"There is something more here," he said, his voice low. "Something more than epilepsy. Do you agree?"

"I don't know, sir. Perhaps."

"But what did he see?"

The following day, the sun shone so bright into the room that the white of the walls almost glowed. Vincent had slept most of the day, the darkness shrouding him, weighing him down. He tried to fight it, his eyes scanning the room, of how the sunlight shone on the walls and how, if he looked long and hard enough, he could see the blue in them, and yellow now too, tiny flecks of yellow sunlight amongst the blue. But it made him feel no better, and so he went back to sleep.

Doctor Rey came into the room late in the afternoon.

"Ah, you're awake. I thought you were going to sleep all day."

Vincent did not look up.

"How are you feeling?" Doctor Rey asked. He waited a moment then cleared his throat a little. "You've reverted back to not talking?"

Silence.

"Can you tell me what you saw yesterday? Do you remember?

Just before you had the seizure?"

Still, Vincent did not look up.

"I'm only trying to help." He cleared his throat again. "I would like to keep you here a few more days, to ensure it is healing properly, that there's no infection. But might I suggest a longer stay? It would be voluntary, of course." He shrugged, half to himself. "Peace of mind. Some fresh air." He peered down at his notes. "Very well, then. I will see you tomorrow."

For the next two days Doctor Rey saw him, and Vincent did not utter a word, preferring to sleep, or pretend to sleep when Doctor Rey came into the room. But then, one morning, Vincent sat up.

"I know you think I'm mad. Many people do."

"Well, bonjour," Doctor Rey said.

"Truly, I'm not mad," Vincent continued.

"That's good. I believe you. But were you mad when you sliced off your ear? Even but for a moment?"

"In a brief moment, perhaps, yes," Vincent said. "But now that I'm here, bandaged like a buffoon, I realize it was a stupid thing to do, a rather embarrassing thing to do."

"Then why did you do it?"

"There is no point," Vincent said. "That's for me. That's mine."

21

Doctor Rey had convinced Vincent to remain in the hospital a week longer and Vincent finally returned to the yellow house on January 7th. The house was quiet. Paul had left and taken many of his paintings with him and there were now bare spots on the walls. The house smelled musty and stale. Vincent climbed the stairs to his bedroom.

The bedroom was a scene of silent chaos, the blur of that terrible night now clear: the bloodied sheets and the pillow and the blood on the wall and the blood on the floor. He picked up the pieces of the water jug. He rolled the bloodied sheets into a ball and placed them at the foot of the bed.

He remembered what Doctor Rey had said and so he opened all the windows. The chilly January wind whirled through the house. At first it was refreshing, lifting his mood, the gloom suctioned out with the warm, musty air, the past whisked away and nothing but the cold and clear future ahead. But it got cold quickly. He put on his coat, then his fur hat, pulling it gingerly over his bandaged head.

He went into the studio where he sat and studied his face in his small shaving mirror which hung on the wall. He'd lost weight in the hospital. His cheeks were thin, his face almost skeletal, and the nurse had done a rough job shaving him, leaving bits of scruff about his cheeks and chin. His eyes, tired and tortured, stared back at him. This is the perfect self-portrait, he thought. A genuine portrait of the artist for what he is, and *who* he is. He smiled and felt the tug of the bandage against his jaw. It was the first time he'd smiled with the bandages and he liked that they tugged at his jaw, that they were there, and that he felt them. He gathered his paints and set up his easel. He worked quickly, feeling the familiar rush once he settled into it. His breath showed white in the cold room while he worked, but he did not shiver, he was not cold. He included in his portrait the Japanese work he'd hung not long after he'd moved into the yellow house, along with Gauguin's easel, behind him. Right where Paul belongs, he thought.

Once he was finished, he knew he'd captured what he'd seen in the mirror, the harshness of his face, the gaunt, broken man before him, and he was very pleased with it. You've got it, he thought. Exactly as it is. His eyes scanned the room.

"Do you see this, Paul? Enjoy your memories. I have what's here and now. What *is*!"

He remained inside the yellow house for the next three days.

All the windows stayed open. Passersby glanced inside, hoping to get a peek at the *fou roux*, the redheaded madman who'd cut off his own ear. Indeed, the incident morphed from town gossip into printed news. From *Le Forum Republicain*:

> Last Sunday, at 11:30 in the evening, Vincent van Gogh, a painter of Dutch origin, called at the Brothel No. 1, asked for a woman called Rachel and handed her ... his ear, saying: 'Guard this object with your life'. Then he disappeared. When informed of the action, which could only be that of a pitiful madman, the police went the next day to his house and discovered him lying on his bed apparently at the point of death. The unfortunate man has been rushed to hospital.

Vincent kept the windows open all the time, even through the night, wearing his coat and fur hat while he slept, and of course when he worked. And all the neighbourhood kept their eyes on him. But Vincent did nothing to excite anyone except to live in a frigid house. Then one morning, after shivering in his sleep all night, he awoke to a world in grey. He rushed into the hall, rubbing his eyes, trying to fix upon something, anything with colour. He ran to the kitchen, to the side of the house that faced the morning sun, but it was the same: a dullness, a nothingness, a hopeless grey. He ran up the stairs and into Gauguin's old room and there, miraculously, glowing yellow as the sun, was his painting of the yellow sunflowers. It lit the room with a warm, concentrated glow. He sat on the floor and fixed his eyes upon it, staying there the entire day and into the evening, drinking the last of a bottle of wine and falling asleep in Gauguin's bed. When he awoke the next morning, the world was back to normal, and he wondered if it had all been a terrible dream. Outside his window was the blue of the sky and the creamy white of the clouds. And he started to laugh. It was absurd, how the world made him suffer so.

By mid-January his ear was healing well. He'd visited Doctor Rey who'd told him he no longer required the bandage.

"Besides," Doctor Rey had said, stroking his goatee into a point. "Exposure to fresh air will do it good."

Vincent set out on a stroll through town, his gnarled ear exposed for all to see. And there was a skip in his step. It felt good to be outside, and he absorbed everything he saw. The colours were more revealing than ever, even the road, the different yellows of the stones, the blue-grey mortar of the buildings. Everything sparkled like tiny stars for only him to see. But the instant he turned the corner to his house it struck again. It was no longer a yellow house, but grey. The dreaded grey. Not again, he thought. Please not again! He ran toward his house, eyes half-closed, hoping, praying it wasn't so.

Just then, a neighbour stepped out from his building and into Vincent's path, and Vincent grabbed him.

"It's you! You've poisoned me. IT'S YOU!"

The man pushed him away.

"Get away from me, you crazy fool!"

"I KNOW IT'S YOU!" Vincent cried.

The man was a muscular, solid man of the fields with wide shoulders and big coarse hands, now clenched into fists. He took a second, deciding whether to engage Vincent or not, then he shook his head and carried on across the square.

Vincent was breathing fast, his heart racing. He didn't care that people were watching; the hotelier unloading crates from a horse-pulled cart, a woman dragging her child around the corner, eager to move on, and an older man up on his second-storey balcony, holding a cup of coffee and watching with a curious grin, trying to figure out what to make of his redheaded neighbour everyone talked about.

Vincent dropped and sat on the curb. He picked a few pebbles and played with them in his hands. Then he took a long deep breath, knowing he could not shake it out of his head. One breath, then another, long and smooth, just as Doctor Rey showed you, he thought. He did it. One breath. Then another. It began to work. The world was trickling in, first as bits of dulled-down hues, then brighter, until the yellow of his house showed in full. The hotelier carried on with his work, and up on the balcony the man still stood with his cup of coffee, watching him. Vincent picked himself up and went into his house where he planted himself in front of the yellow sunflowers and stayed in bed for the next three days.

Many Arlesiens were talking about him now.

Have you seen the madman today?

He keeps his windows open through the night.

I saw him yesterday, drunk at ten o'clock in the morning.

The children are afraid of him.

He's dangerous.

He needs to go.

His only supporter was Joseph Roulin. Vincent knew whenever Joseph was visiting because he would holler at those he caught peering into the yellow house, his voice carrying down the street. Vincent would look out his window and see him cutting across the square, between the rows of leafless platanes along the street, his huge, gorilla-like arms flailing about.

"HAVE YOU NO DECENCY? LET ANY ONE OF YOU HAVE A TRAGEDY IN YOUR LIFE AND THE WHOLE DAMNED NEIGHBOURHOOD TREATS IT LIKE A SPECTACLE! YOU SHOULD ALL BE ASHAMED!"

Once he screamed at a group of children who'd gathered and sniggered and threw stones at the house, trying to get a glimpse of Vincent.

"GO ON, ALL OF YOU LITTLE BASTARDS! I KNOW YOUR PARENTS!"

The children would laugh and throw more stones and wait until Joseph was nearly upon them before running away.

And though Joseph was an imposing figure, he was far outnumbered. The children kept coming, kept throwing stones, and the eyes of every townsperson inevitably veered toward the yellow house.

It wasn't long before the police knocked on Vincent's door.

Vincent answered in his coat and fur hat.

It was Inspector Robert. He twirled his moustache.

"Monsieur Van Gogh?"

Standing beside the inspector was a much younger officer, who was smaller, and whose face was clean-shaven, with boyish rosy cheeks. He leaned ever-so-slightly to get a glimpse of Vincent's gnarled ear, and when he saw it his eyes widened before straightening himself again.

"Oui?" Vincent said.

Inspector Robert peered beyond Vincent, to the cluttered walls, the stacks of canvases, the smell of turpentine wafting from the house.

"Monsieur Van Gogh, I have a petition…"

❦

The fire burned bright. Satan's feet were still out of the blanket, the flames tickling his toes. There was a flatness to his body under the blanket, as though he were deflated. When he breathed, the blanket would rise a little then fall flat again.

"Thirty residents had signed a petition. They took him that day, and the yellow house was closed up. Doctor Rey offered him a place to store his paintings and what few belongings he had."

Hemingway uncorked a bottle of wine and emptied it into his wineskin.

"But he wasn't insane," he said. He squeezed a mouthful of wine. "This is damned good."

Satan coughed bits of blood into the rag.

Outside in the darkness, the land sloped and there were steeper climbs and steeper descents, and the train's engine pushed and thrust up the hills until the brakes fought the weight of the cars as it descended again.

Satan gathered his strength and sat up. Then he nodded out the window.

"It is not long now."

Hemingway pressed his face against the window. The black outlines of the mountains were high and jagged.

Satan coughed into the rag.

"After the petition, Vincent admitted himself to the asylum at Saint-Rémy where he stayed for a year. I would strike him only once over the course of his stay. He struggled dearly with it; indeed, it took him nearly two months to recover and I feared perhaps I had ruined him."

Hemingway frowned.

"How so?"

"To the point where he would never paint again."

"It was that bad?"

"He had gone truly mad. He slept days at time. He heard voices. He did not talk to anyone for weeks. Nor did he lift a brush. I feared I had overstepped. But then, slowly, he began to emerge from his cell. He began talking to the other patients, who, in their own madness, suffered similar episodes, and this had comforted him and eventually brought him back to where he was painting again."

"And you left him alone?"

"Not entirely alone. I visited him, to be sure he was himself again."

"You weren't worried you'd do him in for good?"

"I did not strike him at the asylum," Satan said. "Though I doubt it would have mattered; his work had reached a level even I had underestimated—and its power too."

22

THERE WAS A NEGLECTED GARDEN ON THE ASYLUM GROUNDS; overgrown fig and olive trees, hundred-year-old cypresses, ivy and periwinkle and bunches of wildflowers strewn messily among the weeds. Nobody went into the garden, instead preferring to walk around it or sit on one of the stone benches at its periphery.

Vincent liked it best inside the garden, among the colours and the sunlight and the smells. In the early afternoon the sunlight covered the entire garden and lit it in such a way that he often imagined that this must be what the Garden of Eden looked and smelled and felt like. For Vincent it was solace, a place of pretty flowers, a place where his head was clear. Each day he would set up his easel and paint or sketch. He was especially drawn to a patch of irises that had recently formed in the southeast corner, and he knew he had to paint them, that he only had a small window because the pity with irises, though one of the most beautiful flowers, was that they came and went in little more than ten days; the flower itself its own destructor, growing too quickly and blooming brilliant blue and yellow and violet until the stem folded or broke, unable to hold its own weight. These irises had just about peaked, and he knew, sadly, that soon the weight of their beauty would be too much to bear, and they would be lost. But if he captured them on canvas just as they were now, well, they would live forever.

"Those were my mother's favourites," Satan said, peering down at the patch of irises. He was dressed in the stock, light blue jumpsuit some patients wore.

Vincent, his pipe stuck firmly between his lips, splashed the paint onto the canvas.

"She said they reminded her of the moonlight," Satan said.

"There are many different blues, but the yellow is its heart," Vincent said, still laying the paint on thick. "Every flower has a heart."

"I have heard about your studio next to your sleeping cell," Satan said. He smiled. "I listen to the doctors when they talk. May I see it?"

"Not now," Vincent said.

"Goodness, no. I meant when you are finished."

Vincent slapped down the paint.

"When I am finished," he said.

Satan smiled.

"The nurses say the room has healing powers."

Vincent said nothing and continued to work.

Satan made his way over to the asylum's shaded terrace and sat and watched from a distance. He had seen how much Vincent had changed over the year. There was a controlled intensity about him now. A calm, cleaner focus, withdrawn from the outside world, faded, like a ghost, and fully absorbed in the world of his work. From where Satan sat, Vincent seemed illuminated. Sunlight on sunlight. Yellow on yellow.

When Vincent was finished, Satan walked over to have a look at the painting: a cluster of irises that leaned, almost sweepingly across the canvas.

"Do you suppose your mother would find the moonlight in these?" Vincent asked, finishing it with dabs of sparse brushstrokes.

"Perhaps," Satan said. "And the stars and the night sky too."

Vincent stepped away from the canvas.

"Come with me."

His studio was next to his sleeping cell. All four walls were covered with paintings and drawings. A lone, high-arched and barred window let in some light from outside. The window was set deep in the thick wall and Vincent had placed a variety of coloured bottles in the windowsill. There were paintings of just about every kind of flower in the garden and on the grounds, and cypresses too, and beyond the grounds, the gold of the fields and the peasants who worked them, and beyond that too, to the distant countryside and the mountains.

Vincent sat on a stool in the corner of the cell. He had set up his work so that there was a flow; colours faded in and out as you looked from one to the next, and all were brash in thick gobs of colour and heavy brushstrokes of his impasto style, some as vibrant as anything he'd done to this point, but others, landscapes, dark, with blues and greys and blacks, the contrasts sharper. But there was something else. Satan felt the glow of the room, the warmth of it, and the light it produced.

"Remarkable," he muttered.

Vincent pulled his pipe from his vest pocket, packed it with tobacco, struck a match, and lit it.

"You did all of this in one year?" Satan asked.

"Eleven months," Vincent said, puffing on his pipe.

"Do you have a favourite?"

"Do *you?*"

Satan did a quick turn about the room.

"I like them all," he said. "But I prefer the brighter ones."

"What about that one?" Vincent said, pointing to a night scene with a swirling sky. "It's the view from here; from out the window. Many of the landscapes are of this same view, at different times of day and night. But that one," he said, a hint of pride in his voice. "It is my favourite. It had been on my mind for some time and it fulfills me more than any other. It appeared to me as if by magic. I found myself in a dream state and suddenly the sky opened, revealing herself, the way she moves, in waves, in constant motion, and I saw more light than on the brightest of days and I painted it in a fury. Truly, I don't remember much of it. It's my Xanadu, my Kubla Khan."

Satan spotted a straw hat on the floor in the corner of the cell, next to Vincent's folded easel. Secured to the hat by string were two half-melted candles, sticking straight up, like worn horns, the melted wax forming a smooth coating along the brim and over the string.

"And that is how you see at night?"

"It is," Vincent said.

Satan kept his eyes on the hat.

"It's quite an invention."

"Tell that to the locals," Vincent said. "They know I am living here. When I go out to paint with that on my head you can only imagine what they think of me. But I don't worry about that anymore. I worry only about the work."

"As you should," Satan said. He spotted another night scene and held his stare for a moment.

"That is over the Rhône," Vincent said.

"I like it," Satan said. He paused. "But the brighter ones—"

"Yes," Vincent said. "You can *feel* them."

"Yes," Satan said. He pointed to a vibrant bright landscape with a peasant working the field, fiercely yellow and gold. "What do you call this one?"

"*Wheat Field with Reaper and Sun.*"

"Reaper?" Satan said.

"The peasant," Vincent said. "We are the grain he is cutting down."

"Who?"

"Humanity."

"But it's so bright, and in broad daylight."

"Death isn't always about darkness," Vincent said.

Satan grinned. He closed his eyes and let the light soak in. Soon he began to feel a tingle in his bones, and he lost himself in it, a feeling of fullness, buzzing, swimming through him.

"I have a confession," he said. "I know who you are."

Vincent frowned.

"From where?"

"Arles."

"The *fou roux* from Arles?"

Satan didn't reply.

"Wonderful," Vincent said with a smile. "Even the crazies think I'm crazy."

"I don't think you're crazy," Satan said. "I think you are a saviour."

Vincent was amused now.

"To whom?"

"To me," Satan said.

He did not know why he'd said this, and suddenly a cloud of vulnerability swept over him. He stepped out of the room, into the sleeping cell, embarrassed with himself, for this rare moment of weakness.

The train sped through the gloom. The fire burned. Satan squirmed lower under the blanket.

"Never had I felt such vulnerability."

"Art is powerful stuff," Hemingway said.

"Indeed," Satan said. "I underestimated it. The room itself had healing powers, something I had not expected." He shivered. "But within this realization came the assurance that my plan would succeed."

"The Boulevard," Hemingway said.

"Yes."

"It was a damned good plan," Hemingway said. "Any operation requiring patience and seen through to the end has a better chance at success than some half-ass blitzkrieg. But it is more difficult to do—to hold the line when you see the fight in front of you—to hold it until the perfect time. The patient generals are the ones who win in the end."

Satan lifted his chin from under the blanket and coughed into the rag.

"The end was near. Vincent was almost ready. It had its hold on him. There was no turning back." He tucked his chin back under the blanket. "Do you see, Ernest? I did not do much. There was no need. Nature had run its course."

Hemingway laughed.

"That's like saying the rummy isn't to blame for putting the bottle to his own mouth."

"The rummy is born a rummy, Ernest."

"But he's not a rummy without the rum."

"And what kind of a world would it be without rum?" Satan asked.

Hemingway laughed again.

"Or rummies."

A burning log crackled. Satan stretched his legs so that his feet were right in the fire, his heels resting on the burning coals. Then he withdrew his feet from the flames and started coughing, then hacking, and slumped over the side of the chair. Hemingway scooped him up and carried him to his sleeping quarters and placed him in his bed. Mr. Gregory came with the doctor.

Satan raised his hand from off the sheets and motioned

toward the doctor, who stood near the door, next to Mr. Gregory.

"Go away," he said.

"You should let him check you out," Hemingway said.

Satan closed his eyes and shook his head. Every movement was in slow-motion.

Mr. Gregory escorted the doctor out.

Satan tapped the sheets for Hemingway to sit.

"Not long now, Ernest."

Hemingway lifted himself onto the foot of the bed, his back resting against the window, his feet dangling over the side. The train braked and descended into a steep valley covered in dwarf shrubs, sedges, lichens, heath, and other small plants. It was dark here, a gloom shrouding the land as dense as fog.

Satan continued to cough, his face contorting. Then, once it had passed, his body settled, and he was ready to talk again.

"After Saint-Rémy, Vincent had reached a point of no return."

23

Vincent checked out of the asylum and went to Paris to see Theo, his wife, and their infant son. Three days later, upon Theo's insistence, he took the train to Auvers-sur-Oise, about an hour away, where he rented a room at the Ravoux Inn.

Eating his first lunch at the tavern—bread, cheese, a beef broth, and a beer—he thought back to his work while at Saint-Rémy, at how he'd allowed for darker colours to creep in, and now, after three days in Paris, he was determined to use the boldest colours he could find—deep violets and crisp yellows and burning reds. The reds must burn, he thought. And the blues and greens must cool. And the yellows breathe. The yellows and greens and blues and reds must all breathe and move and be more real than the real thing.

After lunch, he walked up to the church, then over to Daubigny's house and garden, and then down to the Oise River where he sat in the shade of the trees, watching the river flow by. He walked into the countryside. There were flowers everywhere, and they sang to him. He returned to the inn late in the afternoon. The tavern was busier now. He drank a bottle of wine and stumbled up the narrow winding staircase to his room.

The following day, he made the twenty-five-minute trek to meet with the homeopathic doctor Paul Gachet for the first time. Theo had contacted Gachet to look after Vincent, after their friend Camille Pissarro had recommended him.

Gachet's house sat high above the road, behind an eight-foot stone wall. Vincent peered through the barred door, atop the stone steps, to the three-storey house, high and white in the sunlight. He opened the gate and climbed the narrow stone steps up to the front garden. The garden was bright and warm and filled with roses and marigolds and chrysanthemums and daisies. Thuja trees provided some shade near the front of the garden, where a cat emerged and scampered around to the back of the house. Vincent knocked on the door and waited. Gachet appeared and smiled.

"You must be Vincent," he said. "You resemble your brother."

The house was cozy with its narrow main hallway and cluttered rooms. In one room, unfinished stained glass was perched on a windowsill next to a vase of wilted flowers. In another, two cats slept on a couch covered in quilts. Artwork filled every available wall space, some good, some clearly by an amateur hand. Vincent recalled what Theo had told him of the doctor; that he was a painter too, and had worked with many artists, including Cézanne and Pissarro. Vincent spotted a small, framed Pissarro of a streetscape, the canal and the cottages on either side. He spotted another painting. Cézanne's.

Gachet led him past a room with green wallpaper and a red rug and a dark piano in the corner. Vincent loved these contrasts and promised himself to paint this room one day. They stepped out to the back of the house and into the small courtyard, shaded by trees and a limestone cliff. Two large dogs lay flat on a small patch of grass. One lifted its head to look at them, then fell lazily again. In the dark of the shade at the foot of the lime cliff stood a row of pens with chickens and rabbits. A chicken wandered out from behind one of the pens and Gachet scooped it up, its wings flapping and a few feathers falling as he placed it back into the pen and clicked the small gate.

"Don't let anyone tell you chickens aren't intelligent. They have somehow figured out the latch. Half the time I can't figure it out. They rule the roost indeed, and the yard too." He then stood a moment, looking around the space. "There is more sunlight in the front. Perhaps you'd prefer that?"

"It's your house," Vincent said.

Gachet led him around the house to the front garden and Vincent now saw it from a new angle; he spotted some colourful potted plants amongst the lush greenery, and string fencing with vines and batches of tiny raspberries and tomato plants just beginning to bud. A hen clucked and pecked at the ground. Two more cats roamed for mice, in and out of the sunlight. Facing the road now, Vincent could see the orange rooftops of the houses on the street below, and beyond them, to the river and the hilly countryside in the valley of Oise, with its long stretch of forest in the distance, black and green and grey under the wide country sky.

They sat in two chairs at the corner of the house. Gachet had a strong jawline and high forehead and ruffled hair.

"You look more like a painter than a doctor," Vincent said.

Gachet perked up.

"What a lovely thing to say."

Vincent noticed the prominent nose and the goatee and the sad eyes.

"I didn't do many portraits at the asylum and am realizing now how much I've missed them." He began packing his pipe when a girl appeared, seemingly from nowhere, with a tray of lemonade.

"Ah," Gachet said. "My daughter, Marguerite."

Marguerite was nineteen years old with big eyes and thick

blonde hair and shapely hips. She bowed her head and placed the tray on the table.

"How I've missed it," Vincent said.

Marguerite slipped back into the house as quickly as she'd appeared.

As Gachet sipped his lemonade, Vincent noted his comical routine, holding the glass out, arm extended, pinky extended, mouth open as if to gulp it down, but pursing his lips at the last second for a quick sip.

"Theo showed me your work," Gachet said. "Impressive. I would like to have a few of your paintings in my house."

"I plan on working hard here," Vincent said.

"Cézanne has painted all around here; the house, the garden, the street."

"I saw him on your walls."

"You can do the same," Gachet said. "Feel free to work wherever you want."

Vincent bowed his head.

"Thank you. I shall find myself quite content to paint in this garden, if it's no trouble."

"Good. How are you feeling? You seem anxious."

Vincent was surprised at how abruptly the pleasant conversation ended. He wanted to talk more about his work and the shift had caught him off-guard. He struck a match and lit his pipe to let the moment pass.

"My trunk hasn't arrived."

"How does that make you feel?"

"Frustrated, naturally," Vincent said. "I didn't have it in Paris, and not here still." He paused. "You have spoken to Theo. I suppose you know more about me than I do."

"My apologies, Vincent. Sometimes I come across a bit brash." He took another sip of lemonade, with the same comical routine.

"Apology accepted," Vincent said.

Gachet looked around his property.

"I've tried to paint my garden here many times, but alas, I'm merely a painter of will. I've no talent."

"Will goes a long way," Vincent said. He puffed on his pipe, the smoke whirling between them.

"You're speaking of passion," Gachet said. "I can tell you're a man of great passion. Perhaps in that way we're similar. I'm passionate about things too, about how I feel too. Two or three days a week I travel to Paris for work. But it's only work. I do not care for the bustle of Paris, and perhaps that's why I don't care for the work there."

"I'll trade you," Vincent said. "Job for job."

Gachet smiled. He took another sip of lemonade.

"My daughter, do you like her? She makes wonderful lemonade. I'm sure she will leave me one day and take her lemonade with her."

His mind is as cluttered as his house, Vincent thought. He wondered why Theo had recommended him to such a strange fellow, but he liked him, his oddness somehow appealing, and he told himself to give the doctor a chance. He would paint him, and his garden, and his daughter too.

❧

When he returned to the inn later that morning, he stumbled upon a young girl in his room, making his bed. She jumped in surprise when he appeared at the top of the staircase.

"Bonjour, monsieur."

She was a girl of about thirteen, Vincent guessed, with a crooked, awkward frame, long skinny arms and legs, and a prominent nose.

Vincent remained in the doorway.

"You must be Adeline Ravoux."

"Oui, monsieur."

Vincent noticed his trunk against the wall.

"It arrived shortly after you left," Adeline said. "My father had it brought up to your room."

Vincent opened it and grabbed a canvas, his easel, and paints.

And then he bowed.

"It was a pleasure to meet you, young lady."

The girl curtsied and went back to making the bed. Vincent descended the narrow, winding staircase, holding his easel in front of him, careful not to scrape the walls.

He was pleased his trunk had arrived, undamaged, and he knew exactly what he wanted to paint. The church stood on the hill, where the steep road wound around and up to the clearing of the wheat fields. The church had dominant rooftops and magnificent, high, arched windows.

Vincent hurried to get there, anxious to begin, skipping up the alley and up the huge medieval steps at the back of the church. He walked around to the front and set up his easel along the steep road, pressing himself against an old stone wall, sheltering him from the blazing sun. The sky behind the church was pure blue, not a cloud, and though it was not ideal to have his easel standing slanted on the steepness of the road, he was excited to paint today, and he was smiling as he began with a charcoal outline. But his pleasant day did not last long.

❧

"I struck him in front of the church, not long after he had begun sketching," Satan said. "He remained calm, closing his eyes and breathing. He lay down and gripped the stones of the wall."

Hemingway crossed his arms.

"I thought you said you were gonna leave him alone."

"That was then," Satan said. "Auvers was a new place, a new beginning. I wanted to see if he was still adapting, and I felt it safe to try."

"And was he?" Hemingway asked.

"He was," Satan said. "He did not have a seizure. But he did not paint that day." He coughed, meekly. "It was the aftereffect which counted most. It left him defeated. He gathered his things and lugged them back down to the inn where he buried himself in his bed until evening, when he went downstairs and drank himself into a stupor. Two patrons, under the direction of Monsieur Ravoux, carried him up to his room, where he remained in bed for the next two days."

24

Vincent awoke to a knock on his door.

"Go away," he said.

"Biscuits and tea, monsieur. My father asked that I bring it to you."

Vincent wiped the sleep from his eyes. His mouth was dry, and he was sweating through his shirt.

"Come in."

Adeline cautiously stepped into the room and placed the tray on the small table next to the bed.

"Merci," Vincent said softly, guiltily.

Adeline curtsied and closed the door behind her. Vincent struggled to sit up, the weight in his chest feeling like a bundle of stones. The room was very small, the walls close and colourless and bare, but oddly enough, it was the bareness of the room, the hopelessness of it, that gave him the strength to fight it, the refusal to let it defeat him again, that the sun through the small skylight was calling to him, telling him to come out into the light. Sit up, he told himself. Sit up and eat. He fought the weight of his body and lifted himself out of bed and sipped the tea until the cup was empty. Then he ate the biscuits, crumbs and all, that each crumb would help, each little crumb lifting the weight, until he found the strength to gather his things and make his way down the staircase, into the outside world, and up the road to the church again.

He worked vigorously, pushing the weight aside, focussing only on the canvas, shutting out everything around him, everything in him. When he was finished, he sat on the road, resting his back against the coolness of the shaded wall—the same stone wall he'd reached for and had grounded him during his episode two days earlier—and breathed. He was pleased with himself, to have won this fight, to have emerged from it, but now that he was finished, he could feel the weight creeping in again. He returned to the inn, ate a bowl of stew, drank a bottle of wine, and went back to bed.

Slowly, the weight trickled away, and he painted seven more canvases over the next ten days. Auvers, it seemed, was what he'd hoped it would be. He was scheduled to meet with Dr. Gachet again, and he arrived at Gachet's door with his easel, canvas, and paints. He was excited for it, to paint Gachet, to paint any portrait, and he'd jogged all the way to Gachet's house.

"I am going to paint you," he said.

Gachet looked down at his shirt and pulled on it a little, straightening it.

"Where do you want me?"

"In the front garden," Vincent said. "With the countryside behind you."

"Marguerite—" Gachet called into the house. "Lemonade!"

Gachet sat in the chair at the corner of a long orange table while Vincent set up his easel.

"How do you want me?"

"Just relax," Vincent said. "Be natural."

Marguerite appeared with two glasses of lemonade.

"Not on the table," Vincent said.

"Put them on the ground," Gachet said. He grunted and sat up straight. Marguerite knelt and placed the glasses at their feet. A cat came over to investigate, tail raised, purring, sniffing about.

Vincent eyed Gachet.

"Rest your elbow on the table, please."

Gachet did, and then rested his head in his hand. Vincent took a moment and studied the scene. There were two yellow books at end of the table, and he slid them next to Gachet.

"Too much orange?" Gachet said, running his palm over the table.

"Not enough yellow," Vincent said. "Never enough yellow."

Gachet rested his elbow on the table again, head in hand.

"Stop smiling," Vincent said. "Just be yourself."

"Do you think I am someone who doesn't smile?" Gachet asked.

"Not a lot," Vincent said.

"And what makes you say that?"

Vincent shrugged.

"I don't know. A hunch."

"I smiled the moment we met."

"You do, sometimes," Vincent said. "You've got a good memory."

"I'm a doctor," Gachet said. "A good memory is required."

"Yes," Vincent said. "One requires no memory to paint. You only need eyes."

"Vision indeed," Gachet said. "And talent."

Vincent held up a finger.

"Vision without talent is nothing."

"And so is talent without vision," Gachet said. "A healthy balance then. But what does one do who has neither vision nor talent?"

"He becomes a doctor," Vincent said.

"Ha!"

Gachet leaned a little to the side, rested his head on his hand and tried not to move.

"Tell me, Vincent, how was your first week in Auvers?"

"I worked very well last week."

"That's wonderful."

"I had another attack."

Gachet perked up.

"Be still, please," Vincent said.

"When?"

"Let's not talk about it," Vincent said. "I am fine today and I've been fine the last few days and I am working well again and that's all I care about."

"I'm only curious," Gachet said.

Vincent knelt for the glass of lemonade and took a long drink.

"I haven't done many portraits lately, so this makes me particularly happy."

"Happy?"

Vincent shrugged.

"I am *pleased* today."

"It is okay to say you are happy."

Vincent said nothing. He took another long drink, finishing the glass, then, frowning, he examined Gachet again.

Gachet was frowning now too.

"What is it?"

Vincent stepped over to a bunch of purple foxglove.

"May I?"

"Anything you need," Gachet said.

Vincent snapped off two sprigs of the herb and laid it on the table, over the books, then stepped behind the canvas. He started with a rough sketch, then squeezed the tubes of paints onto his palette.

"You work quickly," Gachet said.

It was not a criticism, but a curiosity, and Vincent was not offended; Gachet was not judging him as Gauguin had.

"Cézanne is very articulate with his brush," Gachet said.

Vincent nodded.

"I admire his work."

"Who else do you admire?"

"Millet for certain," Vincent said, his head popping out from behind the canvas then ducking behind it again. "And Delacroix, and Rembrandt, of course. But one cannot come to Auvers without Daubigny."

"And your friends in Paris?"

"Some, yes," Vincent said. "Others, not so much."

"How was your time with Gauguin?" Gachet asked. "Theo said it didn't go as planned."

"That is an understatement. Let's save that conversation for another day."

"Why not now?"

Vincent shrugged.

"Another time," he said. "Please."

"Very well," Gachet said.

Vincent stepped back, and allowed himself a chuckle.

"You're a strange doctor. Do you know that?"

"I do," he said, clearly not offended.

"Perhaps I was mistaken about you," Vincent said.

"About what?"

"Not smiling."

"It depends on the company."

Vincent paused.

"You're a revolutionary."

"But of course!" Gachet said. "We both are. And you, you smile a lot too."

"Today, maybe, yes," Vincent said.

"Does it have to do with the company?" Gachet asked.

Vincent shrugged, and kept painting, and they talked more of art, and of Paris. Vincent was not thinking but just talking, his focus on the canvas. When he was nearly finished, he stepped back.

"I will finish it tomorrow," he said. "Would you care to meet for lunch at the Ravoux? I can show it to you then."

Gachet sat up and clapped his hands together.

"Wonderful. Tomorrow then. May I see it?"

"Tomorrow," Vincent said.

The next day they met at the Ravoux Inn. Gachet sat opposite Vincent. Gachet stretched out his arms.

"You look good."

"I feel good," Vincent said.

"Is it always this way after you are finished?"

"No," Vincent said. "But today it is."

"It's important that you work, to keep your balance," Gachet said. Then he grinned. "I might use it to prescribe to my other patients."

Vincent nodded.

"It's a temporary fix."

"So is morphine," Gachet said, and laughed.

They were sitting next to the front window, facing the street and the square with the straight, symmetrical town hall building with its whiteness clean in the blue sky behind it.

"I painted the town hall two days ago," Vincent said. He looked down at the menu. "The food is good here. The vegetable soup is hearty, and the fish is fresh, and the bread is fresh."

"I've dined here many times," Gachet said. "When I come in from Paris, I eat here before I go home." He smiled. "I can tell Auvers is serving you well."

"Yes, indeed," Vincent said.

"Is it the work or Auvers?"

"Both, I think."

"I am looking forward to seeing my portrait."

"It's upstairs in my room," Vincent said. "It's still drying. I've only just finished it an hour ago."

It was a more extravagant lunch than Vincent had planned for: a bottle of chilled white wine, herring and salmon fillets in oil with capers and asparagus, followed by potatoes and lamb, and finished with a chocolate mousse. Gachet had insisted on paying.

After lunch, Vincent led Gachet upstairs to his tiny room where he'd placed the portrait on the bed, perched so that it faced them from the doorway. Gachet stood a good while before he spoke.

"Is that how I look? Truly?"

"It's not just you," Vincent said. "It's an expression of our time."

Gachet ran his fingers through his goatee.

"Is the whole world heartbroken?"

"It is," Vincent said. He paused. "Do you not like it?"

"It's a very good painting," Gachet said. He sighed. "It is indeed me, sad and confused. It's difficult to see yourself, your true self so clearly portrayed. And we've only just met." He grinned. "You'd make a fine physician, Vincent."

"It's because we are alike," Vincent said.

Gachet chuckled.

"Marguerite says you are a younger version of me."

"We have the same nose," Vincent said.

"A strong nose," Gachet said. "Better to smell the flowers with."

"Or shit," Vincent said.

Gachet laughed, and stood, arms crossed, staring at the portrait.

"Can you paint one for me? The same as this? You must, please, for my house."

"Of course," Vincent said.

Gachet could not look away from the painting.

"I do like it."

He stood for a few minutes, just looking at it, and then his face became serious.

"Marguerite has the same eyes, the same sadness. I suspect you'd like to paint her too?"

"Very much so," Vincent said. "At the piano or in the garden. Or both, with your permission, of course."

"Paint whomever or whatever you please," Gachet said. "But when you paint Marguerite, can you promise me something?"

"Anything," Vincent said.

Gachet sighed.

"She is a young girl, and she is fond of you—"

Vincent blushed.

"No, I don't think—"

"I'm her father," Gachet said. "I saw how she acted last week after you left—smiling too much—too much for a father not to notice. But I'm not talking about that." He sighed again. "When you paint her, can you not show her face? As beautiful as it is, her eyes, sad beyond anything a father can do to bring joy to them, would make me too sad to see." He paused, then grinned, sadly. "Perhaps you are right, Vincent; perhaps the whole world *is* heartbroken."

25

"I LEARNED MORE ABOUT WRITING THROUGH CÉZANNE THAN anyone else," Hemingway said. "He stripped it down to the essence. Rinse-repeat. No bullshit."

"Certainly, Vincent learned the same thing," Satan said. He was too weak to lift his head off his pillow, but he was comfortable in bed. "He and Gachet spoke of him often."

"He was good for him; the doc, I mean."

"For a while, yes," Satan said. "Little by little, disclosures trickled into the conversation, bits at a time. Gachet was good at making Vincent feel comfortable and they talked of many things—the garden, the countryside, local gossip, and sometimes that was all, for which Vincent was grateful, and for that, after a while, he began to open up. They talked of Gauguin. They talked of many things. But I do not believe it was all Gachet's doing. I think Gachet was fortunate he came into Vincent's life at a time when Vincent was ready to release some of his pain. It had built up for too long, and Auvers, with the purity of the countryside, offered a cleansing of sorts."

"Did that concern you?" Hemingway asked.

Satan coughed meekly.

"A little," he said. "But his work in Auvers, it was magnificent. He produced masterpieces daily. How was I to interfere with that?"

***

"Tell me about your seizures," Gachet said. It was early morning, but the sun was fierce and the dew in the garden had already dried.

"Epilepsy runs in my family," Vincent said.

"Yes, but tell me about *your* seizures," Gachet said.

A butterfly fluttered from a flower and settled on the edge of the table. Vincent, smoking his pipe, noted the pattern on its wings, how the orange and black accentuated so sharply, so harmoniously against the other.

"I've learned how to handle them."

"How so?"

"I breathe."

"You breathe? That's it?"

"The seizures are nothing," Vincent said. "I can handle the attacks, but it's the afterward, when it settles in, which is most unbearable."

"Settles in?"

"I have no better way to explain it," Vincent said. "It settles inside me and stays there and then it is just a matter of waiting it out."

"And how do you wait it out?"

"I sleep," Vincent said. "It is very heavy in the beginning and there's no other way to cope."

"How do you cope later?" Gachet asked. "Once it has lessened?"

"Drink and work," Vincent said.

"I see," Gachet said. "Would you think me mad if I said I don't believe you have epilepsy?"

"Not at all," Vincent said. He paused, then took a sip of lemonade. "I thought I was being poisoned."

"By whom?"

"I don't know," Vincent said. "The devil, perhaps."

The butterfly fluttered away.

"The devil?" Gachet said.

Vincent shrugged.

"Who else could it be?"

"But why the devil?"

"To corrupt the soul," Vincent said. "But what other reason is there?"

Gachet nodded.

"Do you think Saint-Rémy served you well?"

Vincent bent low to pat one of the cats that had rubbed against his leg.

"For a while."

"Why did you admit yourself?"

"*La tristesse* had become too much to bear. That is what comes afterwards, and that is what is most difficult to lift."

"Melancholy."

"Yes," Vincent said. He looked down at the cat, which was purring now, and he scratched around its ears.

"It's interesting that you've given it a name."

Vincent straightened up.

"It is what it is. It's its own thing."

"Let me recommend no alcohol or tobacco," Gachet said.

Vincent laughed.

"Other than my work those are my only pleasures. I shan't deny myself that." Suddenly his face became serious. "Besides, when sleep no longer works I drink and it numbs me, and I feel better."

"Alcohol is never a cure," Gachet said.

Vincent smiled.

"It's an effective tonic."

"La tristesse," Gachet said. "Do you know what triggers it?"

"No. But it doesn't take much," Vincent said. "I did a painting of my bedroom before I went to the hospital the first time. It is one of my favourites. When I returned home, I discovered it had been damaged by humidity, and so I had to wrap it in newsprint and send it to Theo in Paris. It was very upsetting."

"Did it cause a seizure?"

"No," Vincent said. "But it made me very sad."

"For how long?"

"Long enough to seek help."

"Do you think you're still being poisoned?"

"No," Vincent said. His eyes followed the butterfly as it went from flower to flower. "But since then, things upset me more easily now. It seems the simplest of things summons it."

"Melancholy is of the mind," Gachet said.

"Yes, but it is a real thing," Vincent said.

"The feeling of it is real, yes."

"Then it is real," Vincent said. "Just as you feel the sun on your face; that warmth is real."

"Yes, but you can see the sun," Gachet said.

"I know that," Vincent said.

"Do you?"

"I do." He looked up the sky and squinted hard and pointed. "It's right there."

"Well, that's good," Gachet said. "And that?" He pointed to Vincent's missing earlobe, healed in a way that it looked as though the side of his head had melted. "You know that was part of it? That it wasn't just a moment with Gauguin? That it was much more?"

Vincent turned his head away.

"I do."

"Good then," Gachet said. "Tell me, Vincent, what exactly happens when they come?"

"The seizures?"

"Yes."

"I see the world as it is," Vincent said. "In black and white."

"How do you mean?"

"Exactly as I said. It's as though a filter has been placed over my eyes. As dull and as grey as a daguerreotype."

"But you can see clearly?"

"Yes."

"Are you sad all the time, Vincent?"

"No," Vincent said. "Maybe."

"When are you happy?"

"Happy?"

"Yes."

Vincent took a moment to think.

"When I paint. I think."

"And when are you sad?"

"When I don't paint."

"Are you sad right now?"

The corners of Vincent's mouth uplifted a little.

"My earliest memories are of being sad in some way. It has always been in me."

"Do you still believe that?" Gachet asked.

"I do," Vincent said. "It cannot be acquired. It is in me and certain things bring it out."

"You speak frankly of it," Gachet said. "That's good."

"How else am I supposed to speak of it?"

"No, no, you speak of it as you wish. Forgive me, by now you must never find it awkward to be frank with me." In the garden, the birds and the flowers and the sunshine made it an easy and pleasant place to talk. "So you believe you were born with it?"

"As I was born with flesh and blood," Vincent said. "It is no different."

"You were also born with two ears," Gachet said.

Vincent puffed on his pipe.

"I like you," he said.

Two chickens appeared from the back of the house, clucking and pecking at the ground, and Gachet got up to put them back in their pen.

❧

Hemingway climbed off the bottom of the bed and stretched his back.

"I'm stiff as a board," he said.

"A chair, perhaps?" Satan said.

Hemingway grabbed a chair from the dining car and returned and placed it near the headboard, beside Satan.

"I know what he was getting at," Hemingway said. "The Black Ass, or *tristesse*, as he called it. And I know why Gachet couldn't grasp it. I bet it frustrated them both. If you don't have it, you don't understand it. It's as simple as that. Yet just about every person of artistic merit has tried to explain it but can't—not fully anyway—not in a way that others who don't have it would understand. And once he grows tired explaining it, or trying to beat it, it's then that he gives in. And once he gives in, it's over."

"He was growing tired, yes," Satan said. "And to my delight, he was giving in, to be certain."

Just then the train slowed and there was a steady screech of the brakes. The train stopped. Hemingway sat up straight to see out the window. The faint outlines of the mountaintops loomed ominously in the darkness.

Mr. Gregory appeared in the doorway.

"I'm afraid there is a delay, sir. It appears a flow of lava has crossed the tracks. Crews are working to clear it. It shouldn't be long."

Satan's breathing was laboured, each breath a heavy, weighted sigh. His eyes shifted to Hemingway.

"Vincent was growing tired, yes," he said again. "He worked fiercely in Auvers to drown out his pain." He took a deep, long breath. "There was a new urgency, a reckoning, and the fiercer he worked, the more deeply he dug himself into his depression. And I could see, finally, the end was near. The church was the last time I struck him. There was no need anymore. Despite the solace of Auvers and the efforts of the good doctor, nothing at this point could stop the inevitable."

"Makes sense," Hemingway said. "When you've won you withhold your troops and allow your enemy to surrender on his own, with some dignity."

Satan managed a grin.

"I do not practice such mercies, Ernest." He strained and coughed meekly. "But this was different. I had come to gain a great deal of respect for him."

"Sounds merciful to me," Hemingway said.

"I had already won, Ernest."

26

Almost two months had passed. The mid-summer sky was wide and blue and Gachet's front garden was hot and bright. The escaped chickens pecked at the ground, and Gachet let them be. The cats wrestled in the dirt, rolling around and swiping playfully at each other. The dogs slept in the sunlight. The string fencing drooped from the weight of the raspberry and tomato bushes, now in full bloom.

Marguerite had picked a bunch of raspberries and had placed them in a small bowl on the table. She brought lemonade, as she always did, and Gachet took a sip, as he always did, extending his arm and bringing it toward him in some grand, theatrical gesture. He sighed, satisfied.

"How many times have we sat out here together now?" Gachet asked, squinting in the sunlight. He adjusted his chair, sliding it back so that his face was in the shade.

"I don't know," Vincent said. "Too many to count."

"Break it down then," Gachet said. "How many Sunday dinners have you joined?"

"I haven't missed any since my second week here," Vincent said. He smiled. "But how could I miss your cooking? Six courses? I don't need to eat until mid-week!"

"Time passes quickly."

"Yes, it does," Vincent said. "I've been painting for nearly ten years now. Sometimes it is hard to imagine."

"You are still averaging a painting per day these past two months?"

"Yes."

"Remarkable," Gachet said. "Would you say you have never painted better?"

Vincent thought a moment.

"That's fair to say. I owe that to Auvers. And to you."

Gachet smiled at this.

"We've come to know each other well, yes?"

"I see you as a brother," Vincent said.

Gachet smiled again. He sipped his lemonade.

"You've painted me, sitting right here. And you've painted Marguerite just as you said you would."

"Yes," Vincent said. He scooped a few raspberries from the bowl.

"We have made progress," Gachet asked. "*You* have made progress."

"As an artist or a patient?" Vincent asked.

Gachet scratched at his cheek.

"Does it matter which? I thought the two went together."

"Yes, well, perhaps they do. When I suffer, I work well. When I don't work well, I suffer."

"Then do you think you've made progress?"

"We have had good talks," Vincent said.

"Yes, we have," Gachet said. "A bloodletting of sorts."

"Of sorts," Vincent said.

"Have they done you well?" Gachet asked. "Have I lessened the weight?"

"For certain, yes," Vincent said. "But progress? I don't know what that would look like."

"It's not something you can see," Gachet said. "But something you feel."

"You sound like Gauguin."

Gachet chuckled.

"Let's not go down that road again."

"Agreed," Vincent said.

"And what about Theo? Are you still concerned that you burden him?" He smiled quickly. "Your words, not mine."

"That cannot be helped," Vincent said.

"Yes," Gachet said. "But now that he has a child—"

"—and he wants his own gallery," Vincent said.

"That costs money."

"He is worried," Vincent said. "Money. His family. His business. Me."

Gachet nodded.

"Theo has never disclosed that he is struggling. He looks happy to me."

"He is my brother," Vincent said. "He is not happy. And he doesn't have the heart to tell me."

"Then talk to him," Gachet said.

"And say what? *I'm sorry?*"

"If that's how you feel."

"It doesn't matter how I feel anymore," Vincent said. "In that I have progressed."

"That's not the progress I was hoping for," Gachet said.

Vincent huffed.

"What's the point? There is no victory. My work is my work and that's all I care about. I don't feel any different. In that there is progress too."

Gachet tapped the table in thought, then scooped a few raspberries.

"I understand."

Vincent watched the cats playing and frolicking in the dirt then running down into the shade of the stone steps at the gate, then back up again, and chasing each other around to the back of the house.

"No words of encouragement?"

"You're right," Gachet said. "There's no point fighting it. You'll never win. You either live with it or—"

"Or what?" Vincent said. "Give in?"

"No," Gachet said. "I was going to say *suffer on*. You're not thinking of that again, are you?"

"Always," Vincent said. "You know that."

Gachet shook his head a little, almost in disappointment.

"But I thought Auvers was serving you well."

"It is."

"But are you giving it thought? I need to know that—if you are."

"Why?" Vincent said. "So you can write *suicidal* in your notes?"

"That's precisely why."

"What good is that?"

Gachet sighed.

"It is a necessity to record such things."

"Death isn't necessarily a bad thing," Vincent said. "Sometimes just the thought of it is a great comfort."

"And why is that?"

Vincent shrugged.

"It just is. Maybe to get it over with."

"Life?" Gachet said.

Vincent nodded.

"And then what?" Gachet said.

"I don't know. That isn't for me to decide."

"Some believe suicides don't get into Heaven."

"I don't know what Heaven is anymore," Vincent said. He looked around the garden. "What if this is Hell? I have suffered my whole life. Whatever Hell is, it can't be worse than this."

"Okay," Gachet said. He was grinning now, and he spoke loudly. "Forget everything I've ever said. You are indeed mad."

Vincent laughed.

"I like that we can joke."

"Laughter is good," Gachet said. "But if you're thinking something like that, you must tell me. This is why I'm here."

"I thought we were friends," Vincent said.

"We are, certainly," Gachet said. "I'm not just a doctor to you, Vincent, but a friend indeed, and between friends there should be nothing but honesty. It's the only way."

"So, no prognosis?" Vincent said, grinning now.

"None," Gachet said.

"Some doctor you are."

"Okay," he said, pausing a second to think about it. "You should laugh more."

"I'm being serious," Vincent said. "What conclusions have you drawn of me to this point?"

"No conclusions," Gachet said. "Just observations." He paused again, a bit longer this time. "You've martyred yourself to your art. Perhaps it has already killed you."

"Art is but a means to cope."

"With la tristesse?"

"That," Vincent said. "And life."

"What do you find difficult about life?" Gachet asked.

"Everything," Vincent said. "All of it."

"Perhaps it's art," Gachet said. "I've often wondered if it is the personality that is drawn to art, or the personality that is drawn out *because* of art."

"Art isn't to blame," Vincent said.

"You're right," Gachet said. "It's you, Vincent."

Vincent whisked away a fly that was bothering him.

"That was quick."

"It's true," Gachet said. "Had you stayed in the Hague and became a man of the Church or a man of the fields then maybe, just maybe you'd have been okay." He took another drink of lemonade. "But I doubt it. No matter what path you chose in life I doubt it would have made any difference. It's who you are. You are unable to do anything without passion, whether that be with your work or your love of your brother or something as simple as what wine you choose for dinner. You are passionate in everything you do."

"Correction," Vincent said. "I choose my wine by what I can afford." He became serious again. "What's wrong with passion?"

"Nothing at all," Gachet said. "But it can be dangerous."

"It hasn't killed me yet."

"And I pray it never does," Gachet said. "But passion is what drives you to create; what lets you see what others don't; what makes you *you*, the very good and the very bad all rolled into one. Imagine yourself without passion. What would that look like? What would the ordinary man named Vincent van Gogh be then?"

"I would be nothing," Vincent said. "Dust. I wouldn't exist."

Gachet scooped another handful of raspberries and jiggled

them in his palm.

"Precisely."

Vincent took a moment.

"Not bad, doctor," he said. "But Auvers is a place of solace, and I believe here I am as happy as I will ever be."

"I don't believe you are happy," Gachet said. "And neither do you."

Vincent said nothing.

Gachet used a serviette to wipe the sweat from his forehead.

"You are nobody's burden but your own, Vincent. And only once you can live with yourself, and love yourself, will you be truly happy."

"If I'm not happy here, then where?" Vincent said.

"It doesn't matter where," Gachet said. He tapped his forehead. "You need to be happy here first." Then he placed his palm on his chest, over his heart. "And here too."

The two cats came around from the back of the house and settled near the front door and flopped lazily in the sunlight. The two dogs, still laying flat, their bodies warmed by the sun, never moved.

With the lava on the tracks cleared, the train came to life with a sudden jolt and a loud clunk, inching forward, the engine pulling hard, straining against the weight of the cars. Bit by bit the train began to gain momentum, until it was moving steadily along.

"If you are thinking about life, you are thinking about death," Hemingway said. "All artists think about life—it's what we seek—so naturally, death too. And that's why every artist is unhappy—the true artist anyway. A happy artist is a fraud."

Satan's voice was weighted, laboured. He would take a breath, and in one swoop, speak a sentence or two before breathing again.

"Vincent did not experience happiness as others do. It came in spurts and did not last long. But it came more frequently while in Gachet's garden."

"I could've used Gachet for myself," Hemingway said.

"Vincent's lucky they didn't have shock treatments. Goddamned things fried my brain."

Satan breathed.

"Auvers was too quiet of a place for you, Ernest. The temptation to take the train back to Paris would have been too much to resist."

"And the horse track too, along that route, not too far from the Gare du Nord," Hemingway said. "I'd have stopped there a few times before getting to the city. But you're wrong. Gachet would've done me some good too."

"You say that now, Ernest, but you were stubborn. What would you have done had Mary brought you to such a person?"

Hemingway chuckled.

"Oh, I don't know." He leaned back in his chair and crossed his arms. "I'd have likely told him to go fuck himself."

Satan grinned. He took a few moments to breathe, keeping the words in until he was ready to speak.

"In this way you and Vincent were much alike. He did not disclose *everything* to Gachet."

Hemingway looked out the window.

"There is no lonelier man than the suicide. Anyone who advertises it will never do it. Those are the phonies, and they're a dime a dozen. But the true suicide, he never tells anyone. It becomes his best-kept secret, and it's only once he feels someone has figured him out, does he act upon it, to keep it his own."

Vincent was sitting at one of the small round tables outside the inn, in the warm morning sunshine, drinking a cup of coffee, when Gustave Ravoux joined him. Ravoux held a basket of warm biscuits which he placed on the table.

"A fine day," he said. He was a heavy-set man, with a thick moustache and a receding hairline and small spectacles which made his face look more swollen than fat.

Vincent sipped his coffee.

"It is a fine place, Auvers."

"I am glad to hear that," Ravoux said.

"How is Adeline?" Vincent asked.

"She worries about you, Vincent."

"She is a lovely girl."

Ravoux smiled.

"She has a heart like her mother. She opens it to everyone."

"Does she like her portrait?" Vincent asked.

"Very much so," Ravoux said. "She calls you The Master."

Vincent smiled.

Ravoux leaned in.

"She worries about you, Vincent. She came to me the other day. She said, *Papa, he drinks too much. For the two months he has been here he drinks himself to sleep every night.*" He sat back and picked a biscuit from the basket and tore it open with his finger. The biscuit steamed a little. "Now I know another man's life is none of my business, but she made me promise that I would speak to you, to express her concern."

"A lovely girl," Vincent said again, and sipped his coffee.

"She asked me about this—" Ravoux touched his ear. "I told her it was a farming accident."

Vincent took a minute before he spoke.

"Do *you* know what happened?"

"I've heard stories."

"Farming accident," Vincent said, and they shared a quiet smile.

Birds chirped in the trees and there was a cool, soft morning breeze.

"I can assure you," Vincent said. "And although many may disagree, I'm not mad."

"I know," Ravoux said. "And so does Adeline."

"Do you know Doctor Gachet?"

"I know who he is, yes."

"You know that I see him often?"

"Yes," Ravoux said. "It is a small village. Everyone talks." He nibbled his biscuit, the crumbs catching in his moustache. "We all have our vices, and you're a fine painter. And Adeline adores you, and because of that, she worries."

"Tell Adeline she has nothing to worry about," Vincent said.

"I wish I could believe that," Ravoux said. He paused. "She found a pistol in your room, under the bed."

"For my protection," Vincent said.

"From whom?"

Vincent shrugged and sipped his coffee.

"I have a pistol too," Ravoux said. "But Adeline, she is a firecracker. She says your room is cluttered with paintings, though it doesn't take much to clutter such a small room. Have you no more space in the shed? She says you bring home a new painting every day. She has counted almost seventy. Most artists I know do more talking than anything else. But you, as Adeline says, *Tu es un vrai artiste*, and she's right. Your talent is extraordinary, my friend."

"Merci, Gustave. I am fortunate to have the company of such a wonderful family."

Ravoux finished his biscuit and spoke with his mouth full.

"And you get along with the fellow in the room next door?"

"His focus is too much on women," Vincent said.

"Anton is young, yes," Ravoux said, laughing a little. "And you are right. But I expected you two to get along, both being Dutch, and painters."

"He is a fine young man," Vincent said. "But as for a career in painting, I'm afraid he doesn't have it."

Ravoux rubbed his hands together to clear them of crumbs. "You are a far better judge of that than I." He stood up. "Take care of yourself, Vincent."

Vincent closed his eyes and tilted his face toward the sun.

27

Later in the morning, while up in his room, Vincent thought deeply about what Ravoux had said. He knew *la tristesse* was winning, but how did Adeline know? Over the past several days it was with a heavy heart he'd come to realize he was in the evening of his life, that everything had come full circle, that all he'd learned was right in front of him, dark to light, light to dark, and now as he lay in bed he marvelled at how profound and how powerful life was, how steady it was in its pursuit, and how hopeless he'd been in his fight against it all along. And the girl, Adeline, in her simplicity and her innocence, was the only other person who saw it. Gachet didn't even see it for what it had become.

In the afternoon, he made his way past the church and up around the steep winding road to the wheat field, where the sky was usually a deep blue against the gold of the wheat. But today the blue mixed with the clouds, almost violently, so blue it looked black. He'd already completed two big canvases of this field and was determined to paint it again to get it exactly right. He studied the scene before him; the dark of the sky and the light of the earth represented everything in his own life, and he knew, he could feel it, he was meant to be here today.

By the time he'd set up his easel the clouds had taken over the sky and a brisk summer wind swept across the field in gusts and made waves in the wheat. Vincent worked through this, changing his palette to match what he saw—more black, and darker blues.

He worked quickly to capture it, and once he was finished, he stepped back for a better look. With the dirt road splitting the field and the wheat swaying under darkened skies, it was a beautifully painted scene. But there was something about it that irked him, something incomplete.

He returned to the inn and placed the canvas on his bed and went down to the tavern for his supper. He found the young Dutch painter, Anton Hirschig, eating alone in the corner. His face lightened when he saw Vincent.

"Sit, please, dear Vincent."

Ravoux brought an extra plate to the table and placed it in front of Vincent. There was a small pot of herring in oil, with capers, and Anton scooped a bit of the fish onto Vincent's plate.

"You worked today, yes?"

"I work every day," Vincent said.

"Yes, you do," Anton said. He took a piece of bread and placed it on Vincent's plate. "I am tired. Marie LePen, who lives by the train station, do you know her?"

Vincent shook his head and ate the herring. He picked a small bone from his mouth and wiped it on the edge of his plate.

"She is a wild woman!" Anton said. "Three nights we have met beside the riverbank. And tonight, after I've eaten, I will go there again. I eat the fish for stamina."

Vincent sighed.

"You are here to paint, Tony, yes?"

Anton grinned, lapping up the oil on his plate with the bread. "And other things."

"I am here to paint," Vincent said.

He ate quickly and took a bottle of wine up to his room where he sat on the edge of his bed and drank and stared at the new painting as it dried. He decided to call it *Wheat Field*. But it bothered him, the imbalance in it. He knew he'd captured something. There was the field before him, earth and the sky, light and darkness, life and death, but still, something was missing, and, troubled, he drifted off to sleep, bottle in hand.

Hemingway felt the train slowing. Out the window were a few miners' huts scattered about the darkness. He turned to Satan and leaned in close to listen, so close he could smell the sickness on his breath. Satan coughed meekly into the rag.

"Vincent returned to the field a week later with the unfinished canvas. He had waited for the same troubled sky to return. I hid in the treeline at the end of the field, under an oak tree." He coughed again and wiped his mouth. "The tree was filled with crows. They cawed and flapped their wings and shit onto the ground. I whisked them away and they flew into a frenzy, circling the field within the gusts of wind. They cawed and drifted in the wind, soaring and gliding, flapping their wings to climb and fight it then ride the current that swirled over the field."

⁂

When Vincent saw the crows, he immediately splashed them onto the canvas and then stood back to examine the painting again. That was it! *Wheat Field with Crows*. He was finished, truly finished with it now. He assembled his things, organized his various paints, brushes, easel, and canvas, and then, leaving them behind, he wandered into the middle of the field. His chest rumbled with *la tristesse*. It rumbled in the wind and the clouds and the swaying wheat; it rumbled in everything. No more, he thought. No more and not ever again. The crows circled overhead, the sky a blur, the wheat swaying all around him. He gripped the pistol with both hands and pointed it to the ground. It was heavy in his hands. He closed his eyes and squeezed the trigger and fired a single shot into the ground. He'd never shot a pistol before and he was surprised at the kick, and the crack that echoed over the field.

Satan stepped out from under the tree. He could see the top of Vincent's head, that speck of orange in the wheat. He hadn't shot himself. Or had he?

Vincent stared up to the sky, to the clouds and the crows circling overhead. He closed his eyes and took a deep breath, and then, without hesitation, he placed the barrel of the pistol against his abdomen and squeezed the trigger and fell back into the wheat.

When Satan heard the second shot and saw the crows scatter, he rushed across the field and found Vincent on his back, holding his belly, coughing up blood. And Vincent saw him. At first, he mistook Satan for an angel, and he'd smiled, but suddenly, all at once, he saw, in Satan's face, Pierre Gagnon, then the farmer in the orchard, the charwoman from the yellow house, the drunk in the café, the old man fishing the creek under the bridge, the patient in the asylum garden, and his eyes flashed wide with terror. He grunted, reaching up to the clouds, desperately, achingly trying to grab them, before his eyes rolled back and his whole body sighed and everything went black.

"He was reaching for Heaven," Satan said. "But it was too late."

"He'd already punched his ticket," Hemingway said.

The train approached the platform, the brakes a long, constant squeal before the train came to a stop.

"I had been too anxious," Satan said. "I heard the shot and saw him drop and I rushed over; a foolish mistake."

"Did he know it was you?" Hemingway asked.

Satan's head was sunk into the pillow.

"People do not mistake me, Ernest."

The wheat swayed across the field as water in the ocean sways, in velvety gusts, fluttering and swirling. Overhead, clouds loomed low and black and moved quickly across the sky. It was evening now, and the air was cool. Vincent had been unconscious for more than an hour, and when he awoke, he was shivering. A sharp, shrieking pain in his gut pulsed throughout his body, like strikes of lightning.

Slowly, he managed to get to his feet. He was dizzy, and he stood in place a moment to steady himself. But the pain struck and gripped him, like claws, forcing him down onto his knees. He pressed his fingers into the earth, managing the pain, the sharpness of it. He breathed. This was a different kind of pain. It was not *la tristesse* at all. This was palpable. He got to his feet again, his hands bloodied, his fingernails black with dirt, and placing one foot in front of the other, he staggered back through the wheat. In his wake, the wheat was smeared with blood and he could not help but note to himself how red-blue the blood was in the gold of the wheat in the moonlight.

He stammered down the road, struggling to keep his balance along the steep descent, hunched forward, coughing up blood, one laborious step at a time, until he got to the inn and climbed the stairs to his room where he fell onto his bed.

Gustave Ravoux had been sitting with his wife and Adeline outside the tavern when Vincent had passed. Adeline saw him first, and then her mother. Vincent was clearly in pain. It was too dark to see the blood, but she knew he was distressed, the way he was hunched over.

"You'd better see to him," Ravoux's wife said.

"He's probably drunk," Ravoux said. "He will sleep it off."

A short while later, Anton appeared at the front of the tavern.

"There is something wrong with Vincent," he said. "He is moaning. I can hear him through the wall. I knocked on his door, but he doesn't answer."

Ravoux took his gas lamp and climbed the stairs to Vincent's room, with Anton behind him. He knocked.

"Monsieur Vincent?"

He could hear Vincent moaning and he knocked again before letting himself in. Vincent was curled in a ball on his bed, knees against his chest, face buried in the pillow. Ravoux saw the blood on Vincent's shirt.

"What happened? What is wrong? Are you okay?"

Anton remained in the doorway. It was sweltering in the room, and Vincent was sweating profusely, the sweat soaking his hair, droplets of sweat on his face glistening in the lamplight.

"I shot myself," Vincent groaned. "I only hope this time I've succeeded."

Ravoux glanced back at Anton, whose eyes were wide and white in the yellow of the lamplight.

"Succeeded in what?"

Vincent didn't reply.

Ravoux placed the lamp on the end table.

Adeline came up the staircase and, standing in the doorway, she saw Vincent and the blood, and she gasped.

"Mon dieux!"

Vincent murmured something, grunted, and twisted himself onto his back. The side of his shirt was wet with blood, and his pants too, where it had trickled down his leg. To Adeline, it seemed to be everywhere.

"Vien ici," Vincent said to her. Bits of blood bubbled from his lips.

Adeline, slowly and stiffly, stepped around Anton and into the small confines of the room, where she nestled herself next to her father.

"Do you know the wheat field above the church?" Vincent asked.

Adeline nodded.

"I left my supplies there," Vincent said. "And a painting. Be a good girl and get them for me."

Adeline looked at her father for approval before scuttling down the staircase.

Vincent winced and gripped his chest and curled into a ball again, his face pressed into the pillow, muffling his coughs.

Ravoux looked up at Anton.

"Fetch Doctor Mazery right away."

Ravoux placed his hands gently on Vincent's shoulders and helped him onto his back. Vincent did not fight it. Ravoux could not see exactly where Vincent was injured, only that it was on his torso. Or was it his groin? He didn't know. He left the room and returned with a bowl of water and a bundle of rags and bandages. Ravoux unbuttoned Vincent's shirt, trying to do it as carefully as he could, delicately working his fingers around each button. Vincent coughed and blood sprayed in tiny flecks around his mouth.

Within the hour, Doctor Gachet rushed up the staircase and into the room with his medical bag. His eyes were wide with excitement and his hair, as it usually was, was wild too.

"Where is Mazery?" Ravoux asked.

"I don't know," Gachet said, looking down at Vincent. "A boy sent for me and I came straight away."

Anton appeared in the doorway a moment later. He was winded.

"I could not find Mazery."

Ravoux was holding a bandage to Vincent's belly and he removed it, revealing the wound just below the ribs, a tiny black hole about the size of a pea, and around it a brown ring. Blood trickled from the hole and Ravoux wiped it away.

"He said he shot himself," Ravoux said.

Vincent winced.

"I can speak for myself. I'm not dead yet."

Gachet turned to Vincent.

"Very well then, what happened?"

Vincent grunted.

"I shot myself."

"Don't worry," Gachet said. "We will fix this."

"Then I'd have to do it all over again," Vincent said.

Gachet's face dropped. His eyes had suddenly become sadder than they'd ever been, the corners of his mouth low. He placed his finger close to the wound, near the brown ring.

"Gunpowder burn."

"Forgive me," Ravoux said. "But I did not think you were a doctor for such things."

"I treated much worse during the Prussian Siege," Gachet said. "But that was twenty years ago." He leaned over so that he hovered over Vincent. "Can you turn over?"

Vincent, in slow, tiny movements, twisted onto his side. Blood had absorbed into the sheets. Ravoux wiped away a trickle that had settled on Vincent's ribs. He held the lamp close as Gachet examined Vincent's back.

"The bullet is still in him. We must wait on Doctor Mazery

who is more current in his surgical decisions than I." He managed a slight grin. "My current vocation is to prevent those from doing such things as this." He sighed deeply and sadly and shook his head. "My dear, Vincent."

With careful lifting and turning and groans of pain with every move, they managed to get a bandage wrapped around Vincent's torso. Gachet, sweating in the hotness of the room, took a rag and wiped down his face and the back of his neck.

Adeline, her eyes red from crying, squeezed past Anton in the doorway. She perched Vincent's easel and the painting against the wall and left. The room was crammed with drying canvases and it smelled of paint and of the humid, stale air of a windowless room in the middle of summer.

"My pipe," Vincent said, nodding toward the end table.

Gachet packed the pipe with tobacco, lit it, and handed it to him. The tiny room quickly filled with smoke.

"Does Theo know?" Vincent asked.

"Marguerite is drafting a letter," Gachet said.

"Not a telegram?"

"I don't want to panic him." He turned to Anton. "Will you go to Paris and take it to him?"

Anton, eyes still wide with fright, nodded, almost frantically.

"Yes, of course, yes, I will take the first train in the morning."

Later in the evening, the local practitioner, Doctor Jean Mazery arrived. In the lamplight all Vincent could see of him was his sunken eyes and the dark crevasses of his huge nostrils as he examined the wound. Vincent's coughing had ceased, though his breathing was more laboured, queasy, and he was still spitting up blood.

"Are you feeling any more discomfort than before?" Mazery asked, showing no emotion.

Vincent shook his head.

Mazery nodded in thought.

"Can you turn onto your side?"

Vincent rolled over. Mazery leaned over and placed both his hands to Vincent's skin and pressed down on Vincent's ribs.

"Does this hurt?"

Vincent winced.

Mazery moved his hands to Vincent's belly and pressed.

"And here?"

Vincent winced again.

Mazery, like a man reading a map, prodded and pressed, running his hands along Vincent's side, chest, and abdomen. He pressed firmly on his lower back.

"Here?"

Vincent gripped hard the sheets and grunted. His eyes watered.

Mazery stood up straight.

"You've likely broken a rib. But in any case, you're fortunate to be alive." He turned to Gachet. "The bullet hasn't hit any vital organs, nor any arteries. It may have grazed his lung, which explains the coughing and the blood, and has settled somewhere deep in his abdomen, too deep to remove. I fear we'd only cause more harm than good if we tried. I suggest we leave it there and let his body mend itself."

Gachet nodded in agreement.

Mazery peered down at Vincent.

"Stop smoking. Drink plenty of fluids. And, if possible, avoid any such future mishaps."

And with that, Mazery gathered his bag and left.

"Nice fellow," Vincent said, wincing.

Gachet did not smile. His face was still broken.

"Anton has gone out for now," Ravoux said. "God knows where he goes at night, but he will inform your brother tomorrow."

"Tony is a man of commitment," Vincent said. He tried to smile but then winced, the pain striking him.

Just then, two gendarmes appeared in the doorway.

"Monsieur Van Gogh," the first gendarme said, stepping into

the room. The other, realizing the room was too small for him, his partner, Gachet, and Ravoux at the same time, remained in the doorway. "Are you well enough to answer a few questions?"

Vincent tried to sit up a little, but it was too painful, and so he lay flat.

"Monsieur Van Gogh," he began. "Tell us please what happened."

"I shot myself," Vincent said.

"By accident?"

"No."

The two gendarmes exchanged quick looks.

"What did you use?" the first gendarme asked.

"A pistol," Vincent said.

"Where did you get the pistol?"

Vincent didn't answer.

"He borrowed it from me," Ravoux said.

The first gendarme looked down at Vincent again.

"Why did you borrow it?"

"Why do you think?" Vincent said.

"To shoot crows," Ravoux cut in. He stepped aside, so they could see the painting perched against the wall. "He'd just painted this. You can see them. Dreadful things."

"Where is the pistol now?" the gendarme asked.

Vincent waited a moment before he spoke.

"I threw it away."

"Where?"

"I don't recall."

"Where were you when this happened?"

Vincent stared at the wall.

"I don't recall."

The second gendarme stepped into the room from the doorway and peered over his partner's shoulder. He too was mechanical, his arms at his sides.

"You are not in any trouble."

Vincent cringed and very slowly pushed himself up in bed.

"Did you wish to commit suicide?" the first gendarme asked.

"Yes, I believe so."

"It is a crime, you know—against the state."

"And against God," the second gendarme added.

"I thought you said I wasn't in trouble," Vincent said.

The two gendarmes glanced at each other again.

"We are investigating a shooting."

Vincent lifted his shirt, showing the bandage.

"Well, here it is," he said. "You've found it. Congratulations. A fine piece of investigation, gentlemen."

The two gendarmes stood a moment without speaking. Then the first leaned slightly sideways.

"What happened to your ear?"

Vincent sighed heavily and slunk back down under the blanket.

28

Satan struggled to keep his eyes open.

"Vincent did not say anything further to them. He was irritated, and so he closed his eyes until they left. When Gachet returned the next day, Vincent's condition had unexpectedly deteriorated. He could no longer sit up in bed." Satan coughed into his blanket then grinned, painfully. "The irony."

"You gonna be okay to get off this train?" Hemingway asked.

"Do not concern yourself with me, Ernest."

"You really don't look good," Hemingway said.

"Vincent instructed Gachet not to send for Mazery again. It was not until the second day that Theo arrived from Paris."

Theo burst into the room, panting, as though he'd run all the way from Paris. Vincent was lying flat, his head propped up by two pillows. Theo looked over at Gachet, who stood under the sky-light, in the beam of sunlight that lit the room.

"You said he'd only wounded himself."

"His condition has worsened," Gachet said. "If I'd known I would have sent a telegram."

Theo sat on the edge of the bed and took Vincent in his arms. He was crying.

"Vincent, what have you done?"

Vincent moaned and opened his eyes.

"I have done it, brother," he said. "You need only worry about your family now. Not me. I am free, at last. As are you."

"Free of what, Vincent?"

"La vie," Vincent said, then closed his eyes and rested again.

Theo remained at Vincent's bedside all that afternoon and into the evening. The room was terribly hot, and Theo's clothes were drenched in sweat, but he never left his brother's side. Adeline brought him a tray of tea and biscuits at lunch, and a bowl of broth, ham, bread and cheese at dinnertime. Vincent slipped in and out of consciousness. By one o'clock in the morning, his breathing had slowed considerably. The moon shone through the skylight, sending a faint blue light onto Vincent that gave him an angelic glow. His face glistened in sweat. His pillow was damp, and his clothes too. Gachet stood alongside the bed, in the moonlight, sketching Vincent's face.

Theo, sitting in the chair beside the bed, had drifted off a little, his eyes heavy, and he perked up when Vincent spoke.

"I saw him," Vincent whispered. A line of sweat trickled from his brow into his eye and he blinked it away.

Theo leaned in close. "Who? Who did you see?"

"The angel of death," Vincent said. "In the field." His arm dropped over the side of the bed. "La tristesse," he muttered. "It will last forever." Then he exhaled a long quiet breath, and his body went still.

July 30 was stifling, a blanket of heat beginning at dawn. By ten o'clock in the morning the sun shone mercilessly, beating down on the dried-out countryside. The Ravoux Inn's front doors had been propped open, but it did little good.

In the back of the room sat Vincent's closed coffin, a white cloth draped over it. Bunches of sunflowers and yellow dahlias had been placed upon it, and many of Vincent's paintings hung on the walls around the coffin.

Émile Bernard and fellow painter Charles Laval arrived from Paris and, having walked up from the train station, their faces glistened with sweat. Julien Tanguy stood in the corner of the room with a glass of water and chatted quietly with Gustave Ravoux, and he nodded at the pair. Laval made his way over to him, but Émile went to the coffin, where Theo, hands clasped, head down, wept quietly. Émile placed his hand gently upon Theo's shoulder.

"I'm so sorry, Theo." He pulled a handkerchief and wiped his forehead and face and neck. "He was a beautiful soul. So good-hearted. So human."

Theo sniffed.

"He spoke highly of you, always."

"I am honoured for that," Émile said. He eyed the paintings. "Look at his work. It glows. Like a halo." He wiped the back of his neck again and placed the handkerchief in his pocket. "He will be remembered."

Doctor Gachet came out from the back room. His eyes were bloodshot. He sat in one of the chairs and stared down at his feet. Another man stepped in from the street. He was not sweating and did not seem bothered by the heat. He approached Theo and stood on the other side of him, opposite Émile.

"My dear Theo," Satan said. "I am so very sorry."

Theo turned and his eyes widened.

"Pierre!" he said, his voice raised a little. They shook hands. "How did you know? I haven't seen you since Vincent—" His lips trembled, and he wiped his wet eyes with his hand. "Since Paris."

"Forgive me," Satan said. "Business has taken me abroad. I should have written."

Theo wiped away more tears.

"Claude was wrong about you."

"Monsieur Monet?"

Theo nodded.

"He told me to keep you away from Vincent. He didn't say why, but to just keep you away from him." He looked around the room, then wiped his eyes again. "But where is Claude today?" He placed his hand on Satan's shoulder. "Thank you for coming, Pierre."

❧

A few passengers began to appear on the platform. Mr. Gregory poked his head into the room.

"He has fallen asleep," Hemingway said. "I think we should leave him be for a bit, before we go. He needs the rest."

When Hemingway returned to the dining car, there was an assortment of meats, cheeses, breads and fruit on the table. He sat, ripped a bun in two and slopped three slices of ham, a slice of cheese and squirted a healthy amount of mustard then slapped it together. Mr. Gregory stood with his hands behind his back.

"Can I get you anything else while we wait, sir?"

Hemingway took a big bite of his sandwich.

"Sit," he said.

Mr. Gregory frowned.

Hemingway kicked the chair from under the table.

"Sit down."

Mr. Gregory sat, stiffly, his hands in his lap.

"Tell me about Vincent after he got here," Hemingway said.

Mr. Gregory adjusted his glasses.

"I'm afraid I'm not at liberty to discuss such things, sir."

"Horseshit," Hemingway said. He took another bite of his sandwich. "You think he cares?"

Mr. Gregory glanced back in the direction of Satan's sleeping quarters.

Hemingway finished the sandwich with another bite then reached across the table, picked an apple from the dish and bit it in half, core and all.

Mr. Gregory glanced over his shoulder again.

"Spit it out," Hemingway said.

Mr. Gregory lowered his voice.

"He waited for Monsieur Vincent at the Gates."

"Satan?" Hemingway said.

Mr. Gregory nodded.

"He was very excited…"

❧

An endless line of souls emerged from the darkness outside Capital City, snaking slowly toward the Gates. Satan stood at the entrance, just inside the Gates. In the darkness it was difficult to decipher one soul from another and he did not know where Vincent was, only that he was there somewhere, and he did not see him right away, hunched among the others, his frame bent round as he held his chest, his head low. Then Satan's eye caught the red hair and he stepped in and plucked him from the line and put his arm around him.

"Welcome," he said.

Vincent said nothing. His face was expressionless and grey, like that of a weathered statue. Satan turned Vincent so that they faced each other, then, gently, he unwrapped the bloodied bandage from around Vincent's torso.

"You won't need this anymore."

Vincent glanced up, for the first time, at the gloom of Capital City.

"Are you hungry?" Satan asked.

Vincent nodded.

Satan escorted him to his carriage, where they were driven down the Boulevard, straight to Satan's tower.

Vincent was given a hearty stew, a bottle of wine, a new pipe, and a pouch of tobacco. Satan sat across from him, not speaking, just watching. When he finished eating, Vincent packed and lit the pipe. The brown scent of tobacco filled the air, the smoke hovering between them.

"Do you know where you are?" Satan finally asked.

Vincent looked around the room, at the floor-to-ceiling windows and the dim lights of the city below.

"Do you know who I am?" Satan asked.

"In the field," Vincent muttered. "Everywhere."

Vincent smoked his pipe and rubbed his chest.

"Does it hurt still?" Satan asked. "It shouldn't."

Vincent thumped his hand lightly on his wound.

"Here, no." He raised his hand to his heart. "But here, very much."

"It will pass," Satan said. He got up from the table and led Vincent to one of the windows. In the darkness the Boulevard was nothing more than a long grey line slicing through the center of the city.

Mr. Gregory was more comfortable talking now that he'd begun, which pleased Hemingway; where Satan's voice had grown increasingly hoarse, his words laboured and slow, Mr. Gregory's flowed like a fresh breeze.

"I was there when Satan made his proposal to Monsieur Vincent," he said. "And he was, I believe, afraid."

"He doesn't seem the fearful type," Hemingway said, to which Mr. Gregory grinned.

"He is afraid of only one thing, sir."

"God," Hemingway said.

"Yes, sir. Perhaps a better word is *anxious*. He was anxious. Yes, that's a more suitable word." He leaned in and lowered his voice. "He was worried Monsieur Vincent wouldn't do it. Satan had much pressure; the Boulevard had consumed him for centuries."

"How'd he convince him?" Hemingway asked.

Mr. Gregory nibbled the skin off a grape, discarded the skin, and then ate the grape.

"Actually, it did not take much convincing, sir."

⁂

Satan and Vincent stood at the window looking down upon the stretch of the darkened Boulevard.

"It is yours," Satan said.

Vincent took a moment, smoking his pipe, then finally he spoke.

"I don't understand."

"There is much to unlearn," Satan said. "I am not who you think I am."

Vincent turned.

"You are not… Satan?"

Satan shook his head.

"Not the Satan you know."

Vincent frowned. The brown pipe smoke curled against the window.

"I still don't understand."

"Give it time," Satan said.

They stood, silent, just looking down upon the long dark line of the Boulevard. Satan rocked a little back and forth. Vincent, on the other hand, was calm.

"Would you like something else to drink?" Satan asked. He snapped for Mr. Gregory who scuttled over to them. "Fetch a good bottle of red from my personal collection."

"No thank you," Vincent said.

"But just a drink," Satan said.

Vincent peered over to the half-drunk bottle on the table.

"I've drunk enough."

Satan turned to Mr. Gregory again.

"Never mind."

A minute passed in silence.

"Why do you paint?" Satan finally asked.

Vincent thought, then shrugged.

"Why do you breathe? It is no different."

"A necessity," Satan said.

Vincent nodded.

"I want you to paint it," Satan said.

"It?"

"The Boulevard. All of it. Every building."

"Is that why I'm here?" Vincent asked. "For a commission?"

"It is not for me," Satan said quickly. "Not for me at all."

Vincent huffed in disbelief. He saw his reflection in the window.

"Why do you paint?" Satan asked again. "It is in you, yes, but do you do it solely for you? For your own pleasure?"

"I take little pleasure in it," Vincent said.

"Then why do you do it?" Satan asked.

Vincent turned to Satan again.

"Why am I here? Is this not for you?"

Satan looked down to the Boulevard again.

29

MR. GREGORY PEELED THE SKIN FROM ANOTHER GRAPE AND sucked it into his mouth.

"I think at that moment they came to an understanding. Monsieur Vincent knew Satan was the reason for his being here, like most do, and, like most, he hated him for it."

Hemingway reached across the table for another apple.

"They never talked about it?"

"They rarely spoke after that," Mr. Gregory said. "I think it was Monsieur Vincent's way of communicating how he felt of the whole affair."

Hemingway finished the apple in two bites then scooped a handful of grapes into his mouth, his cheeks bulged full.

"But he still painted it."

Mr. Gregory nodded.

"It was in him, sir. Surely you understand it better than I."

"It's a curse," Hemingway said. "A goddam curse to have it in you. It just keeps filling and you do your best to drain it, but it keeps filling until you're unable to drain it and then it either ruins you or kills you."

"Is that what happened to you, sir?"

Hemingway looked sharply at Mr. Gregory.

Mr. Gregory slunk in his chair.

"I apologize, sir. I overstepped."

The corners of Hemingway's mouth uplifted slightly.

"Nah," he said. "Fair question." He paused. "I had my reasons." He paused again, then he shook his head as if to shake away what he was thinking. "Tell me about the Boulevard. How did he start it?"

Mr. Gregory straightened up and helped himself to some more grapes, eating one at a time, peeling the skin with his teeth.

"It was a daunting task, sir, and I was placed at his disposal."

Mr. Gregory and Vincent stood at the foot of the Boulevard. Fifty feet away, the mighty Gates loomed ominously. The Boulevard was all cobblestones then, and so old and worn that it dipped in places from centuries of pedestrians and oxen and horse-drawn carriages.

Vincent sighed long and loud and scratched at the stubble on his cheeks. He stepped out to the middle of the street and looked northward, to Satan's tower in the distance. A man on a bicycle nearly rode into him and he cursed at Vincent, but Vincent never flinched. He stood, staring up the Boulevard.

Several minutes passed before Mr. Gregory spoke.

"Monsieur Vincent, are you alright?"

Vincent did not respond.

Mr. Gregory stepped out onto the street, skipping to avoid a cyclist, and tapped Vincent lightly on the shoulder.

"Monsieur?"

Vincent took another minute, just staring up the darkened Boulevard.

"I used to have episodes," he said.

Mr. Gregory frowned.

"Monsieur?"

"All colour disappeared," Vincent said. "Poof! Gone in an instant." He quietly huffed. "I've now just realized it was this I was seeing—this place. Hell." He held his stare up the long stretch of the Boulevard. "To think that now I am expected to remedy it."

Mr. Gregory rolled on the balls of his feet.

"Yes, well, monsieur, if it is any consolation, we are most pleased that you are here. We have been waiting a long time for you."

Vincent held his stare a moment more before he blinked, and he was back.

"Right then," he said. "We have work to do."

Mr. Gregory straightened and clasped his hands.

"I am at your disposal, monsieur."

"I need this to stop," Vincent said, gesturing to a horse-drawn cart filled with manure as it passed. "Is that possible?"

❧

Mr. Gregory puckered his thin lips and sucked in another skinless grape.

"His first request had been to eliminate any traffic on the sections he would work. Satan closed the entire Boulevard so that it was empty, so that Monsieur Vincent could see the length of it, sixty blocks in all. Every building a blank canvas, some fifty stories high, and beyond anything he could have imagined."

"Quite a daunting task," Hemingway said. "Just to set himself up mentally for it. Any new project takes mental prep more than anything. I took me months to get myself ready; it's a marathon and you can't just strap on a pair of running shoes and go. You gotta train."

⁂

At the foot of the Boulevard, shadowed by the mighty Gates, was a seven-storey brick mid-rise that housed much of the Immigration Department's files.

"This one," Vincent said, looking up at it. "This is where I will begin. It's not as big as the others." He patted the brickwork with the palm of his hand; the rough brickwork and the plastered grooves. "And I thought Paul's jute was coarse." He turned to Mr. Gregory. "I am going to paint over the windows; I hope that is okay."

"We can board them up if you prefer," Mr. Gregory said.

Vincent ran his hand along a smooth pane of glass.

"That won't be necessary."

"Anything you wish, monsieur."

Vincent stepped back from the building, far enough so that he stood in the middle of the Boulevard and could see the face of the building in its entirety.

"Tomorrow I will provide you with a list," he said. "Materials, brushes and paints. The paints will be specific."

"Anything you wish, monsieur."

But Mr. Gregory did not receive a list the next day, nor the day after that. Mr. Gregory tracked him down in a tavern two blocks off the Boulevard. Vincent was alone, slumped over a table.

"Monsieur Vincent," Mr. Gregory said. "Where have you been? We have been looking for you."

"I am painting," Vincent said. There was a slur, a drawl in his voice.

"Painting what, monsieur?"

"The Boulevard."

"But monsieur—"

"Fucking Paul," Vincent said. He tilted his head forward, just enough to pour the beer into his mouth.

"Paul Gauguin?"

"He would know what to do," Vincent said. "He would love this. Ha! Do you hear me, Paul?"

Mr. Gregory looked around the tavern.

"I don't understand, monsieur."

Vincent drank the last of the mug of beer. His stubble, which had since grown into a beard, foamed along his upper lip.

"A painting a day," he said. He looked at Mr. Gregory, though in his drunkenness his eyes seemed fixed upon Mr. Gregory's forehead. "Do you know in Auvers I was averaging a painting per day?"

Mr. Gregory sat opposite Vincent.

"A fine accomplishment, monsieur."

Vincent belched, catching it in his mouth.

"It came easily at the end," he said. "It found me. I would walk into the countryside until it found me—it was that easy. But here, there is nothing to find. Just death and darkness." He chuckled drunkenly. "But what else would it be?"

Mr. Gregory leaned across the table.

"That's why you are here, monsieur. To lead us out of the darkness."

Vincent sighed loudly and rolled his eyes.

"I am no saviour."

"But you are, monsieur. You are the chosen one."

Vincent slammed the empty mug on the table.

"I never asked for this."

"I know, monsieur."

"And he wants me to paint the whole thing? The whole damned thing! It will take me a lifetime—and that is if I can even begin."

Hemingway perked up and snapped his fingers.

"He needed a plan."

"Yes," Mr. Gregory said. "And so there he was, with nothing in front of him; no choice but to think everything through, to imagine each piece in his mind, to work from memory. And he did not know how to begin."

"Getting shitfaced is a good start," Hemingway said. "Gets the juices flowing."

"He was not in a good state, sir."

Hemingway scooped a handful of grapes from the dish and shoved them into his mouth.

"So, he needed a plan," he said again. "The very thing he'd fought against with Gauguin."

"Indeed, sir."

"Welcome to Hell."

"Yes," Mr. Gregory said. "But oh, how he wished Monsieur Gauguin were with him. He'd regretted not listening to him, to not practising more from memory."

"How'd he do it then?"

"How did you do it, sir? How does any artist do it?"

"You just do it," Hemingway said. "You don't have a choice."

Mr. Gregory nibbled the skin off another grape.

"You eat like a fuckin squirrel," Hemingway said. "I used to take out the .22 in the mornings up in the backyard in Ketchum and blow their heads off from fifty yards out. Buggers picked clean my strawberries. And they ate just like you."

Mr. Gregory sucked the skinless grape into his mouth.

"Does it bother you, sir?"

Hemingway sighed.

"Carry on."

"I waited two more weeks before Monsieur Vincent gave me his list. All the colours you could imagine: cobalt blue, Prussian blue, emerald green and so many yellows I cannot recall them all—cadmium, zinc, and chrome—colours I never knew existed."

"He's a pro," Hemingway said.

"I provided him with a team of assistants," Mr. Gregory said. "All young and eager demons who stood, awaiting their orders. I had scaffolding built in such a way that at any given time Monsieur Vincent could access any section of the building he wanted."

"Good idea," Hemingway said.

Mr. Gregory nodded in agreement.

"It was solidly built, attached firmly to each building, allowing him to move freely, climbing to any level with relative ease. Initially it was built from steel, but he found that it bothered him—it creaked, and he said it felt like being in a cage. And so we imported bamboo which he adored. It was equally solid, and as he put it, *organic*, like his work."

"Makes sense," Hemingway said. "I used to write in an open-air room above the property. It relaxed me. Allowed me to think."

Mr. Gregory nodded again.

"He'd conceded to working from memory, but he was determined to be able to splash his paint at any point on any given section. In this way he convinced himself that he'd still be working in the moment, still capturing each image as it was, whether it came from memory or not."

"What was the first one he did?" Hemingway asked. "The brick building—which one is it?"

Mr. Gregory peeled and ate another grape.

"After much thinking and preparation, he decided the first mural would be a cluster of purple violets."

Vats of paint lined the sidewalk, their colours labeled in bold letters.

Vincent was working three floors up, on the scaffolding. He was covered in paint, his face and hair and arms a mess of colours. Buckets of paint lined the scaffolding. Teams of demons mixed the colours on the ground then hauled them up by pulleys to wherever Vincent was. Pulleys and gears formed an intricate web all over the scaffolding.

Vincent dipped a big brush into a bucket of green and slapped it onto the brickwork. The paint splashed about. He splashed on more paint. Then he leaned over the scaffolding, holding the brush high.

"This isn't enough," he said. He dropped the brush and it fell to the ground and landed at Mr. Gregory's feet and splatted paint over his shoes and pants.

Mr. Gregory looked up at Vincent.

"Bigger," Vincent said.

"Monsieur?"

"Look at the size of this canvas," Vincent hollered, waving his arms as if to sweep them over the face of the building. "I need a bigger brush. I need big and bold strokes and those piddly brushes are too small."

Mr. Gregory brought Vincent many brushes; larger ones, those used to paint walls. But in the grand scope of the work from afar his brushstrokes were still too small to see; no longer the bold, dramatic strokes Vincent had grown accustomed to.

Then Mr. Gregory brought him a huge, broom-like brush.

Vincent laughed.

"Are you serious?" He took the brush and held it with both hands and moved it up and down in the air. "This might actually work." He climbed back up the scaffolding, dipped the brush into a bucket of cobalt blue, and slapped it onto the brickwork. Then he turned and looked down at Mr. Gregory who was waiting below. "This will do," Vincent said, holding the broom-brush. "But no more buckets. I need bigger. Troughs." He looked at the stretch of scaffolding he stood on, then back down to Mr. Gregory again. "They can be built into this, and some more assistants to mix the paints in them."

"Certainly, monsieur," Mr. Gregory said.

More construction began on the scaffolding; troughs lined each level, and buckets of paint were hauled up using the various systems of pulleys. And with that, Vincent set about to capture his bold brushstrokes, slapping the paint on thick and waiting for it to dry before slapping on another layer, and another, until he'd achieved his impasto style. In some places, the paint was six-inches thick. In other places, the paint was so heavy it broke the windows, which had to be boarded up and painted again. Vincent's arms and shoulders ached constantly, and Mr. Gregory brought in a masseuse whenever needed. The scaffolding was covered in gobs of paint. Along the ground, the spilled and dripped paint was so thick that shovels had to be used to remove it.

⁂

Mr. Gregory smiled.

"The scaffolding was a work of art in itself."

"You speak proudly of it," Hemingway said.

"Indeed, I am proud, sir. I was also part of the design team. We used Michelangelo's structure, the way it allowed him to move about, but on a much larger scale. It took Monsieur Vincent eighteen months to complete the first piece."

⁂

Vincent and Mr. Gregory stood along the Boulevard. The first mural was finished, scaffolding removed. A bright cluster of purple violets swept across the building and onto the next building, with a vibrant yellow background. The purples and blues of the flowers, along with the sharp greens of the stems, popped from the yellow behind them.

"*Purple Violets in Spring*," Vincent said, smiling. His hands and arms were stained with paint, and his face too, with bits of paint in his beard. His hair was matted, and dried flecks of paint peppered his scalp. "I love violets. They remind me of home."

Mr. Gregory clasped his tiny hands together. He was grinning wide.

"It is most impressive, monsieur. Most impressive indeed." He turned to Vincent. "Can you see it?"

Vincent frowned.

"See what?"

"Look at it, monsieur. Look at everything but the painting itself."

Vincent did just that, yet he was still puzzled.

"I don't understand."

"It emanates light, monsieur. This end of the Boulevard is already lighter than the rest."

Vincent shrugged.

"But of course it does; isn't that why I'm here?"

"Oui, monsieur," Mr. Gregory said, bowing. "Forgive me, I am just seeing it for the first time, and it is rather overwhelming. I cannot imagine what the whole Boulevard will be like."

"I used half the next building to continue the longest violets," Vincent said. "I couldn't cut them off. I am thinking of maybe using two full buildings for the next piece. Maybe even three."

Mr. Gregory was practically giddy with excitement, and he hopped a little on the spot, his tiny hands still clasped.

"Anything you wish, monsieur."

⁂

Mr. Gregory ate another grape.

"This was something Monsieur Vincent quickly learned to use to his advantage, the limitless canvas, a different kind of spontaneity."

"No project ever goes exactly as planned," Hemingway said.

"After that first mural was complete, Monsieur Vincent absorbed himself into his work," Mr. Gregory continued. "He did not stop for meal breaks, but had food delivered to him on the scaffolding, allowing him to keep working. Indeed, every waking moment after that, Monsieur Vincent was at work. Sometimes he went days, sleeping for a few hours at a time on the scaffolding."

"A new lease on life," Hemingway said.

"More of a distraction, sir."

"A damned good one, I'd say."

Mr. Gregory nodded.

"As the years passed, Monsieur Vincent's methods evolved with each new mural, whether it be the way he held his brushes or learning how different colours settled onto different surfaces. He found that he needed to be extra thick on wood, the paint absorbing into the wood and less vibrant after it settled, whereas brick accentuated the brashness of the strokes, something that gave him great satisfaction. Each new discovery led to new routines, making each building flow more easily than the last, until he was completing a building every few months."

Hemingway stood from the table and made his way over to the fire. Mr. Gregory scooped a handful of grapes and followed and sat his tiny frame in Satan's chair, his feet dangling.

"So, he was happy?"

"I wouldn't say that," Mr. Gregory said. "But he was fulfilled, at least physically. As the years passed, Monsieur Vincent had grown from being scrawny and undernourished, to muscular, his arms and shoulders bulging and tight. He grew so strong he was able to scale buildings without the use of the scaffolding, holding himself with one arm against a windowpane or a narrow ledge and using the other to paint, gripping tightly to the brush that was as long as a broom handle." He peeled another grape with his teeth. "Fifteen years in, the Boulevard was nearly a quarter complete. It was around this time that Monsieur Vincent started working on several murals at once, allowing his instinctual spontaneity to spark in different places on different murals and at different times."

Hemingway leaned forward and threw another log on the fire, then reached to the floor for his wineskin and took a long drink.

"So your scaffolding grew too."

"Yes, sir. It required a bold new scaffolding system that stretched across the Boulevard, allowing him to move from one building to the next so that he could paint several murals at the same time, using the same colours on different murals if necessary. At any given time, the new scaffolding covered four blocks, arching across the width of the Boulevard, which had been paved and divided into eight lanes for the traffic that was to come once it reopened." He nibbled the skin off another grape and flicked it into the fire. "Bit by bit, year after year, the glow from the Boulevard grew more and more vibrant, until, finally, it dominated the cityscape and lit the sky in such a way that it shone, almost, like the sun, as it still does today."

"There's nothing like it," Hemingway said. "I gotta tell you, when I first arrived here and saw that, it changed everything. Made all of this tolerable." He lifted the wineskin again before sitting back, snug once again between the armrests. "How is Vincent now?"

"You will see soon enough," Mr. Gregory said. "The Boulevard took sixty years in all to paint, a year per block. Monsieur Vincent's light is all but diminished now, like a gas lamp after it has run out of fuel, the flame becomes smaller, until, finally—"

"It flickers out," Hemingway said.

"Yes, sir."

"That's a damned shame."

"It was Monsieur Vincent's light to give, not to receive," Mr. Gregory said. "But if you'd seen him when he painted it, for a time he was, dare I say it, sir, *perfect*."

Mr. Gregory ate his last grape, flicked the skin into the fire, then sat back and eyed the bottle of scotch at Hemingway's feet. Hemingway poured some into a glass and handed it to him.

Mr. Gregory sipped the scotch, then nodded.

"By the time the Boulevard was complete, Monsieur Vincent could do no more. There was a grand ceremony. The Boulevard was lined with millions of souls. Every building was draped with giant cloth coverings. When the coverings fell, the light exploded from the murals, lighting all of Capital City, and everyone cheered."

"Where was Vincent?"

"I don't know, sir. Perhaps he was already in the Foothills by then."

"Does he paint anymore?"

"No," Mr. Gregory said. "From what I know, he is unable. He only sketches, and only in black and white. There is no colour in him anymore."

The fire hissed and popped. Out the train window the platform was dark and empty.

"The Boulevard took it all," Hemingway said. "Christ of the coal mines."

30

Mr. Gregory stepped into Satan's sleeping quarters. Satan was awake; he'd pushed himself upward, so that his head was perched against the headboard. His movements were very slow. Even his blinking was slow, his eyelids half closed. Mr. Gregory clasped his hands.

"Sir, I'll send a car for Monsieur Vincent."

Satan coughed into the rag.

"No."

"But sir, you are in no condition—"

"Do as I say."

"Yes, sir."

Hemingway poked his head into the room.

"You alright?"

Satan's eyes rolled slowly toward him.

"The sleep did me well."

"You don't look well."

At first Satan did not even have the strength to pull down the blankets, but once he did, he held out his hand and Hemingway helped him sit up. From there he let his legs fall over the side of the bed and he sat, his hands on his knees.

"Now then, Ernest, shall we go?"

Hemingway peered down at Satan's disheveled nightgown he and Mr. Gregory had put him in when they'd brought him to bed.

Satan glanced down at himself.

"Yes. Give me a minute."

Hemingway waited with Mr. Gregory at the dining table. He poured himself a glass of scotch.

"It's damned fine scotch."

"Thank you, sir."

"Why you thanking me?"

"I picked out that particular bottle," Mr. Gregory said.

"Well, it's damned fine and I must say, you are damned fine at what you do."

Mr. Gregory rolled on the balls of his feet.

"Thank you, sir."

❧

Satan stepped into the car, dressed in a sheer black suit, black shirt, and black tie. Too weak to stand on his own, he braced himself against the wall. Hemingway grabbed him by the arm and swung it around his shoulder. When Satan's legs went limp, Hemingway simply picked him up as if he were a child. It was like carrying a skeleton.

Hemingway stepped off the train and into a wall of heat. He made his way across the platform and down a staircase to a waiting limousine. The chauffeur, a spry young demon with a big, excited grin, stood next to the open door and offered an exaggerated salute.

"Good day, sir! Any luggage?"

"Get a blanket," Hemingway said, placing Satan in the back-seat.

The driver went to the trunk and returned with a thick wool blanket, which Hemingway wrapped snuggly around Satan, who slumped forward and was shivering. Mr. Gregory climbed into the front seat and twisted around.

"Perhaps we should return to the train."

"No," Hemingway said. He motioned to the driver. "Go."

The sky was low and dark. The road snaked through the rocky landscape, dipping and twisting around masses of boulders. They passed a cluster of miners' huts, their put-together rooftops covered black in ash and coal dust. There was heather and protruding rocks, all blackened with ash and coal dust. In some places there appeared an orange glow where molten lava bubbled and pooled from the ground.

"This is what it was like in the beginning?" Hemingway said.

"Yes, sir."

"Jesus Christ."

Satan's head rested against the car window. He coughed into the blanket and spit up clumps of bloody phlegm. Blood covered his chin. Then suddenly he heaved, then vomited, and blood spewed down the blanket and onto the floor. Mr. Gregory twisted around, eyes wide from behind his tiny spectacles.

"We should really go back, sir."

"Shut your mouth," Hemingway said.

"Yes, sir."

The limousine stank of blood and bile. Hemingway pulled his shirt up over his nose and mouth.

"When's the last time you saw Vincent?"

"Not since he painted the Boulevard, sir. But I've heard stories. By all accounts, he is a defeated man."

"But how do you know for certain?" Hemingway said. "Stories are just stories."

"I don't know for certain," Mr. Gregory said. "But could anyone live out here and not be defeated?"

Hemingway grunted from under his shirt.

"It's a damned shame. That's all I'll say about it."

"Perhaps he is as good here as anywhere," Mr. Gregory said.

Hemingway could see the coal dust already shading his window.

"Well, you can never really know," he said. "I don't know the man. But there's something to be said for solitude. There's peace in that. But you can't escape your own head, no matter where you go."

The limousine pulled onto a dirt road and drove a quarter of a mile in before stopping. The driver got out and opened the door. Hemingway pulled the vomit-covered blanket off Satan and tossed it on the ground. Then he lifted Satan out and wrapped an arm around him, under his armpit, holding him up. There was a layer of ash underfoot that cushioned the earth. The dust-thick air tickled Hemingway's throat and lungs.

Satan pointed toward a cluster of boulders about fifty yards off the road. Hemingway squinted and saw the silhouette of a man sitting at the base of the rocks, sketching another man sitting a few feet in front of him. There was an orange glow emulating from the sitting man. Not bright enough for a candle, but more colourful than anything else around it. He was dressed in a plain grey shirt and black trousers, and his skin was black with dirt. The other man was a miner, his face black with coal, his miner's cap and lamp equally black, indiscernible from his skin. As they drew nearer, Hemingway saw that the glow was not a candle, but the sitting man's hair—he was so dirtied that the orange of his hair looked extra bright, and Hemingway remembered what Satan had said, that Vincent's hair was the colour of carrots. Goddamned fluorescent carrots. He leaned Satan against a boulder, and in the gloom they blended into it.

Satan coughed and spit onto the ground. Vincent turned, revealing the piercing green eyes, the pointed nose, and the high, sharp cheekbones. Once Hemingway's eyes adjusted to the darkness, he saw the red stubble on the cheeks and chin, and on the left side of his head, the flat, healed flesh of the missing earlobe.

Satan coughed again, and Vincent perked up and looked in their direction, but in the darkness, he did not see them. He lowered his head again and continued sketching. Behind them, a siren rang and out from the mine came a group of miners, their headlamps flickering.

"What are we waiting for?" Hemingway whispered.

Satan didn't answer. He stared at Vincent.

Vincent's head turned again toward them, and for a few moments everyone remained still, waiting for the other to move.

"Who goes there?" Vincent finally asked.

Hemingway, just as Satan had been when he first met him, was surprised at the softness of Vincent's voice. It did not match those fierce eyes. Hemingway and Satan remained beside the boulder, still as statues, and once again there was the standoff of who was going to blink first. Then Satan coughed, and because Vincent was listening for it, he looked directly at them.

"Show yourself," Vincent said, standing now, facing them. He took a step toward them.

Satan grunted, and then, searching for his last reserve of energy, he stepped out from the boulder and stood on his own.

Vincent's face dropped.

"Oh," he said.

He nodded to the miner who seemed to understand that their time was up. The miner stood, then walked away. Vincent, without looking at them, gathered his drawing pad and charcoal pencils.

"Not here," he said.

Hemingway wrapped his arm firmly around Satan, and they followed Vincent into the darkness. Mr. Gregory scampered over. The ground was so soft Mr. Gregory had moved without a sound, and Hemingway did not notice him until he'd placed himself on the other side of Satan to help.

Vincent led them along a footpath of smooth, hardened ash that shone dimly purple in the dark; what little light there was, reflecting purple from the black, and it was these purple patches that led them through the darkness. They turned a bend around a mass of boulders and came to a cluster of huts. The huts were clumsily built with wooden planks and crooked chimneys and small, uneven doorways. A web of low-lying powerlines connected the huts together. Through the planks you could see the faint yellow lights inside, accentuating each hut's imperfection. It reminded Hemingway of an early Van Gogh painting, the thick, dark lines, the rough brushstrokes of the planks and the purple-black earth.

Vincent held the door to his hut as Hemingway and Mr. Gregory eased Satan through the narrow entry and sat him at a small table on a wooden chair.

The hut had a metal cot in the corner, and an end table beside it, with a lamp that gave off a soft yellow light. Tucked behind the cot was an unused hearth, now filled with boxes, its rough brickwork up the wall and through the low roof. There was a sink and counter, and a stove. Above the sink was a shelf with a few dishes—two plates, some mugs, a bowl, and cutlery. The floor was made of hardened ash, the same as the pathway, and the hut smelled of burnt earth and the dried wood of the plank walls, which had charcoal drawings tacked to them. Drawings were scattered on the table and Vincent gathered the pages and placed them on the end table beside his cot.

A rat scurried out from under the cot and slipped under the doorway through an opening in the planks. Mr. Gregory jumped, startled, then stood, poised, his hands clasped.

Vincent filled a pot with water and placed it on the stove's burner. He took four mugs and scooped a spoonful of coffee into each. He then turned to Hemingway and pulled out the chair opposite Satan.

"Please."

"Thank you," Hemingway said, and he sat, then slid the chair close so that he was an arm's length from Satan, but with his weight the chair's legs sunk a little into the earthen floor and so he lifted the chair and scooted over.

Vincent turned to Mr. Gregory then gestured toward the cot.

"I'm afraid I've nowhere else to offer you to sit."

"I'm fine, thank you, Monsieur Vincent," Mr. Gregory said. The dimness of the room made shadows under his eyes. "It's good to see you."

"You as well," Vincent said.

"It has been a long time."

"Indeed," Vincent said.

The water in the pot came to a boil and Vincent lifted it off the burner and poured it into the mugs and handed them out. He reached under the counter for a tin of milk and placed it, and a glass bowl with sugar, on the table. Then, taking a sip from his mug, he leaned against the counter and looked at Satan.

"What do you want?"

Satan muffled a cough with his hand, and then he swayed and Hemingway reached across the table and steadied him.

Satan coughed again.

"How have you been, Vincent?"

Vincent shrugged.

"What do you care?"

"You are drawing?"

"Sketching."

"That is good."

"And you've come all this way to ask me that?"

Satan's eyelids drooped. He gripped the mug and lifted it to his mouth. The mug shook in his hand. He sipped, then placed the mug on the table. It was all done slowly, and it required a great effort.

"Why did you do it?"

Vincent lifted the mug to his mouth, but lowered it without drinking.

"Do what?"

"The Boulevard."

Vincent crossed his arms and grunted. He dug into his pocket for his pipe, struck a match and lit it. The hut filled quickly with the thick, brown tobacco smoke. He stepped forward and slid the tin of milk toward Hemingway.

"Help yourself."

Hemingway nodded.

"I take it black, but thanks." He sipped. The coffee was watery and bits of grounds caught on his tongue.

"You look well," Satan said.

Vincent shrugged again.

"How am I supposed to look? I have been in these hills for more than seventy years; longer than it took to paint the Boulevard. But what is seventy years to eternity? A drop of a drop."

There was a long silence, and the room simmered in it. Muffled voices came through the planks as two miners walked by the hut. Vincent smoked his pipe, and then his and Hemingway's eyes met briefly.

Satan raised his head. His eyes were red and watery, and he coughed again and he and Vincent held a stare for a moment. Satan then turned to Mr. Gregory and nodded, and Mr. Gregory stepped forward and handed the printed email to Vincent.

Vincent leaned against the counter, pipe between his lips. When he finished reading, he plucked the pipe from his mouth.

Mr. Gregory stepped forward and took the paper back.

"If I may, Monsieur Vincent," he said, and nodded toward Satan. "He is quite ill. He has made a long journey."

Vincent smoked his pipe and kept his eyes on Satan.

"If he has come all this way to say something then he should say it." He looked at Satan. "Out with it."

Satan raised his head again.

"The Boulevard," he said. His head dropped and he stared into his mug, at the steam coming from it. "It must be destroyed."

Vincent showed no reaction, though with his face darkened with coal dust his eyes looked like they were glowing.

Satan nodded.

"It would bring unspeakable trouble."

"For whom?"

Satan didn't answer.

"I thought so," Vincent said.

"This decision was not made lightly," Satan said.

"You came all this way to tell me that?" Vincent turned to Mr. Gregory. "Why did you bring him here?"

"He has come on his own accord, monsieur."

Vincent huffed again and glared at Satan. Then he tossed his pipe into the sink and bits of sparks flashed up into the underside of the shelf. He crossed his arms, took in a deep breath, then looked at Hemingway.

"What say you, Monsieur Hemingway? What do you think of this?"

"It's a damned shame, for sure," Hemingway said. "I've said that already."

Vincent offered a grin.

"But how do you really feel about it? If he were not sitting across from you? If you weren't afraid to say the truth?"

"I'm not afraid of anyone," Hemingway said.

Vincent nodded toward Satan.

"Not even him," Hemingway said.

"Then tell me how you really feel," Vincent said.

Hemingway took a moment. Then he looked up.

"If I'm gonna be completely honest," he said. "It's a fuckin disgrace." He paused. "For what he did to you. And now this. But look where we are. Look who he is. It goes with the territory."

Vincent glared down at Satan.

"You are a coward. Nothing more. It is no surprise you are doing this."

Satan had slouched over, his head low. Vincent stepped closer to him.

"COWARD!"

"Easy now," Hemingway said.

Vincent gritted his teeth, and breathed; then, as if feeling foolish, he shook his head and sighed deeply.

Satan raised his head.

"I am dying."

"Then what are you afraid of?" Vincent said. "What difference will it make?" He grinned. "Ah yes, it's always about you, isn't it? Right to the very end."

Satan blinked, slowly, and looked down to the floor. There was a long pause, until Mr. Gregory stepped over to the counter and placed his empty mug in the sink.

"Perhaps we should be going, monsieur."

Satan looked up at Vincent again.

"You have not answered my question." He swallowed hard, his breath thick in his throat. "Why did you do it?"

"I could ask you the same thing," Vincent said. "Though I doubt I would receive the same answer."

Satan coughed again and leaned back. Hemingway held him up. There was another long silence.

"Darkness needs light," Vincent said. "Just as light needs darkness. It makes no difference whether here or anywhere else. That's why I did it. Not for me, but for everyone else in this god-forsaken place—sinners—for them, not me." He grinned. "This should be no great revelation."

"No, no," Hemingway said. "You're not saying anything

new—I get it." He nodded to Satan, whose head hung low, his eyes shut. "He gets it."

"Does he?" Vincent said. "Is he capable of understanding such a thing? He hasn't a selfless bone in the whole of his body."

"He gets it," Hemingway said again.

Vincent smiled.

"I am sorry, Monsieur Hemingway, but I don't believe that's possible."

Satan raised his head again, his eyes yellow in the lamplight.

"What do you suggest I do?"

"How do you mean?"

"If I kept it," Satan said.

Vincent crossed his arms.

"I speak to you truly," Satan said. He then broke into a hoarse cough, and he keeled over, and Hemingway held him up.

"I don't believe you," Vincent said.

Satan shook his head. He was trying to speak, but his cough choked him, and he spit up blood and wiped it on his sleeve.

Vincent peered over to Mr. Gregory.

"He is dying—truly?"

Mr. Gregory nodded.

"It would seem so, monsieur."

Vincent turned back to Satan.

Satan nodded slowly, then lifted his head. His eyes met Vincent's. There was blood on his lips.

"Tell me not to do it."

Vincent looked quickly to Hemingway then to Mr. Gregory then back to Satan. A few muffled voices passed outside the hut.

"No," Vincent said. He paused. "This is no shared burden."

Satan licked the blood from his lips, then turned to Mr. Gregory, and there was a whimper to his voice, as though the weight of his words were stuck in his throat.

"Call it off."

Mr. Gregory, standing by the doorway, his hands clasped, leaned in.

"Sir?"

Satan grunted, and he took a breath, as if trying to summon the words.

"Do as I say."

"Yes, sir."

Mr. Gregory pulled out his phone and stepped outside.

It was quiet and heavy in the smoke-filled hut. Vincent picked his pipe from the sink and packed the bowl with more tobacco and relit it.

Mr. Gregory stepped inside.

"It is done, sir."

Upon hearing Mr. Gregory, Satan's eyes opened and his head jerked up. He muffled a cough then extended his hand. Hemingway stood and helped him to his feet.

Vincent was still leaning against the counter.

Satan twisted himself around slowly.

"There is one more thing. I shall submit a formal request for your extradition. If permitted, you can return to Heaven with the visiting party."

"No thank you," Vincent quickly said.

Hemingway turned.

"He just offered you the Golden Ticket."

Vincent shrugged.

"Jesus Christ," Hemingway said. "I'd be hopping drunk if I were you."

Vincent smiled sadly.

"Monsieur Hemingway, ask yourself why he makes me such an offer." He winked. "Not a bone in the whole of his body." He walked over to the door and held it open. "Besides, these people need me here." He and Hemingway shook hands. "It was a pleasure, Monsieur Hemingway."

Hemingway and Mr. Gregory helped Satan through the narrow doorway.

"Think about it," Satan said as he passed.

Vincent shook his head.

"I shan't give you the satisfaction."

Once outside the hut, Hemingway and Mr. Gregory, each

holding one side of Satan, trekked back through the darkness, along the smooth, black-purple path, the coal-dust air tickling their throats, until they climbed into the limousine and drove back to the waiting train.

31

By the time they got to the station, Satan could not stand on his own, the sickness smothering him now. Hemingway carried him across the empty platform once again. As they climbed the steps to the car, Satan lifted his head.

"Let us sit by the fire one last time, Ernest."

Hemingway placed him in his chair and wrapped the blanket around him. He added another log and stoked the fire so that the flames grew. Hemingway's face was streaked with coal dust and his eyes and teeth were very white. He reached down beside his chair for his wineskin and squeezed a mouthful. Then he unbuttoned and removed his shirt, weighted with sweat, and wiped his face with it. And there he sat, bare chested. He turned to Mr. Gregory.

"Get me a cold beer. As cold as you can make it."

Mr. Gregory scuttled away.

"Make it two," Hemingway said.

Satan placed his feet in the fire, resting them on the glowing coals. He wiggled his toes, the flames burning around them.

A few moments later, Mr. Gregory returned with two bottles of beer. Hemingway cracked open the first one, took a long drink, then leaned forward and poked at the logs.

"He couldn't resist painting the Boulevard, could he?"

"There was still much light in him," Satan said. "But he was right; he did not do it for himself. It was for him to give. I could never do such a thing."

"I gotta disagree," Hemingway said. "Look at all you've done —the Boulevard, and coming all this way to tell him."

Satan's lips curled into a subtle grin.

"That is as far as it goes, Ernest."

Hemingway finished the beer quickly and cracked the second bottle, drinking it half down in a single gulp.

"What happened back there?"

Satan paused, staring blankly into the flames.

"He was not afraid."

"Of what?"

"Of me," Satan said. "Of anything."

"He doesn't like you much," Hemingway said.

Satan grinned again.

"That is understandable."

"He was pretty pissed."

"To spite me, no doubt."

"Or *in* spite of you."

"Perhaps," Satan said. "But in his spite, he was unafraid. And in that moment, he showed me what I had to do, and so I did it."

His face contorted to cough but only a whimper came. Hemingway sat patiently. Everything Satan did was accompanied by a weighted silence, a stillness between every little thing. A minute passed, a long minute, before he took a deep breath and mustered the strength to speak again.

"Since the beginning of time we have held our tails between our legs." He paused and breathed, gaining his strength again. "I have rebelled, yes, but now I am tired. I am tired of hiding. Tired of being afraid." His face was still. Then he cringed, his small black eyes closing as he took another slow, laboured breath. "I will not do it. I will not destroy all that I have built just to appease him."

The fire burned bright.

"Do you see?" Hemingway said. "You *are* capable."

Satan opened his eyes.

"But what have I to lose, Ernest? Vincent was right: God's

wrath will make little difference upon me now."

The fire snapped and popped.

Hemingway finished the second beer then reached down for his wineskin. The sweat on his chest glistened in the firelight.

"You're really doing it, eh?"

Satan could barely keep his eyes open. It was a struggle even to nod, which he did.

"You got balls," Hemingway said. "I'll give you that." He took a long swig from the skin. "But I get it. It's the right thing to do. How else do you face your maker if not in your own shoes?"

Satan's eyes scanned the length of the blanket, down to his bare feet resting in the burning coals. Hemingway saw them too, and he chuckled.

"Even better," he said.

He looked out the train window, beyond the platform to the gloom of the base of the mountains, where he imagined Vincent sitting, sketching in the candlelight.

Satan wheezed long, low breaths and stared blankly into the flames. A moment later, his eyes rolled back and his head fell to the side. Hemingway lifted him out of the chair and, very carefully, as one does with a sleeping baby, he carried him to his bed.

Mr. Gregory followed him.

"Is he—?"

Hemingway adjusted the pillow, moving it so that Satan's head rested squarely upon it.

"Not yet."

When Hemingway returned to the car, he sat at the small table, which had been cleared, except for the bowl of grapes. Mr. Gregory stood on the opposite side of the car. Hemingway kicked the chair out.

"Have a seat."

Mr. Gregory sat, his hands clasped.

Hemingway leaned back in the chair and crossed his arms.

"What happened back there?"

Mr. Gregory frowned.

"Where, sir?"

"With Vincent; that was too easy."

Mr. Gregory sighed and picked a grape from the bowl and rolled it in the palm of his hand.

"It's a long way to Cabo San Vito," Hemingway said. "I've got all night."

Mr. Gregory sighed again.

"Do you recall what Monsieur Vincent said about Satan? About selflessness?"

Hemingway nodded.

"Said he doesn't have a selfless bone in his body."

"Yes," Mr. Gregory said. He adjusted his spectacles. "Well, that's not entirely accurate."

Hemingway sat up.

Mr. Gregory adjusted his spectacles again and nibbled the skin of the grape. He then lowered his voice.

"Satan hasn't been completely truthful with you, sir."

"About what?" Hemingway said. "Vincent?"

Mr. Gregory shook his head.

"No, sir, that was accurate." He sighed again. Then he leaned forward, his arms on the table. "I'm talking about what came before; when we were in Heaven."

"What part?"

Mr. Gregory peered back toward Satan's sleeping quarters, then to Hemingway once again.

"Most of it, sir."

❧

Eden, with all its beauty, was littered with vials and jars strewn about. Angels tramped on the newly made ground. But over time everything was collected, until there remained only the last few inspectors. Mr. Gregory, Lucifer, and Mr. Graves had worked together and were returning from their third visit to Eden, on one of the last caravans before its official opening. The convoy consisted of a dozen other angels who sat, buckled in, talking amongst themselves. Lucifer sat between Mr. Gregory and Mr. Graves.

Mr. Gregory and Lucifer were chatting quietly when Mr. Gregory crossed his legs and there, stuck to the sole of his shoe, was a dandelion. Lucifer's eyes widened. Mr. Gregory stopped mid-sentence and quietly gasped.

"I didn't—"

Lucifer quickly muzzled him, placing his hand over his mouth. He leant forward and plucked the dandelion then sat up, cupping the flower in his hands. Mr. Graves had been snoozing and Lucifer nudged him and opened his hands, slightly, just enough to show what he was holding.

"What is that?" Graves whispered. His eyes darted around the caravan, but none of the other angels were paying any attention to them.

Lucifer chuckled.

"It was on my shoe."

Mr. Gregory leaned in to speak, but Lucifer held him back.

"Oops."

Mr. Graves spoke in a low but frantic voice.

"You need to report it—as soon as we get back."

"Nonsense," Lucifer said.

Mr. Graves huffed.

"Are you mad?"

"I am keeping it," Lucifer said.

Mr. Graves' whole face dropped.

Lucifer shrugged.

"It is only a flower."

"*Only a flower?*" Mr. Graves said. "Do you have any idea how dangerous that thing is if you get caught with it? It needs to be reported. Immediately."

"But he didn't report it," Hemingway said.

"No, sir. Instead, he placed it in one of the cases we'd used in Eden."

"Then what?"

Mr. Gregory shrugged.

"At the time, I thought that was the end of it."

"But it wasn't," Hemingway said.

"No, sir. It was just the beginning."

"Mr. Graves never asked about it?"

"No, sir. He never expected Satan to lie. Before Eden we had never lied; in Heaven there was only truth."

"But he lied in Heaven."

"Yes, sir."

"You were the only one who knew?"

"In the beginning, yes," Mr. Gregory said.

"And how did you feel about that?" Hemingway asked.

"Naturally, I wasn't comfortable with it," Mr. Gregory said.

"Why didn't you say something?"

"That is more easily said than done, sir."

Hemingway nodded.

"Fair enough."

"On our next visit, he took another flower—a sunflower. He'd stuffed it under his wing, but it was so big the yellow of the petals showed."

"But nobody noticed," Hemingway said.

"No, sir."

"And where did he put it? In the same case?"

"Yes, sir. And he hid it high in the hills. He took me there and showed me. I think he needed me to share the secret—to share the burden."

"And once you were in it, you were in it; no turning back."

"Precisely, sir."

"Why do you think he picked you?"

"I don't know, sir. Perhaps because I can be trusted."

"Can you?" Hemingway said.

Mr. Gregory inflated his chest a little.

"Indeed, sir."

Hemingway grinned at Mr. Gregory's posturing; the tiny demon, who looked more like an elf, doing his best to impress him.

"Who dug the tunnel?"

"That came after our final expedition," Mr. Gregory said. "Satan had collected more flowers, and once he learned we wouldn't be returning, he asked me to help him with it."

Hemingway huffed.

"And you just went along with it?"

Mr. Gregory smiled a little.

"It was fun, sir. Eden had done things to all of us. I wasn't immune to that."

Hemingway leaned back in his chair and laughed.

"You little shit, eh?" He pointed at Mr. Gregory, his arm stretched across the table, not far from Mr. Gregory's face. "You aren't so innocent yourself."

"None of us are, sir."

Hemingway nodded and sat back once again.

"Ok, so you dug the tunnel. Then what?"

"We went in and out to Eden as we pleased," Mr. Gregory said. "We collected as many samples as we could find."

Hemingway was grinning.

"And that was fun too, I suppose."

"It was, sir."

"When did the others join?"

Mr. Gregory quickly peered over his shoulder.

"Satan could not keep it a secret. We had the garden in the valley already planted, and the flowers had spread, but not as explained to you. You see, the valley was well hidden, and it had contained them. They did not spread beyond the valley floor, and from high up in the hills you could not see them through the whiteness—just their glow. But you must understand, sir, there were many different lights and colours in Heaven—everything

glowed in its own way—and so you would not know it was the
glow of flowers unless you trekked down to the valley floor, under
the cloud of white, and saw them with your own eyes."

"But Satan brought others in?"

Mr. Gregory shook his head.

"Every day he brought angels in to see it. He was very proud
of it."

"Who was the first one he brought?"

"Ms. Victoria," Mr. Gregory said.

"He liked her."

"Everyone liked her, sir. She was beautiful then—and is
beautiful still."

"I've seen her," Hemingway said. "Indeed."

The train, having left the station, was well into its gradual
descent from the Foothills, out of the mountains and back into
the open landscape, moving steadily through the darkness. Hemingway ate another grape.

"So how did Graves get mixed up in all of it?"

"As a Team Lead, he had access to the records and he'd
discovered no dandelion had ever been turned in. He confronted
Lucifer, as he was then known, and they had a terrible row,
screaming and yelling, and that is when Satan took him to the
valley to show him. It was his hope that Mr. Graves would be so
taken by its beauty that he would forgive and forget."

"Which he obviously did," Hemingway said.

Mr. Gregory sighed.

"He has yet to do either, sir."

Lucifer took Mr. Graves by the arm and led him to the path that
snaked along the hillside and climbed up and up into the whiteness until it leveled off and revealed the glow of a valley on the
other side. They descended into the valley without speaking, until
they came upon Mr. Steel, Mr. Gordon, and Ms. Victoria a hundred yards off the path, sitting amongst the flowers. The glow of

the flowers had permeated the whiteness, making colourful hues of the air —a patch of irises, a purple hue; sunflowers, yellow; roses, red. And as they walked, the colours swirled in their wake and mixed, creating more colours and more swirls, and it all seemed a rather magical place.

Ms. Victoria fixed her eyes upon Mr. Graves.

"It's okay," Lucifer said.

He turned to Mr. Graves.

"Welcome."

Mr. Graves' eyes shifted to each angel, then to the flowers and the colourful hues around him.

"What is this?"

"It is exactly what you think it is," Lucifer said.

Mr. Graves stepped back.

"Do you not understand the seriousness of this?"

"We do," Lucifer said.

"He knows what he's doing," Mr. Steel said.

"Does he?" Mr. Graves said. "Do any of you?"

Mr. Steel shrugged.

"It's just a few flowers."

"You have defied God," Mr. Graves said.

"Relax," Lucifer said.

Mr. Graves took another step back.

"Eden has gotten to you. Eden has gotten into your heads."

"Yes, it has," Lucifer said. He took Graves by the hand and gently pulled him in. "It has made us free."

Mr. Graves pulled his hand away.

"Rubbish! Do you not know the consequences if you are found out? You will be banished. All of you."

Mr. Steel frowned.

"Banished to where?"

"I knew this was a bad idea," Mr. Gordon muttered.

"Shut up," Lucifer quickly said.

Mr. Graves was shaking his head.

"What idiotic notion brought you to the conclusion that this was okay?"

"It is nothing," Lucifer said. "I thought you would like to be involved. Apparently, I was wrong."

"Does Council know of this?"

"We have already spoken to Council."

Ms. Victoria looked surprised.

"We have?"

Lucifer nodded.

"I took it to them yesterday."

Mr. Steel glanced quickly at Ms. Victoria, then back to Lucifer.

"What did you say? Did you tell them of this?"

"Of course not," Lucifer said. "I merely suggested the idea of such a place. And they rejected us outright."

"What was their reasoning?"

Lucifer offered a sympathetic smile.

"What is their reasoning for anything?"

"He is lying to you!" Graves said. "He is lying to you all. He took nothing to Council."

Mr. Gordon shrugged.

"They are idiots, the lot of them."

"Idiots, perhaps," Mr. Graves said. "But they control your fate. And when they find out about this, may they have mercy on you all."

"Nobody will find out," Lucifer said.

"You better be sure of that," Mr. Graves said.

"Everyone involved has been carefully vetted," Lucifer said. "Everyone is committed. Our bond is our security."

"Was I vetted?"

"Will you go to Council?"

Mr. Graves looked at Ms. Victoria, then Mr. Steel, and back to Lucifer. The flowers surrounded him.

"Who is in charge?"

Mr. Steel, Ms. Victoria, and Mr. Gordon all pointed to Lucifer.

"It belongs to all of us," Lucifer said. He placed his hand on

Mr. Graves' shoulder. "And it is yours now too."

Mr. Graves looked down at the flowers. His eyes could not look away.

Lucifer took him by the hand again.

"Come," he said softly. "Don't be afraid."

Mr. Graves kept his eyes on the flowers. Then, slowly, his wings drooping over his shoulders, he breathed deeply.

"This is madness," he said.

"But it is *our* madness," Lucifer said. "Just ours."

32

THE TRAIN PUSHED ON.

Mr. Gregory nibbled the skin off the grape, discarded the skin onto a napkin, and sucked the skinless grape into his mouth.

"The valley was raided that day, and we were taken into custody, along with Mr. Graves."

"Any idea who leaked?" Hemingway asked.

Mr. Gregory shook his head.

"It could have been anyone, sir. Many angels were in the mountains then. We will never know." He slumped in his chair now, remembering it. "After the raid, Council did a broad sweep—anyone associated with us was included, and everyone was declared guilty. We were collected and taken away."

"Then what?" Hemingway asked.

Mr. Gregory swallowed hard.

"The guillotine, sir."

"FOR THE CRIMES OF CONSPIRACY, TREASON, AND INCITING A REBELLION, THE AFOREMEN-TIONED PARTIES HAVE BEEN FOUND GUILTY AND ARE HEREBY SENTENCED TO BANISHMENT, WHERE THEY SHALL BE CAST DOWN INTO THE PITS OF HELL. HEREWITH, ON THIS DAY, SUCH PUNISHMENT SHALL BE EXECUTED."

Lucifer, Mr. Graves, Ms. Victoria, Mr. Steel, Mr. Gordon, and Mr. Gregory stood side by side, shackled by chains, facing the guillotine.

Mr. Graves leaned over and whispered into Lucifer's ear.

"I will never forgive you for this."

Lucifer said nothing.

Mr. Graves tugged at his chains.

"How are you so calm? This is all because of you. YOU are the reason we're here!"

Lucifer's face dropped. He knew this already, but to hear it brought real weight to it, and the words hit him with a thud.

"It is done. There is nothing I can do. They have chosen their side."

"And what side is that?"

Lucifer peered over to the hole.

"Not ours."

"We never had a choice," Mr. Graves said. "You decided for us."

The angel rolled up the scroll and turned to another angel posted next to the guillotine.

"PROCEED."

The angel stepped forward.

Ms. Victoria cried. Next to her, Mr. Steel, shaking like an infant. Mr. Gordon had vomited, appearing half-mad with his teeth, and Mr. Graves snarled and tugged at his chains. Mr. Gregory went unnoticed, his small frame overshadowed by Mr. Gordon. Lucifer, however, stood still, his head low. He did not move; not until Mr. Graves pressed his shoulder into him and shoved him and he stumbled forward from the line.

The angel grinned.

"We have a volunteer."

Lucifer turned and eyed Mr. Graves, who stood stoic, his gaze ahead but not seeing the crowd.

The angel stepped forward and, along with another angel, they took Lucifer by the arms and led him to the guillotine. Lucifer did not fight them when they strapped him down and folded his wings under the blade. Neither Mr. Graves, Ms. Victoria, Mr. Steel, Mr. Gordon, or Mr. Gregory would look at him. They had all straightened up and, in Lucifer's eyes, their sudden calmness was more a satisfaction in seeing him go first. As they strapped him down, Lucifer kept trying to make eye contact with them, but they all looked away. When the blade fell and Lucifer grunted loud and deep, Mr. Graves sniggered; on the ground, Lucifer's wings fluttered erratically, the last of the nerve endings quivering until there remained only a lifeless pile of blood-soaked feathers.

Later, as the demons dropped into Hell, Lucifer awoke with his face pressed into a bed of ash. The wound on his back throbbed. His hair, once golden, was now jet-black, and his blood too, dried black along his hairline and down his face. Those who had already fallen began to move, their bodies emerging slowly from the ashes.

Lucifer sat himself up, brushed the ash from his hair and picked at the bits of dried blood in his hairline. Then Mr. Graves was on top of him and had his hands around his throat and was slamming his head up and down, tuffs of ash pluming out from under him.

Mr. Graves toppled over, winded, and they lay side by side in the ash, their bodies black and tired and sore.

"This is your mess," Mr. Graves said. He was calm now. He wiped the ash from his face, and it streaked across his plump cheeks.

Lucifer sat up. Other demons were making their way toward him, encircling him. A blast of lava burst from the ground next to them.

Lucifer stood and staggered back.

"I will make this right," he said.

Mr. Graves shook his head.

"There is nothing you can do, short of bringing Heaven to Hell, that will absolve you from this."

"Then that is what I will do," Lucifer said. "I shall make it my mission; I swear to you—to all of you!"

"And how will you do this?"

"I don't know," Lucifer said. "But we have time. We have all the time in the world."

⁂

Hemingway stuffed a handful of grapes into his mouth and sat back in the chair, and his eyes drifted away.

"So, this whole thing boils down to guilt. And that's why he built the Boulevard?"

"His guilt runs deep, sir. It consumed him."

Hemingway looked sharply at Mr. Gregory.

"And what about you? You started everything."

Mr. Gregory paused.

"It was an accident."

"Yeah, but you still planted the seed."

Mr. Gregory shrugged.

"I did, sir, yes. But in the end, it is up to the flower whether it decides to grow or not."

Hemingway nodded and grinned.

"It was an accident," Mr. Gregory said again.

Hemingway laughed.

"There are two kinds of generals," he said. "Those who feel for their troops, and those who only focus on victory. I'm not saying one is better than the other, but you gotta be a cold son-of-a-bitch to be the latter." He huffed. "You don't take any of the blame?"

Mr. Gregory shook his head.

"None whatsoever, sir."

Hemingway nodded again.

"Probably just as well."

Mr. Gregory looked down at the bowl, at the few remaining grapes.

"Are you hungry, sir? Can I get you anything else?"

"I'm fine," Hemingway said. He twirled the bowl on the table. "So that's why he built the Boulevard."

"Yes, sir."

"And if he destroys it, he's gotta deal with all of you, and if he doesn't, he's gotta deal with God."

"Yes, sir."

"And God ain't gonna like it."

"Not at all, sir. It isn't the Boulevard itself, but what it represents."

"Disobedience," Hemingway said.

"Yes, sir."

"That's a heavy weight."

"Indeed, sir. It is no wonder he is dying."

"You really think he's dying?"

"I believe so."

"So, nothing to lose, eh?"

Mr. Gregory shrugged.

"It seems his guilt has overtaken his fear."

"Ain't that the truth," Hemingway said. "A dying man is afraid of nothing. When he accepts his fate, fear disappears. I saw men in Italy, Spain, France—you name it— run into live fire knowing they were done—really done—and it was fear, or lack of it, that carried them into it."

He turned to Mr. Gregory.

"Why would he lie to me?"

Mr. Gregory was looking out the window too, at the blackness whizzing by.

"He is ashamed, sir. He hasn't told anyone."

"Yeah, but I don't give a shit," Hemingway said. "He knows that."

"Shame has an audience of only one, sir."

"As does guilt," Hemingway said.

"Yes, sir."

Later in the evening, Mr. Gregory went to check on Satan. Hemingway remained by the fire. His shirt had dried and he'd put it back on. He'd uncorked two bottles of wine and had emptied the first into his wineskin, which he'd propped between his feet, and now was pouring the second bottle. He peered over to Mr. Gregory when he entered the car.

"He still breathing?"

Mr. Gregory nodded.

Out the train window there was only darkness.

"Relax," Hemingway said. "He's a tough bugger. He'll be fine."

"And if he's not?" Mr. Gregory said.

Hemingway lifted the wine bottle and held it to the light to see how much was left. There was only a little, and he gulped it down.

"Then he's not."

Mr. Gregory sat at the small table, his head in his hands.

"We still have the Boulevard."

"Yes, you do," Hemingway said.

Mr. Gregory sat up.

"There would have to be an election."

Hemingway nodded.

"Sure."

"Mr. Graves, I suspect, would be the leading candidate."

"Sure," Hemingway said again. "But don't get too ahead of yourself." He nodded toward Satan's sleeping quarters. "He'll be fine. Don't you worry."

In the middle of the night, the train came to a stop at the village of Cabo San Vito. The village lay below the tracks, its lights glowing up to and beyond the empty platform.

Mr. Gregory saw Hemingway to the platform.

"Good luck, sir."

Hemingway grinned.

"With what? Jean or the cockfights?"

Mr. Gregory grinned back.

"Both, I suppose."

There was the smell of fireworks smoke, the faint sound of music, of guitars and villagers singing. Mr. Gregory watched as Hemingway, typewriter in one hand, suitcase in the other, made his way across the platform and down the path. A few fireworks spit up into the sky and framed his silhouette, tall and lumbering in the faint glow of the light, sinking lower over the bank with each step, until he was out of sight.

⁂

The train sped past the land and the darkness outside. Then, just before dawn, with the train in full throttle toward Capital City, Mr. Gregory checked on Satan again. The sheets were soaked. Mr. Gregory wiped him down with a cold cloth, which woke him up.

"Your fever has broken, sir."

Mr. Gregory placed a cup of water to his lips. Satan lifted his head, slightly, and took tiny sips, the water trickling down his chin. His head sunk back into the pillow. His eyes were yellow and waxy.

"I dreamt," he said, his voice coarse, his lips cracked and dry. "It was bright, the whiteness, and there were flowers everywhere, and all the land was beautiful." He stared at the ceiling, lost in the memory. "Do you remember it? How it was?"

Mr. Gregory refolded the wet cloth and dabbed it lightly along Satan's forehead.

"I do, sir."

Satan sipped more water before resting his head on the pillow again. Then came a long, drawn-out sigh.

"Do you think of it?"

Mr. Gregory refolded the cloth again and wiped down Satan's cheeks and chin.

"Every day, sir."

Satan's eyes watered, and he blinked, and a tear rolled down the side of his face.

Mr. Gregory dabbed the cold cloth on Satan's forehead.

"Rest up, sir."

33

In the morning, Satan lay awake in bed. Out the train window the land sped past. He yawned and stretched. His body no longer ached, and he felt the relief that comes upon awakening and knowing you've overcome an illness. He took a deep breath and exhaled. His lungs were clear. He stood up. His bones creaked and his legs were weak, but he was in good spirits, knowing it had passed. He made his way into the dining car, toward the table, now filled with bacon, eggs, potatoes, beans, and toast. Mr. Gregory slid out a chair.

"You look better, sir. How do you feel?"

Satan sat, gingerly.

"How would Hemingway put it?"

"Like a can of smashed assholes, sir."

Satan looked up with a smug grin.

"Very good, Mr. Gregory."

He ate without speaking, each mouthful fuelling him further. He drank two cups of coffee.

"Hemingway got off in Cabo San Vito?" he finally asked.

"Yes, sir," Mr. Gregory said. "He said he will see you when he returns to Capital City, if he survives Ms. Rhys." He rolled on the balls of his feet. "He also took your medicine."

"All of it?"

"Yes, sir."

Satan grinned again, and poured another cup of coffee.

❧

Satan remained by the fire all day as the train pushed on. By late evening he had recovered much of his strength. All the land was dark outside. Then a speck of light appeared in the distance, a lone, bright-burning star amid the black abyss, and the train pushed on, moving steadily toward it. Slowly, steadily, the light grew brighter, and the land grew less gloomy, less dim, until Satan could discern the suburbs and the outlines of Capital City's buildings. Just the thought of the Boulevard's glow invigorated him with a new, raw energy.

He turned to Mr. Gregory.

"Call Mr. Graves and tell him to meet me in my office."

❧

High up in Satan's tower, Mr. Graves was sitting in one of the wingback chairs in front of the fire. It was the middle of the night and his hair was dishevelled and his eyes puffy. The elevator door opened and Satan stepped into the room. Graves cleared his throat.

"What happened to you?"

Satan made his way over to the bar and poured himself a glass of scotch.

"Nothing."

"You look like you've lost thirty pounds."

"I have never felt better," Satan said.

He strode over to the fire and sat on the edge of the hearth, facing Graves, and swirled the scotch in the glass. The black of his shoes shone in the firelight.

"So, you've come to your senses," Grave said.

Satan nodded.

"How was the trip?" Graves asked.

Satan took a moment.

"Interesting."

"Care to tell me about it?"

"The details are not necessary," Satan said. "What matters is the outcome. You are to round up every artist you can find. Every building is a blank canvas and they must use only the brightest of colours. Mr. Capone's crews can clean up the Boulevard and restore anything they have already destroyed."

Graves was rubbing his palms together.

"This is good. Very good."

"I knew you would be pleased," Satan said.

"They've only just begun," Graves said. "I don't know if I've ever seen a Capone-run project move more slowly."

Satan sipped his scotch.

"He'll likely try to renegotiate," Graves said.

Satan shrugged.

"Just tell him to get it done." He took another sip. "If we are doing this, then we must do it right. We need more light along the river. Every street swept and cleaned. Triple the production of copper and wooden flowers. I want them everywhere, in every window and every storefront. I want this city to shine." The fire crackled and burned. "It is time."

"Indeed it is," Graves said.

Satan looked at the flickers of firelight through the glass.

"I was a foolish kid. Grown more foolish still."

"Kids make mistakes," Graves said.

"Yes, they do."

Within a few days Capital City had transformed into a sparkling metropolis. Not a piece of trash could be found. Sidewalks were swept, walkways and streets scrubbed, windows washed, foundations restored, graffiti painted over. Painted flowers bloomed everywhere.

The Boulevard was shut down and a massive, manic restoration project began. Thirty thousand workers were spread over its length, averaging five hundred workers per city block. Scaffolding covered every building and was covered with massive tarps. Each mural's glow escaped through slits in the tarps.

Thousands of drums containing emulsion cleaner, neutralizer and other various chemicals were trucked in and lined the Boulevard. Vats of emulsion cleaner were applied using paint rollers, then the neutralizer was applied before the cleaner would eat away at the paint. In the worst places where the varnish had cracked or was stained beyond repair, a varnish remover was used, carefully with brushes, and then a fresh layer of varnish reapplied. Much of the varnish along the street level of the murals was either damaged or dirtied. Along the tops of the highest buildings where the air was thick with smog and had settled and solidified, it was all replaced with a new, clean and clear layer of varnish.

Capone had personally overseen the project, always making himself visible along the Boulevard, and in the end, he had come through, earning him ownership of his own borough, a concern Satan would deal with at a later date. Indeed, it was a tremendous success, and a minor miracle; a project that should have taken months was completed in just under four days. Once all the scaffolding had been removed and the tarps taken down, the murals shone as bright as the day Vincent had painted them, and a sense of renewal, of rebirth, spread throughout Capital City, which only escalated the anticipation of God's arrival.

As the days passed, makeshift eateries began to spring up on the streets. T-shirt vendors set up shop on just about every corner. Jugglers, musicians, and mimes appeared along the Boulevard. Crowds started camping out in lawn chairs along the route, until finally, the day arrived.

Carlos Castro fell into his couch exhausted. The whirlwind of the past week had taken its toll.

After Mr. Steel's visit to his apartment, Castro had gotten straight to work. He'd headed down to the Boulevard and quickly realized what a daunting task it would be. The Boulevard seemed endless. Sixty blocks. Supplies from scaffolding was already being trucked in. Capone's crews had already begun to arrive. He needed bodies. Lots of them. And fencing. And barriers. And the equipment to put it all into place. He went back to his apartment.

Upon opening his door, he found, on the floor, a folder. In it was information regarding contacts for everything he needed: names and numbers and companies to call. There was also a personal note of assurance from Mr. Steel saying that everyone was expecting him, and that there will be full cooperation from all those involved. In short, he would get whatever he wanted. He sat down and started making calls. And before he knew it, things were moving. Within a few hours, crews were assembled, and materials and equipment were already on route. He spent his first day on the Boulevard overseeing the instillation of the first sets of barriers. He made adjustments, made more calls, and things were going as planned. When he returned to his apartment that evening, as soon as he opened his door, he heard the floor squeak behind him in the hallway.

Appearing as if by magic was a man dressed in full military attire, polished buttons, grey-black lapels, and standing straight as a board. He had sharp features, slicked hair, a pointed nose, and small, thin lips.

"Carlos Castro?"

Castro nodded.

"I am Colonel Olaf Hess. Mr. Steel has informed you of me?"

Castro nodded again. He remembered the name Hess on his list of contacts, though he'd yet to call him.

"You and I are to work together," Hess said. "May I come in?"

Castro backed out of the way, allowing for Hess to step inside.

Castro removed a newspaper from the armchair.

"Sit, please."

Hess sat.

"Something to drink?"

"A beer, if you have it."

Castro went to his fridge and retrieved two beers, twisted off the caps and handed one to Hess, who took a quick drink and placed the bottle on the coffee table.

"We have quite a task ahead of ourselves," Hess said. "It is imperative that we work together."

"Certainly," Castro said. He stepped into the kitchen and placed some corn chips in a plastic bowl, along with a small jar of salsa, and placed it on the coffee table. He took a swig of beer and sat opposite Hess, on his couch.

"As you know, I am overseeing the itinerary," Hess said. "And since you are security, we must coordinate our efforts. It is the best way."

"I agree," Castro said.

"I see you have already begun work on the Boulevard."

"Of course," Castro said. "We have limited time."

Hess reached for his beer and took a long drink.

"How much is he paying you?"

"Enough," Castro said.

"I do not like him," Hess said.

Castro smiled.

"He's a demon. Puta. All of them."

"Yes," Hess said, grinning a little. "But we must do as we are told."

"Of course," Castro said.

"Good. In that we are in agreement; that we work as one."

"As one," Castro said.

"Good," Hess said again. He pulled an envelope from his breast pocket and tossed it on the coffee table. "You will find in here the itinerary. It is all you will need to know. Times and places. That is all. I will provide the transportation, including the motorcade for the grand entrance. You may make the necessary changes to ensure it is safely done. But I assure you, all possibilities have been considered."

Carlos leaned forward and scooped up the envelope from the table.

"Certainly. Good. Yes." He held up his beer. "Salud." He stood up, as did Hess, and they shook hands and Hess left.

Together they had coordinated everything. The whole city, it seemed, was at their disposal.

�

Castro, sunken into his old couch, sighed, thinking back on it, exhausted yet relieved the preparations were complete, and that he'd done his job and had done it well. Everything he'd envisioned had been put into place. Hess had been meticulously organized from the beginning, and Castro had let him oversee any security issue he wished, and in doing that, Hess had inadvertently overseen the entire project, which suited Castro just fine. And now he could rest.

He turned to his patio garden. He'd neglected it. Between his garden and the flower shop, it was a constant upkeep—painting, repainting, making more flowers, placing them in different spots, in different bouquets. He hadn't constructed a single new flower for the shop, orders hadn't been filled, and a backlog awaited him. He knew he would have to take some from his garden. But not today. All he wished to do now was sleep. He managed to lift himself off the couch and put on a record, *Los Fabulosos Cadillacs*, then plopped back onto the couch. He was just drifting off when a knock on the door awoke him. He opened the door to a courier holding a small box.

"Carlos Castro? Please sign here," the courier said, offering a pen.

Castro signed and closed the door behind him, placed the box on the coffee table and returned to the couch. He did not want to open it right away. He simply sat and stared at it. He went to the fridge for a beer and grabbed a paring knife from the drawer. He sat again and took a drink of beer. A moment like this, he knew and feared, would be wonderful and brief, wonderfully brief, but what exactly would happen he did not know. And so, he sat and stared at it and drank his beer.

Two beers later, paring knife in hand, Castro cut open the package and unwrapped the box. It was a solid, black box, with a silver handle. He flicked the handle and opened the lid. Inside was a glass case, and inside the case was a single dahlia, upright and alive, its petals a soft violet-pink. Then, as carefully as he could, Castro lifted the glass case from the box and set it on the coffee table. And he sat back, and he was crying.

❦

Hemingway, fiddling with one of his cufflinks, stepped off the elevator. His tuxedo was tight around the girth of his belly, and so he walked stiffly across the room toward the fireplace, each step of his shining black shoes a pigeon-toed thump. When he plopped into the wingback chair, a button popped off his jacket and fell into his lap.

"Dammit," he said, fingering between his thighs, searching for it.

Mr. Gregory came with a glass of scotch. Hemingway took the glass and continued digging between his legs.

Satan sat in the other chair, staring into the fire. Black tuxedo, black shirt and tie, hair slicked.

"Goddam tuxedo," Hemingway said. "I told Jean it was too small. But no, she says it slims me down. I can't breathe in this thing." He gave up on the button, took a deep breath, and a sip of scotch, and grinned. "Big day."

Satan nodded.

Hemingway took another sip.

"I got one question—"

He waited for Satan's eyes to shift his way.

"You having the chicken or the fish?"

Satan grinned, a little.

"Ah shit," Hemingway said. "You've come this far—no point worrying about it now. The Boulevard looks great. The whole damned city looks great."

Satan closed his eyes and breathed.

A minute passed in silence, just the crackling of the fire.

Hemingway leaned stiffly forward in his chair.

"Look," he said. "Every man must face his judgment and it doesn't matter the outcome. What matters is how you face it—how you handle yourself on the way out—if it's your way out—I'm not saying it is—but *if* it is, then how you handle yourself is all you've got."

He felt the warmth of the fire on his pantlegs. He sipped his scotch and sat back.

"I remember it was just me and the Pilar out in the Gulf. I was making a run back from the Keys. They called for the storm but I'd tried to beat it, and about halfway out—in that place where there's just water and sky—it hit. Swells so big they'd swallow you whole. When it's like that there's nothing you can do. So, I steadied her straight and held on. Mother Nature will do what she does. There's no convincing her otherwise."

Satan stared into the fire.

Hemingway leaned over and tapped him on the knee.

"You listening to what I'm saying?"

Satan blinked, and then sighed, long and loud.

"Set your course and see it through," Hemingway said. "Let the storm come—it comes no matter what, and there's nothing you can do about it now."

"I have done things, Ernest."

"We've all done things," Hemingway said. "But most never get the chance to atone for it. You should consider yourself lucky."

He finished the last of his scotch, handed the empty glass to Mr. Gregory, and lifted himself to his feet. His tuxedo jacket was opened now, which relaxed his posture, and, spotting the button on the chair, he knelt and retrieved it, tossed it into the air and caught it.

"Just keep yourself together, eh?"

And with that, he walked back across the room, stepped into the elevator, and was gone.

Far below, the long stretch of the Boulevard was crammed with souls. Everyone peered toward the Gates. The usual line entering Hell had been rerouted. Nobody would be coming through today. Whenever any movement occurred around the Gates, everyone rose from their seats, followed by a collective sigh when they realized it was nothing. Then the anticipation would build again.

Some had abandoned their places, only to have them quickly refilled. Every now and then someone would jump the barriers and was quickly escorted back. As more time passed, whispers began to circulate that God was not coming. But then, just as it seemed that nothing was going to happen, without warning, the Gates opened, and the Boulevard fell silent.

God entered Capital City as a ball of brilliant light, as though he were the sun itself. The gloomy overcast suddenly dispersed and the sky opened far and wide, a pure and endless blue. The light poured over the Boulevard and lit up the murals in all their glory, so bright even the furthest corners of Hell felt their glow. Fireworks shot into the sky but were barely visible, just booms echoing off the buildings and a few faint smoke trails sputtering into the blue.

Satan, watching from high above in his tower, quietly gasped. There it was, at long last, Heaven's glorious light, and it filled him with a warmth he hadn't felt since the beginning, soothing him in such a way that he lost himself, his mind swimming, dreaming, and his fears vanished.

But it did not last long.

As God inched his way along the Boulevard, closer toward him, the reality of what was about to come, what he was about to face, dropped into his gut with a thud, and the warmth he felt a moment ago was quickly replaced with a cold, hard panic.

Mr. Gregory grunted a little to break the silence.

"It's time, sir."

Satan looked down at his trembling hands. He'd never felt fear like this and he did not know what to do, except to straighten his tie and take a deep breath and try to muster some courage; from there he would find grace. But when he breathed his chest tightened and he found neither. He thought of Hemingway, of how he would handle this, this stepping into the ring. He actually grinned, amused with himself for using that analogy. What had Hemingway said? A storm? He hadn't been listening. It was always an analogy with him. But he wished Hemingway were still here with him, to comfort him, to tell him of the storm again, but he wasn't, and he suddenly felt very alone. He breathed deeply and let another moment pass. Then, still trembling, he walked over to the bar, poured himself a good stiff drink, and gulped it down.

Acknowledgements

First, for my wife, Leigh. There is too much to write to rightly thank you for all you are to me. Being a writer's wife isn't easy, and though you signed on before I was ever published, how you've put up with me all these years, I'll never know.

For my two girls, Hadley and Harper, for being interested in your dad's books but still too young to read them. I love you more than everything.

For my publisher and friend, Lee D. Thompson, for taking a chance on this project; for believing in this story, and in me.

For Bethany Gibson, who'd offered her expertise on several occasions, reassuring me this manuscript was worth the grind; this book would not be what it is without you.

For Warren Layberry, my friend since my Chapters days many years ago when I'd first thought of this story; for your unwavering support during the down times, I'll always be grateful.

For Lucy Robinson and David Williams, old neighbours who always listened to my ideas as early drafts played out.